FATEWAKER

J.R. MCCULLOUGH

Fatewaker

Cover design by Jennifer R. McCullough
Interior design and formatting by Lucas E. McCullough

Printed in the United States of America

ISBN: 979-8-9989197-1-8
U.S. Copyright Registration Number: TX 9-511-787
First Edition
www.Fatewaker.com

To my Luke

My heart

The air I breathe

My comfort and peace

My home

I love you—forever

Thank you for being mine.

CHAPTER I

Colin Aedric shifted uncomfortably on the stone floor. He had been standing for over an hour, waiting for his audience with *him*. He sighed deeply, thinking how strange it seemed that he didn't even like to say *his* name in his head. He had such an extreme dislike for the man that the mere thought of *him* made his skin crawl—a highly inconvenient sentiment for someone who served as *his* protector and a captain of the Royal Guard.

Another five minutes passed, and Colin adjusted his stance again. He had been offered a chair, but declined, wanting to be in the most suitable position for making an escape if necessary.

Now he regretted that decision as the minutes stretched on.

He had started his day looking forward to spending it away from the palace. Days off didn't come often, so when they did, Colin tried to make the most of them.

Today, he had planned on heading into the nearby village of Houck to do some fishing. He was more than a little annoyed when he got the message at six in the morning that he had been summoned.

The memory still had him scowling when the door to *his* private chamber flung open and a tiny man announced that he could go in.

Making a concerted effort, he pulled his face back into a mask of cold indifference that went so well with the uniform and stepped inside.

The pungent scent of sulfur assaulted his nose. As his eyes adjusted to the dim lighting, he could see puffs of smoke slowly rising from a vessel on a table against the back wall.

Next to the table was a tall figure he recognized. Robed in deep crimson from head to toe stood *his* personal sorcerer, Kaz. Colin had never liked the man. Suffering and death were gifted to any that crossed his path.

A low moan slid across the room, coming from a darkened corner on his left. He turned his head slightly in that direction, but didn't look too closely. Some things were best left unseen.

"Ah! Captain Aedric!" came a high-pitched voice from the opposite corner. Colin turned sharply to face the voice and forced a curt bow.

"My lord," Colin answered. He tried to keep the disgust from his expression.

Slinking into view, Lord Draegor Mordane came to stand a few feet away from Colin. He was shorter than Colin by a few inches, but pulled himself to his full height and stood with practiced confidence.

His eyes were a deep brown with hints of something else Colin could not distinguish—his hair dirty blonde and slicked back.

Lord Mordane had been ruler since the death of his father twenty years ago. He was in his thirties when his father died, yet he still looked much younger than the fifty years Colin estimated he had lived.

Colin wondered what the man was doing to preserve his youth, suspecting that Kaz was surely involved.

Never one for wasting time, Lord Mordane got straight to business. "I called you here because I have a very important task for you."

This made Colin's unease sharpen. What *he* considered an 'important task' could range from the assassination of a rival king to the destruction of an entire village. Colin prepared for the worst.

"My lord?"

"I need you to go on a journey to pick up a very important package."

A sudden sensation of relief swept over Colin, followed immediately by a feeling of impending disaster. What kind of 'package' needed a captain of the Royal Guard? Having one do your fetching for you was overkill, to say the least.

Apparently sensing Colin's confusion, Lord Mordane continued, "You and the Guard will travel to Pyete. There is a monastery there in the mountains. My future wife and Queen is there."

Colin struggled to keep his features neutral. This was the first he had heard of any marriage plans. Lord Mordane, although having many mistresses, had never sought marriage to anyone—at least not publicly. Colin wondered what kind of woman would agree to marry the man, and what she was getting in return.

Collecting himself, Colin replied, "Congratulations, my lord."

Lord Mordane's lips curled up on one side, as if contemplating something wicked. "Yes—thank you! I think she will serve her purpose well."

If Colin had not known the man so well, he would have thought this an odd thing to say. But he did know him—too well—so this comment was barely noticed.

The ruler wasn't known for having a kind heart. People were his playthings, and it didn't surprise Colin that his future bride was being viewed as a commodity.

After a pause, the unpleasant smile on his face finally turned into his normal sneer, and Lord Mordane's voice squeaked. "Now! For the details! The journey to Pyete will be a long one. I expect you to go the fastest route there—directly over Trew Mountain. On the way back, however, you are to take the Lake Road."

Colin blinked. "My lord?"

While the journey over Trew Mountain would only take a week, the Lake Road would take a month, barring any issues. The Lake Road was also far removed from most towns, with few places to stop and rest. Not exactly easy traveling for the future Queen.

Lord Mordane waved his hand in the air, dismissing Colin's apparent confusion. "She is far too valuable—it must be this way."

Looking behind him to the darkened part of the room where the moans were still emanating, Lord Mordane barked, "Kaz!"

The sorcerer slithered out of the shadows and into view, bowing deeply to his master.

"I want you and your men to be protected on this journey. Kaz here will do a... prayer... over you," Lord Mordane ordered with another wave of his hand.

That was out of character for him. At no time in his years at the palace had Colin ever heard Lord Mordane even remotely suggest that he had concerns over another human being. The hairs on the back of his neck stood on end—a sure sign that something was amiss. Whatever was happening here was not for his benefit. Of that, he was sure.

Before Colin could process it, the doors swung open and his troop of twenty men, his lieutenant among them, marched in.

The Royal Guard was an impressive sight, decked in black with a gold falcon embroidered on their capes. They each had gold helmets signifying their allegiance to the crown. Their gear didn't do much in the way of camouflage in the event of actual combat. It served more to impress and intimidate—each man of the Guard standing at least six feet tall and powerfully built.

As the men stood at attention in formation, Colin went to join them, taking position up front. Pulling a book out of his large cloak, the Royal Sorcerer began to mumble words in some long-forgotten ancient tongue.

If the objective was to make them all feel better protected, Kaz had failed.

His shrill voice repeatedly rose and lowered several octaves as he read the verses.

Colin had spent enough time in the halls of the palace to know a spell when he heard one. He silently praised his men for staying motionless and expressionless through it. He was sure they all knew the truth of it as well.

Colin only wondered why. Why bother with a spell? What was it for? Why were they going on this "package" pick-up mission?

After Kaz had done his "prayer" and his men had been dismissed, Colin stayed back to get any remaining details about the trip from Lord Mordane.

When he was finished, Colin bowed to take his leave. The ruler's dark eyes focused intently on Colin as he said, "I expect that you will return here with my bride *safely in hand*, Captain."

Colin did not immediately respond, choosing to wait a few breaths before answering. It was a quiet act of resistance, a reminder that he wasn't some wet-behind-the-ears recruit.

Nodding slowly, he answered, "Of course, my lord."

Lord Mordane took a moment to analyze him before waving his hand in dismissal.

Colin didn't wait around for him to change his mind and sharply turned on his heel, then strode out of the room.

Once outside, Colin made his way over to his lieutenant, Bren Holt, who was standing just outside the gate to the palace.

Bren glared at him as he approached, clearly having something on his mind. Colin knew Bren well. If he didn't give him an opportunity to voice his concerns, there wouldn't be any peace on the trip.

"Spit it out, Bren," Colin grumbled.

"I don't like it."

Colin didn't need to ask what he was referring to, and he wasn't going to argue with him—he felt the same way, so he let him continue.

"Sending us to pick up his bride? And why the slowest route possible on the way back? And why the spell?"

Colin nodded. "I'm guessing he is expecting some sort of trouble and wants us as far off the main road as possible. Doesn't exactly make for an easy trip. Even the long route isn't completely without its dangers. We'll have to be extra vigilant. Be sure you make this clear to the men. As for the spell, your guess is as good as mine."

Bren nodded quietly and sighed as he looked out toward Trew Mountain. "I have a really bad feeling about this."

Colin didn't reply, but his lieutenant and lifelong friend knew him well enough to know that he had his own reservations.

As they walked back to their quarters, they discussed the upcoming journey but kept any remaining doubts to themselves.

CHAPTER 2

A week later, Colin woke up in his sleep sack at the base of Trew Mountain. It had been an easy journey with pleasant weather and no real threats on the road, aside from a bear unwise enough to approach their camp one night. The thought of the bear's demise—and its subsequent donation of dinner—made Colin's stomach rumble with hunger.

They were making good time and would reach the monastery by nightfall, so he grabbed a quick bite of whatever was cooking and packed up his gear. In under twenty minutes, the Guard was on their way along the last stretch to Pyete.

Colin spent the time thinking about the information he had gathered during his final conversation with Lord Mordane before they departed. Not surprisingly, the future Queen would be traveling with a companion—someone *he* described as a sort of teacher. The "package" herself was off-limits to everyone except Colin, and even he was under strict orders to keep conversation and contact to a minimum.

Her name was Lady Elaris Vaelora. That was all he learned about her. Lord Mordane would say no more. Colin figured a month on the road would give him plenty of time to get a better sense of who she was. She was probably some spoiled brat from a neighboring country that *he* was trying to conquer, Colin thought. The idea made him scowl. The last thing he needed was to play nursemaid to a pampered royal.

"What's the problem, Captain?" Bren asked, noticing the change in his face.

Colin glanced over his shoulder to make sure the men were out of earshot. He and Bren were friends, but he didn't want the others mistaking that for permission to speak to him as equals. "I'm wondering what she's like," Colin said quietly.

"I'm guessing some rich daughter of a rival king. I don't see him marrying someone unless he's getting something for it."

Colin thought for a moment and nodded slowly. "Perhaps." It never ceased to amaze him how much he and Bren thought alike.

Bren knew the look on Colin's face well enough to know that he was deep in thought. Still, he felt the need to lighten the mood. Speaking loud enough for all the Guard to hear, Bren declared, "Sir, I hear that Corporal Nurburg ate the last of the venison you shot yesterday, leaving none for the rest of the men!"

The corporal in question groaned loudly as his fellow guards laughed raucously, slapping him on the back. "Sir, I swear, I didn't touch that venison!" he argued.

Colin's scowl turned into a look of reluctant amusement. Bren grinned even wider, waiting for a reply. Colin sighed and laughed. "I suppose we need to punish the lad."

The corporal groaned even louder as his comrades cheered the idea.

"Oh, I agree, Sir. What do you suggest?" asked Bren with mock innocence.

Colin turned to catch a glance at the poor corporal, who wasn't a day over twenty years old and was the youngest soldier to ever enter the Royal Guard. He had earned the position by impressing Colin with his integrity and strength of character. "Clearly, we must gut him like a fish!" Colin teased.

More laughter ensued as the young man protested, "Sir!"

Bren seemed to like where this was going. Corporal Nurburg had kept half the Guard up last night with his snoring, and now he was going to pay. "Excellent idea, Captain! Who should have the honor of performing the gutting?"

Colin feigned deep thought and stopped to survey his men. All were waiting anxiously for his answer. "Briggs."

Whoops of laughter arose again as everyone turned to Sergeant Briggs—possibly the largest man ever created, but with the kindest heart. He was known for constantly stopping to feed stray dogs and for sending his mother every penny of his salary that he could manage each month.

"Don't worry, Corporal, I'll be gentle." Briggs grinned at the corporal, who finally started laughing himself.

Colin took one look at Bren and got a wink in return. The man was a menace.

Their revelry was soon interrupted by the sight of two men on the road ahead. Colin stiffened and barked, "Look sharp!"

The laughter died and was replaced immediately by twenty stone-faced elite soldiers and their Captain. As they approached, the tallest of the two men on the road stood and greeted them. "Happy day, good sirs!"

Colin dismounted from his horse and replied with measured command, "Good day. What business have you?"

The tall man visibly gulped. "We are travelers heading to Kilkane."

Colin nodded once, stiffly. "You head north, then."

Although it was more of a statement than a question, the man still nodded nervously. A bead of sweat trickled down his temple.

Colin glanced at their horses and noticed something strange. "You pack light for such a long journey. Kilkane is at least five days away."

The tall traveler looked to his companion, as if seeking help, but received none. "We are men of simple means, Sir."

Colin grunted in reply while still analyzing them. The Royal Guard was known for striking fear into anyone who crossed their path, so their nervousness wasn't uncommon. Colin still felt uneasy about the pair, however.

"What business have you, Sir?" the man asked with another gulp.

Colin raised an eyebrow at this. The man had nerve asking such a thing of the Royal Guard. "Our business is our own," he growled with deadly authority.

The man stepped back and folded his arms protectively across his chest, saying nothing further.

Colin continued to glare at him as he mounted his horse and turned to leave, barking, "Step aside!"

The taller man jumped back and practically landed on his companion. As the troop marched past, Colin caught a look of hatred on both travelers' faces.

After twelve hours of riding, Colin and the Guard finally climbed the steep mountainside that was host to the monastery. It had rained for the last three hours of the trip. Both men and horses alike were wet, tired, and ready to be fed.

Colin squinted into the dark at the imposing structure. It didn't look much like a holy place. If he didn't know better, he would think it was a prison. A dark black wall surrounded the entire complex. Matching black bars could be seen in every window. Guards stood watch in small sentry posts every few hundred feet. Nothing about this monastery said "welcome." In fact, he was sure it was designed to say the opposite.

Approaching the door, he was greeted by a very tall, exceptionally large guard who asked with great authority, "What business do you have?"

Colin felt himself tense in agitation and growled, "I am here to escort Lady Vaelora to her groom."

Not exactly the most formal response, but Colin was tired and didn't care about the niceties. The sentry did not respond except to open the door for him. When he entered, he was met with a large, cavernous room with not a soul in sight.

The walls were mostly void of any decoration, and the few carpets that littered the floor were threadbare.

He stood motionless for a moment, wondering where to go next. After a pause, he muttered, "As friendly as the weather."

A sharp bark of laughter rang out above him, and he could see a shadowed figure move from behind a screen on the balcony.

The figure cleared its throat and spoke with a soft voice, "Hello—I assume you are my escort?"

Before Colin could respond, a stout woman, probably in her sixties, swiftly came into the room and grabbed his hand, shaking it warmly. She threw a stern look up in the direction of the shadowed figure for the briefest of moments before curving her lips upward. "Hello, my dear. I am Hatti Abro, Lady Vaelora's companion."

Colin heard footsteps above, moving away from the balcony. He had no time to dwell on the exchange, as his hand was still being grasped by the older woman.

Warming his features, he replied, "Captain Colin Aedric, Ma'am. I'm here to escort you and Lady Vaelora to Lord Mordane."

Hatti smiled up at him, though it didn't reach her eyes. She slowly let his hand go. "Of course, Captain—and I'm sure you are anxious to meet your charge. Let us first talk about the next month and the journey ahead."

Colin found this reasonable and nodded in agreement.

"I am assuming we will be departing tomorrow, as scheduled?"

Colin nodded again. "We are, Ma'am, unless you have some reason for delay?"

He silently prayed she wouldn't keep them there longer. He wanted to be back on the road as soon as possible.

Hatti waved her hand, dismissing the idea of a delay. "And I believe you and your men have been briefed on proper protocol where Lady Vaelora is concerned."

Colin knew what she was asking and thought about acting obtuse but decided against it. "Lady Vaelora will have minimal contact with my men."

Hatti gave a gentle grin, seeming to appreciate him getting straight to the point. "I'm glad to hear it, Captain. You may not have been told, but Lady Vaelora has never been exposed to outsiders."

"Outsiders?" Colin asked, confused.

"Outsiders, Captain. Lady Vaelora has lived in Pyete since she was an infant. She has never stepped beyond the outer walls, nor has she received visitors. Her teachers and the staff here are all she knows. So, I am hoping you can understand my concerns."

Colin struggled to keep the surprise off his face.

What possible reason could there be for shutting someone up in this oppressive fortress? Clearing his throat, Colin emphasized, "My men won't be a problem."

Hatti adopted another half-smile and touched his arm lightly. "Good. Now—let's go find the lady in question."

Hatti guided Colin down a dark corridor that led toward the back of the monastery. Candles were placed every fifty feet, making it difficult to see down the many hallways they passed. Colin's nerves were on high alert. It was cold and damp, and he wondered how anyone could live in a place like this.

He noticed how Hatti's pace slowed as their journey progressed. He wondered why she was hesitant.

Finally reaching a door at the end of the corridor, Hatti paused with her fingers on the handle. Colin waited patiently as she collected herself and slowly swung the door open to reveal a small, warmly lit room. In the center of the room was a veiled figure in a chair—the same figure he'd seen on his arrival.

Moving into the room, Hatti turned to Colin and announced proudly, "Captain Aedric, may I present Lady Elaris Vaelora."

Colin bowed deeply while keeping his eyes fixed on Elaris. He started to talk but was interrupted as she rose from her chair.

"So pleased to meet you, Captain. I hope you had a safe journey."

Hatti coughed in disapproval, and Elaris sat back in her chair.

Colin hesitantly answered, "I did, my lady. Fortunately, we were blessed with good weather and fast roads."

Colin wished he could see the woman's face. Her veil was too dark and thick to make out any distinguishable features. He found it odd that such an accessory was in use considering her cloistered existence. Who could she possibly be shielding herself from?

During her brief escape from her chair, he could tell that she was quite tall—just a few inches shorter than him—and she possessed a fully developed womanly figure.

Beyond that, little else was discernible, as she was draped head to toe in a dark dress.

Noticing his gaze linger, Hatti stepped protectively between them. "Captain, I'm sure you and your men would like to eat something after such a long journey."

Elaris's head snapped to the woman, and she interjected in a disgruntled tone, "I have not finished my discussion."

Hatti turned to her in silence. Colin watched as the two seemed to communicate without words. Finally, Hatti stepped back and mumbled, "My apologies."

Elaris turned back to Colin and leaned forward. "I am very much looking forward to our journey, Captain. Will we have the opportunity to visit many villages on the way? I was hoping to see Timbrow—or perhaps Glendale! I hear both have extensive libraries, and Glendale has a temple dating back three thousand years, thought to be built by the early settlers of Ashcar before they migrated South."

Hatti coughed again.

Colin looked at Hatti in confusion but responded hesitantly, "Unfortunately, no, my lady. The route we will be taking is very removed from most of the villages. It should be a very *quiet* trip."

Even as he spoke the words, Colin regretted them. He probably just cursed them all.

Even through the veil, Colin could hear Elaris's sigh as her shoulders slumped. She was clearly disappointed. Despite her seclusion, it was clear she had studied much of the world she hadn't seen. He suddenly felt sorry for her— trapped in this cold tomb with no one for companionship except scholars and staff.

"I'm sure there will be an opportunity for you to see much wildlife, my lady."

Elaris seemed to perk up a bit with that news, tilting her head to the side with curiosity. "Do you think so? I have studied many of the species that are native to the mountains and had hoped to catch a glimpse of them."

"I believe that is a wish easily fulfilled, my lady."

Elaris nearly sprang from her seat, barely able to contain her excitement. "Thank you, Captain."

Colin bowed again in response.

Hatti cleared her throat as Colin stared at the dark figure in front of him, wondering again what was hidden beneath all that fabric. On the second throat clearing, Elaris spoke up.

"It's time I finish preparing for our departure tomorrow, Captain. I welcome you and your men to a warm meal. Our chef is truly amazing, and I'm sure you will like what he has prepared."

Colin bowed his head slightly and replied, "Thank you, my lady. My men will surely appreciate it."

With that, Elaris rose from her seat and moved to a door in the back of the room. She paused at the door for one final glance, then disappeared.

Colin was left alone with Hatti, who instantly recovered from her interruptive coughing and came to stand in front of him again. "She has been preparing her whole life for this, Captain."

"I'm sure she has you to thank for the majority of those preparations, Ma'am," Colin responded.

Hatti turned a rosy shade of pink and beamed with pride. "She has been like a daughter to me. I want nothing more than to see her happy—and protected." She paused for a moment as if contemplating her next words, so Colin remained silent.

"She doesn't understand what the future holds for her. I fear she will fall prey to those who would destroy her."

Colin was surprised at the woman's words. Lady Vaelora had been surrounded by scholars her whole life in apparent preparation for her future. Why would she not understand what was coming?

"As Queen, Lady Vaelora will have all the protection needed to ensure her safety. Lord Mordane wouldn't have it any other way."

On this point, he was unsure. The ruler had something up his sleeve and Colin suspected that this young woman was just a pawn in a larger game.

Hatti smiled. Once again, the smile didn't make it to her eyes. "You speak of your master in such complimentary terms, Captain. Perhaps my impressions of the man have been wrong," she murmured as she led him from the room.

Colin was surprised at her blatant honesty about her misconceptions. Anyone even remotely suggesting that Lord Mordane was anything other than perfect in every way often found themselves losing property, family, or their life. She must be either incredibly naive about the world outside these walls or incredibly brave. Colin tended to lean toward brave. Hatti struck him as someone who, perhaps thirty years ago, would have made an excellent member of his company.

The rest of their journey to the main foyer of the monastery was quiet. Hatti seemed to have much on her mind and Colin, who had taken an instant liking to the older woman, decided to leave her to those thoughts.

One hour later, Elaris sat in her chamber, finishing up her nightly preparations. She had been so intrigued by the captain that she had thought of little else since seeing him. The man was handsome, there was no doubt. He was tall, with light brown hair and the bluest eyes she had ever seen. Granted, she hadn't seen many sets of eyes in her lifetime, but she liked to think that his were unique. He seemed kind but reserved. She sensed something from him—doubt, perhaps? She was curious about what occupied his thoughts.

Just as she started to dwell further on this question, a knock came at the door. "Enter," she called.

Hatti had the door open before the word was completely past her lips and was bustling into her room. She made her way to a chair opposite Elaris and met her gaze with kind eyes.

"Big day," she started.

Elaris laughed at this understatement. "Yes—quite!"

"The captain and his men are enjoying dinner and should be departing for their camp within the hour. We shouldn't hear anything more from them tonight."

Elaris didn't know if she was happy to hear this or not. Part of her felt disappointed, knowing the night would pass without further interaction.

She didn't bother to ask if she could join them. That would be ridiculous, and Hatti would probably lock her up for suggesting it. Trying to ignore these thoughts, Elaris said, "I do hope the weather is pleasant tomorrow. I am so looking forward to seeing all the countryside."

Hatti gave her a warm look and replied, "I believe it will be."

"The captain is very handsome."

The words were out before Elaris knew what she was saying.

Hatti gave a short bark of laughter before replying, "Indeed he is. But may I remind you, my dear, that you are shortly to be married."

Elaris grinned slyly at her companion. "One can enjoy the scenery while traveling."

She may not have met many men her age in her lifetime, but she knew instantly that she liked looking at the captain.

Hatti laughed again and shook her head. "Just make sure you keep the sightseeing to a minimum. Now, time for your blessing and then off to bed."

Elaris hated being treated like a child but understood Hatti's protectiveness for what it was—love. Hatti had stopped by her room every night for as long as she could remember to give her a blessing before she went to bed.

Elaris had never thought much of it—it was simply routine. She wondered what would happen once she was wed. Hatti had explained to her that she wouldn't need a blessing anymore after she was joined to Lord Mordane. Hatti had also planned on retiring to her family's home after Elaris was made Queen.

The thought made her both sad and happy—sad that she would lose the one friend she had, and happy that Hatti would finally be able to relax outside the walls of Pyete.

Hatti stood and walked over to Elaris, placed her hands on her head, and began speaking the words.

Elaris had asked once what the foreign words meant, and Hatti had told her it was forbidden to speak of it. Elaris had studied many ancient languages but had never heard anything similar. As the final words were spoken, the familiar warmth coursed through her—from her head to her toes.

"Thank you, Hatti," Elaris whispered as the woman removed her hands and moved toward the door to leave.

"I shall see you in the morning. Try to get some rest," Hatti ordered in her most maternal voice.

As the door clicked shut, Elaris stood to move to the window. She hoped she would be able to see the encampment or perhaps some of the soldiers. She had never been any farther than the outer wall of the monastery grounds. While the grounds were expansive and allowed her ample space to ride her horse or go for leisurely walks, it was still surrounded by a wall that had begun to feel more like it was keeping her in rather than keeping everyone else out.

Colin sipped his ale as he watched Bren finish off the last of the third leg of lamb that he had consumed that night. "Honestly, Bren, I don't know where you put it all."

Bren smiled broadly as he sat back to guzzle his ale and pat his stomach. "I have plenty of room left, but I will restrain myself."

The two men sat with the rest of the soldiers at a long table in the banquet hall of the monastery. Colin wondered how often the room was used since, by his count, there were no more than twenty people that worked or lived there, and he didn't imagine them hosting many dinner parties.

He had to admit, however, Lady Vaelora was correct—the chef had done an outstanding job feeding his men, with plenty of food to spare.

As his troops began to pack up and depart for their camp on the grounds, Bren took the opportunity to get some questions answered that had been plaguing him.

"So, is she the spoiled princess we thought her to be?"

Colin snorted, "Hardly. The girl has been here her whole life, sheltered in this damp fortress."

Bren looked confused. "But why?"

Colin shrugged. "Your guess is as good as mine. It wouldn't surprise me if *he* wanted it that way."

Bren nodded in agreement. While both men were outwardly loyal to the Guard and the royal house they served, they had a shared unease about their ruler and his motives. Lord Mordane was not a good man—of that they were certain. But they never spoke of it other than in vague references unless their privacy was absolutely assured.

Bren tried to lighten the mood a bit, asking with a mischievous grin, "Is she pretty?"

Colin rolled his eyes, answering, "I wouldn't know. They have her draped head to toe in black. It's a wonder she can breathe."

Confused, Bren shook his head.

Colin sighed heavily, leaning back and balancing on the rear legs of his chair.

"She's led a very sheltered existence here but seems quite educated. We should make sure she can see some wildlife on the way."

"Wildlife?" Bren choked.

"Well, she wanted to see villages but seemed content with the idea of birds and squirrels."

"Hmm, good idea," Bren agreed.

"She didn't even ask about *him*."

Bren didn't need clarification on who Colin was referring to. "That's odd," he said.

Sensing the end to their conversation, the men finished the last of their drinks, stood up, and headed to the main door. Colin was looking forward to some fresh air. The inside of the monastery made him feel like a trapped animal—and he had only spent one day there. He couldn't imagine a lifetime in these walls.

As they stepped out into the cool air, Colin felt the hairs on the nape of his neck rise.

He knew instinctively to look up to the windows above. There, in the only lit window, was the shape of the dark figure, hidden behind a sheer curtain, looking down at them.

To Colin, she didn't look like a bride awaiting a royal escort—she looked like a prisoner.

CHAPTER 3

Elaris woke early, the excitement of the day already coursing through her veins. She had dreamed last night of lakes, forests, and mountains, all of them filled with creatures she had never seen before.

Anxious to start her day, she shot out of bed, dressed, and made her way to Hatti's room. Her knock on the door was answered with a sleepy "Enter," followed by a groan as she opened the door and allowed a beam of sunlight from the hallway to hit her companion's blinking face.

Hatti sat up slowly, glaring at Elaris the whole time. "Is the monastery on fire, my lady?"

Elaris laughed. "No, Hatti, it is not."

Hatti smirked at her charge and stood up to get dressed. "I suppose an early start isn't a bad idea."

"Just what I was thinking!" Elaris replied, beaming.

With her objective complete, Elaris returned to her room to finish her preparations for the day. A tray with a light breakfast was brought to her, but she found she was too excited to eat much.

Hatti came to her room shortly after to escort her downstairs and say her goodbyes. Elaris had spent so much time dreaming about getting out of the cold, dreary monastery that she hadn't really given herself much time to consider all the people she was leaving behind.

As she made her way down the stairs, she noticed several crates and bags stacked in the foyer. Her possessions had already been loaded onto the cart. The rest must have belonged to the departing staff.

She knew that, for most of them, their time at the monastery was coming to a permanent close. After all, they would have no pupil to teach or serve. The thought of never seeing any of them again caused a sudden wave of sadness.

As she stepped outside, she was moved to discover all the staff and her teachers standing in a long line, waiting for her. Tears instantly welled in her eyes, and she nearly lost her composure until she noticed the Royal Guard standing in formation at the end of the courtyard.

The last thing she wanted was to be a sobbing mess in front of all the soldiers. Gathering herself, she walked slowly past everyone, stopping to thank them each individually for everything they had done. Each returned the sentiment, surprising her with little stories of times they had enjoyed while she was growing up. Hatti walked by her side, a silent pillar of strength.

Once all her goodbyes were made, Colin stepped forward to lead her to her horse. Elaris took a moment to look over the large group of men at his command.

They were truly impressive. She felt small and fragile just imagining herself riding among them.

After Elaris and Hatti were safely seated on their horses, Colin said the word and they started their journey to the main gate. Elaris had ridden to it before, many times. She would go there as a child and look out, hoping to catch sight of someone riding by.

Often, she could report back the sighting of a new animal to Hatti, who always sternly reminded her to stay away from the gate.

Today, however, she would be passing through it at last—with Hatti at her side.

Colin rode just ahead of Elaris, the Guard behind her. He planned to let her have her moment as she left the property, and then he would reorganize the formation.

As the gate came into sight, Elaris's pace seemed to quicken. Within a few moments, they were clearing the giant iron bars and gathered on the road just outside. When Colin looked at the veiled figure sitting on the horse next to him, it seemed he could feel her happiness. Even her horse sensed it, prancing in circles, wanting to take off in a run.

With a few quick orders to his men, they were back on their way—half of the guard leading and half following, with Colin keeping a watchful eye on Elaris and Hatti in the middle. The cart filled with her possessions followed slowly behind, driven by Corporal Rowan.

As the hours went on and more miles came between the traveling party and the monastery, Colin waited for a flood of questions from Elaris, but they never came. She and her companion shared quiet conversation, often pointing at nearby trees, flowers, and the occasional hare or bird. He wondered at her restraint but assumed that she was more comfortable talking to Hatti than himself.

As midday drew near, Colin ordered the Guard to stop and prepare a fire for lunch. They hadn't covered much ground in the few hours they had been traveling, making Colin wonder if they would make the first planned stop by nightfall. They'd need to keep their break short.

As Bren directed the food preparations, Colin gathered appropriate chairs from the back of the cart for the ladies to sit on. Elaris spoke little to him, leaving him surprised and a bit confused.

"Is Lady Vaelora alright?" Colin asked Hatti once they had a private moment.

Confused, Hatti answered, "Why yes, Captain, she is perfectly fine. Why do you ask?"

"I noticed she was very quiet. I just wanted to make sure she was comfortable and did not want for anything."

Hatti threw her warm smile toward him and grasped his hand in assurance. "Oh, she is very comfortable and very much enjoying the trip! If she is quiet, it is only because of her training. One must be poised and composed when one is Queen, especially in public."

Realization hit Colin. While she may have demonstrated excitement for their journey during their private audience, she now had to be concerned about appearances to the Royal Guard—*her* future Royal Guard.

Seeming ignorant of the world around her may lead some to question her authority in the future. She was right to keep her curiosity in check. He was honestly surprised she had trusted him with her true self.

As the ladies took their seats under a nearby tree that lent a small amount of shade, the Guard quietly took theirs around the fire. His men had never failed him before, and they certainly didn't now. The conversation remained at a respectful volume, and crude jokes were absent.

He could see many of them stealing glances at Lady Vaelora. They probably wondered, as he did, what was hidden behind the veil.

The meal was blessedly short, and Colin—with Bren's help—managed to get everyone back on the road within an hour.

He had hoped to arrive at Lake Rehl before nightfall—and with a modest increase in pace, he believed they could make it. His dreams of an uneventful afternoon were dashed, however, when his soldiers riding point alerted him to something troubling up ahead.

"All stop," he commanded.

Bren, advancing from his position in the back, rode to meet him. "Trouble, Sir?"

"Take a look," Colin growled, pointing to the two men on the horizon. "Recognize anyone?"

"Well, well. If it isn't our travelers. Looks like they seem to be a bit lost."

"Indeed. Watch my back."

Before Bren could protest, Colin took off at a gallop to intercept the two men they had met on the road to the monastery the day before. As he approached, they backed away from the side of the road to stand in the mud, gripping their horses' reins to keep them from bolting. Colin came to a halt at an uncomfortably close distance from them, causing the previously silent one to trip and land on his rear in the mud.

Colin wasted no time getting to the point. "It seems, gentlemen, that you have lost your compass."

"Sir?" the talkative one squeaked.

"You previously reported you were heading north to Kilkane, and yet here you are, several miles south of where we last met. Explain yourselves," he barked.

"Ah... change of plans," the man grumbled, his friend still struggling to get out of the mud.

Colin didn't like how the man's eyes kept darting over to the traveling party, as if trying to catch a glimpse of someone. "I strongly suggest that your plans get sorted immediately and you find yourself out of our path. Do I make myself clear?"

"Yes, Sir! Crystal clear. We will be out of your way!"

Colin waited impatiently as they quickly gathered themselves and mounted their horses to leave. He gave them no option to head back toward the traveling party. Instead, they moved south and took a nearby road to the east, heading toward Glendale.

Once they were out of sight, he rode back to meet Bren.

"I want two men to follow them and ensure they make their way to wherever it is they're going. By that, I mean anywhere but where we are. They can rejoin us at Lake Rehl tonight."

"Understood." Bren nodded. Before he had a chance to say anything else, Corporal Nurburg advanced forward and boldly declared, "I can go, Sir!"

Colin trusted Bren with these decisions but silently hoped he would not allow the young corporal to go. While he clearly trusted him, he wanted people with a bit more seasoning for this mission.

Bren read his mind. Ignoring the corporal's outburst, he assigned Sergeants Grayston and Whilthouse to the task. They left immediately, kicking up a trail of dust behind them.

Turning to the corporal, Bren slapped him on the shoulder approvingly. "I like the initiative, Corporal. Your day will come."

Corporal Nurburg nodded in appreciation and fell back into formation. The rest of the party waited until their captain's order was given and then resumed their journey.

Colin's awareness was heightened for the rest of the day. He spent his time scanning the tree line and keeping a close watch on the road. Bren sensed his unease and would occasionally ride ahead to scout for trouble.

To Colin's relief, they arrived at Lake Rehl about an hour before sunset. As the soldiers got to work preparing the ladies' tent and the campsite, Elaris and Hatti took the opportunity to freshen up at the lake. Colin kept an eye on them closely while giving them as much privacy as possible.

He was pleased to see that Lady Vaelora had become more talkative since arriving at the scenic site. She and her companion seemed to be deep in conversation about the lake, the birds, and the trees nearby.

Without the formality of a military escort, she was positively animated.

Elaris was thrilled. She had never imagined such a beautiful place in her life. Lake Rehl was enormous, sitting at the base of a snow-capped mountain. Evergreens dotted their way from the lake up the mountain's base, while streams of light from the setting sun sparkled on the water's surface. Their side of the lake had a beach littered with polished stones of varying colors.

"Hatti! Just look at this place!"

Hatti chuckled and teased, "What am I looking at?"

Even though the veil was securely covering Elaris's face, Hatti could still sense the annoyed smirk being directed at her. She stifled another laugh.

"I'm glad you're so amused," Elaris chirped.

Hatti waved her hands in front of her in surrender. "I'm very happy you seem to be enjoying the scenery."

Elaris grumbled to herself but couldn't maintain her feigned annoyance. She was too excited to see what the lake had to offer. Walking down to the water's edge, she immediately spotted a brightly colored fish swimming nearby.

Pulling a book from the depths of her thick black skirts, she opened it and started perusing the pages, attempting to find any reference to the creature.

"You brought your *Gillian's Guide* with you?" Hatti inquired.

"Yes—I thought we would have an opportunity to see some fish, and I was correct!"

Hatti stood back and watched her pupil happily studying the creatures in the clear water. It reminded her of when Elaris had been a child, always carrying a book wherever she went, sometimes making up her own. Although she was a grown woman now, Hatti couldn't help but see that young girl, full of curiosity and excitement.

Looking back at the camp, Hatti spotted the captain keeping watch. The sight of him brought back the cold reminder that Elaris would soon be gone. She quickly wiped away the tears that had welled in her eyes.

Elaris, seeming to sense her companion's distress, turned to see her composing herself. "Hatti, are you alright?"

Hatti forced her mouth into a reasonably passable smile and choked out, "Of course, dear. I just got a little something in my eye."

Elaris knew instantly that this was a lie and had her suspicions as to why Hatti was suddenly emotional. "I shall miss you, you know."

Hatti's eyes started welling up again, and she seemed unable to speak. Elaris surprised her by throwing her arms around her and clutching her tightly. Rather than pushing her away, as she should have done in public, Hatti welcomed the embrace.

Once she had composed herself again, Elaris pulled away slightly and joked, "I suppose we could run away!"

Hatti's laughter erupted, sudden and unrestrained. "You shouldn't be talking that way, my lady," she scolded, though still giggling.

Elaris looked somewhat disappointed. "Why must this be my destiny? Why can't it be exploring, or being a teacher— or becoming an *evil sorceress!*" she teased, raising her hands in an impression of someone casting a spell.

Hatti immediately turned serious, and she cautioned, "You must not jest about these things! Someone may hear you! You are destined to be wed to Lord Mordane. It has been so since your birth.

"I would love for you to be able to do what you would wish, but it can't be so. I would love for you to marry any other man..." Hatti stopped abruptly.

Elaris was stunned. Hatti had never spoken in such a way. She had heard nothing but positive things from Hatti and the rest of the staff regarding her future husband. Granted, she had noticed that Hatti's heart wasn't always in some of these conversations. At times, they seemed forced.

"I apologize, my lady. The excitement of the day has made me misspeak."

Elaris didn't know what to say, so she grasped her companion's hands and squeezed them tightly in comfort. "Perhaps we should get back to camp and see if our accommodations are ready. I see the captain there on the hill waiting for us."

In silence, they made their way back up the slope to the captain, who led them to a nicely appointed tent. They both remained quiet as they settled in.

Elaris sighed in relief as she ripped her veil from her face, causing Hatti to throw a look of pity at her. "I'm alright, Hatti. I just hate having my view blocked by that thing."

Hatti hated it too. Elaris had been subjected to the veil since childhood. She was free to show her face in front of trusted staff and her teachers, but all other times she was covered. The restriction made it difficult for her to enjoy being a child who had loved to explore and play.

Hatti had hoped the restriction would be eased when Elaris grew into a woman, but that hadn't been the case. Instead, a fully concealing dress had been added to the ensemble.

As they readied for supper, Hatti wondered how different Elaris's life would be in a month. She feared for her and the future she would have, but there was nothing that could be done.

CHAPTER 4

The sun had fallen behind the horizon, leaving vibrant colors of orange and red in its wake. The Guard had built an enormous fire at the center of the camp, and several men sat around it, enjoying fish they had caught from the lake.

Hatti and Elaris emerged from their tent and made their way to a table Colin had prepared for them away from the scorching heat of the fire.

The camp went quiet with their arrival, conversations ending abruptly, laughter dying away. The men sat stiff and alert. Colin appreciated their military bearing but sensed it was making the ladies a bit uncomfortable. Confirming his suspicions, Elaris boldly addressed everyone by announcing, "Please proceed, gentlemen, with your revelry. We certainly aren't bothered by it."

The soldiers looked to Colin for silent guidance, and they received it in the form of an almost indistinguishable tip of his chin. With that approval, they slowly began talking again, and the occasional burst of laughter could be heard. To their credit, they kept the subject matter and language at an appropriate level for the ladies.

Once Colin was assured the camp was settled and secured, he made his way to the table, where he was welcomed to a seat with the wave of Elaris's hand.

"Thank you, my lady," Colin murmured as he took a seat next to her companion.

"I hope your accommodations meet with your approval."

Elaris nodded in acknowledgment. "The tent is lovely, Captain, but nothing compared to the location itself. I must have seen at least four species of fish in the short time we were by the water—and the mountain! So perfectly situated. It's like something from a painting!"

Colin flashed a wide grin. "I'm glad you enjoy it. Lake Rehl is always a spot we try to camp at when passing through this area—though it doesn't happen that often."

Hatti tilted her head and inquired, "Is it unusual to see men on the road in these parts?"

"Not at all—why do you ask?"

"Those men today—you were clearly unhappy with their presence."

"Ah," Colin sighed. "The men in question were seen the day before heading in the other direction. Normally, we wouldn't worry, but with you under our protection, we don't like to take chances."

This answer seemed to concern Hatti more than appease her. "I hope your men are alright, Captain."

His men had been at the forefront of his mind tonight. Neither Grayston nor Whilthouse had made their way to the camp yet. It was still too soon to send someone to find them, but Colin had significant unease about the situation.

"They should be joining us shortly."

Hatti saw the worry on his brow but left him alone. She recognized the quiet burden of being charged with another's safety.

Finishing their meal, Elaris and Hatti made their way to the tent to get some much-needed rest. Colin, however, wouldn't be able to sleep until he knew the status of his missing soldiers.

Bren approached him from across the camp, sensing his friend's unease. "Want me to send a scout?" he asked, knowing exactly what was on Colin's mind.

"Immediately," Colin answered. "Let's hope they just got lost."

But both men knew the soldiers in question, and they would never get lost—especially in this area.

While Bren handled the scout, Colin ensured the appropriate guards had taken the watch for the night and then headed to his tent.

Several hours later, Colin lay in his sleep sack, waiting for the return of their scout. Bren had come to report earlier that Grayston and Whilthouse still had not arrived, and the scout, Sergeant Pike, had not yet returned. It made him uneasy and put his nerves on high alert.

He could hear everything—the sound of the wind passing through the trees, the low mumbles of the Guard talking by the fire, and Corporal Nurburg snoring five tents away.

Colin also noticed another sound—something familiar. Branches breaking, but softly. No one should be in the woods at this hour, and if they were, they wouldn't be moving at such a slow pace.

Already having his boots on, he jumped up and out of the tent in one smooth movement.

"Report!" Colin barked at the first soldier he came upon standing watch.

Corporal Whyte snapped to attention and replied in a calm, clear voice, "Nothing to report, Sir. Still no sign of our missing men."

Colin's eyes darted to the tree line, hearing another branch crack, this one louder. A cool sweat formed on the back of his neck and every nerve in his body pricked with anticipation. Something was wrong.

"Wake the men," he ordered.

Before the corporal had time to respond, a high-pitched whistle sounded above, ending with a thud in the corporal's chest. Colin had no time to grab the man as he fell to the ground, an arrow sunk deeply between his ribs.

"We're under attack!" he yelled.

Bren and Briggs were the first to arrive. Within seconds, the rest of the Guard was on their feet, out of their tents, forming a defensive line. There was no time to ask questions—arrows flew in by the dozens.

"They're in the trees!" Colin bellowed, pointing to the spot where they should concentrate their attack.

Several of the Guard took shelter under their shields while holding the line as the strike intensified. Colin turned to Corporal Nurburg and barked an order. "Cover Lady Vaelora's tent!"

The Guard began advancing closer to the tree line, swords drawn. Colin was tired of this game of hide and seek.

"Light the trees—burn them out!" he ordered.

Before his men could comply, the attackers, apparently hearing his order and not wanting to burn to death, emerged at once from the woods.

Chaos ensued.

Each soldier found himself in hand-to-hand combat with one of the intruders. Colin immediately recognized at least one of them—the talkative traveler from the road. He had apparently brought friends.

Colin fought his way toward the man, cutting down the enemy one by one. Finally reaching him, he grabbed him by the throat and held a dagger against it until blood trickled down the man's chest. The captive surprised Colin by laughing loudly at his impending demise.

"Go ahead. Kill me. We can't be stopped. She must die, and we will ensure that happens."

Colin had no time for this. He threw the man to the ground, then took his sword and drove it through the man's shoulder and into the ground. A blood-curdling scream ripped through the camp.

"What? No more laughing?" Colin mocked as he went on to his next victim.

Next on the agenda was a tall figure in a black cloak loitering near the tree line. Colin hadn't seen him attack anyone with a weapon yet—just stand and observe. This unnerved him, so he quickly moved to where the man stood and lunged to grab him.

Before he could make contact, he was hit by something akin to lightning, which caused his whole body to seize.

He dropped to the ground and shook uncontrollably. Through the haze of his pain, he could see the cloaked man standing over him, extending his arms. Bright sparks of light flew from him to Colin.

Magic. The man was a wizard.

Colin's pain intensified with every heartbeat, and it took everything he had to continue breathing. Just as he was about to lose consciousness, the pain was gone.

He opened his eyes slowly to see Bren next to him, pulling his sword from the gut of the wizard and cleaning the blood off with the wizard's cloak.

"You alright?" he asked while extending a hand to Colin.

Colin took the hand gratefully, standing up and collecting his sword. "I owe you one," he said as he moved to another target.

His men were still engaged in battle and were holding their own. Colin quickly dispatched a small man wielding a sword several inches longer than the man was tall. He did a quick scan of the area and noticed another cloaked figure on the opposite side of the camp—but this one wasn't idly observing the fray. He was moving toward the ladies' tent.

Colin began running toward the tent, dodging sword strikes.

"Nurburg!" he yelled.

Nurburg stood at his post, sword at the ready, eyes scanning. Upon hearing his captain's hail, he turned to see him running in his direction and knew there was a problem, but his view was blocked by a patch of trees obscuring the cloaked figure advancing toward him.

"Stay down, ladies!" he bellowed through the tent walls, crouching in anticipation.

Colin pushed his way through soldiers and enemies alike, quickly realizing he wouldn't make it in time to intercept the wizard.

"Guard! Nurburg!" he bellowed.

The highly trained team all turned toward Nurburg. Those nearest him attempted to disengage from whatever skirmish they were involved in, while those furthest away worked to occupy the assailants to prevent them from following.

The intruders quickly realized what was happening and moved to stop the Guard from making it to their objective, grabbing limbs and slashing mercilessly at anything they could reach. Colin continued advancing, pushing and hacking with his sword.

As the wizard emerged from behind the patch of trees, Colin could see Nurburg's posture change—ready to fight. Sergeants Downey and Archer managed to gain their freedom from the struggle, but it was too late.

Colin watched in horror as the wizard raised his arms and shot bright lightning at Nurburg.

Nurburg immediately fell, his body shaking violently. Almost in slow motion, Colin could see the life draining from him. Sergeants Downey and Archer readied their swords to strike the wizard down, but this one was quicker than the last.

In one swift movement, the men were down, overcome by the same magic that was taking Nurburg. Colin was still too far away, being held back on every step by the assailants. In mere moments, all three men were dead.

Colin could hear the primal scream of a man on the edge from the middle of the battle.

Briggs.

Colin watched in horror as the tent flap opened, revealing Hatti. She stood rod-straight, staring down the approaching assassin.

"NO!" Colin yelled.

Hatti didn't budge. The wizard adopted an arrogant sneer as he approached—but he had underestimated his quarry. Hatti calmly raised her hands, and the darkened camp was suddenly filled with light. The wizard's advance immediately stopped—his body frozen.

It only took a moment for the Guard to understand what they were seeing.

Briggs wasted no time. Pushing his way through the crowd, throwing bodies left and right, he made his way to the captive wizard. In one swift movement, his sword sank deep into the wizard's chest.

The kill emboldened the rest of the guard, who raged against their attackers, slicing them down one by one.

The end of the battle did not come soon enough, however. As Hatti lowered her arms, a single arrow, fired from within the tree line, found its mark. It plunged deep into her chest, and she fell backward into the tent.

The sounds of battle were broken by Elaris's heart-wrenching scream.

CHAPTER 5

Lord Draegor Mordane, thirty-fourth ruler of Ashcar, stood just out of sight in the darkness, watching. The child in front of him played happily with his toys on the floor. The boy was intelligent, he could tell. He solved puzzles quickly and had started talking much faster than the others. He felt no love for him, of course—perhaps a slight glimmer of pride, but that wasn't enough to spare the boy.

The child's caregiver sat quietly in the corner, stitching away at some article of clothing. In normal households, a child might have his mother nearby, but not here. Draegor couldn't even remember her name. She had served her purpose and was dismissed. He gave her the same consideration a bull might give a cow he had impregnated.

He stepped forward out of the darkness, startling the woman. "My lord!" she squeaked.

"How is my son today?" His tone was warm, but the expression behind it was hollow.

"He is well, my lord. He started his classes today, and his teachers say he has great potential!"

Potential. Draegor sighed at the word.

"He looks small."

The woman visibly puffed up and, barely containing a disgruntled tone, replied, "No, my lord! He is just the perfect size. Why, my son was smaller than he, and he—"

"Yes, yes, I'm sure your son was the model of perfection," Draegor interrupted brusquely with a roll of his eyes.

The woman quickly quieted.

Draegor continued to analyze his offspring. The boy looked up to him and smiled. Draegor noticed one of his teeth was crooked. That would have to be fixed.

"Make sure the royal physician corrects his mouth."

The caregiver once again took a defensive posture and replied, "He has baby teeth, my lord. They will fall out soon, and he will get his adult teeth."

Draegor grumbled something unintelligible. Taking one last look at the boy, he turned on his heel and left the room. He had to admit this one was better. Finding the right breeding stock to give him an acceptable son had become exceedingly difficult. The last child born was not what he would consider exceptional. No potential there. The mother had made an incredible fuss when the boy was killed.

Walking down the hall, he reflected on his impending wedding. The thought made him genuinely smile, something he didn't often do. The time was almost here. He could feel the excitement coursing through him. One month away.

He had been reluctant to delay their union by ordering the Guard to escort her on the long route, but it was necessary. Ultimately, he knew the anticipation would only make their joining more fulfilling.

Rounding a corner at the end of the hall, a pretty young maid stopped abruptly in front of him, coming very close to running into him. "My lord!" she gulped, eyes as big as saucers.

Draegor could smell the fear on her. Reaching out a hand, he stroked her hair slowly downward until he came to her neck. Placing his palm on the side of it, he squeezed gently. "What a pretty thing you are," he drawled.

The girl couldn't find the breath to talk. Draegor assumed that he probably had a bit of a reputation with the staff, and she might have heard of his tastes.

"Why have I never seen you before?" he asked, squeezing her neck harder.

The maid trembled in fear and whispered, "I just started this week, my lord."

"Well, I certainly hope you are enjoying your position."

"Yes, my lord—very much so," she whimpered.

Draegor breathed deeply, drinking in the heightened tension in the air. "I believe my room is in need of cleaning, my dear."

The girl's eyes were unblinking, terrified and fixed on his face. Draegor moved his hand to her lower back and pressed firmly to guide her down the hall toward his chambers. Her feet moved reluctantly, dragging with every step. He could feel trembles moving down her back like ripples in a pond. It only increased his excitement.

As they drew closer to his goal, one of his guards pulled the door open. They were just about to cross the threshold when Kaz emerged from the shadows and his shrill voice stopped them. "My lord!"

Draegor sighed but did not turn. He kept his hand at the maid's back. "This had better be good."

"My lord, I have important news. We must speak."

Reluctantly removing his hand from the girl, Draegor took her chin in his palm, saying, "Another time, my dear." The maid did not wait to be dismissed and hurried down the hall, barely resisting the urge to run.

Walking into his room, Draegor poured himself a glass of wine and sat down in his most comfortable chair. "Out with it!" he barked.

Kaz, undaunted by his master's tone, didn't waste any time on pleasantries.

"She's dead, my lord."

Draegor shot out of his chair, spilling his drink across the floor. "Who is dead?" he demanded.

"The companion, my lord, as well as several members of the Guard."

Unamused, Draegor grabbed his sorcerer by the throat and squeezed tightly. "Are you *sure?*"

Kaz, with barely enough breath to speak, managed to squeak out, "Absolutely."

Kaz's neck was slowly released.

"How?"

"I'm unsure, my lord. I felt the woman's magic die away and sensed my tracking spell departing from the others."

Draegor turned and walked toward the fireplace. He stared at the flames, contemplating this new development. "This complicates matters."

"Indeed, my lord."

"Captain Aedric will have a new challenge on his hands."

Kaz knew his master didn't require a response.

"Let me know of any further developments."

Slinking away without a sound, the sorcerer left his room. Draegor's thoughts turned to Elaris.

She was about to awaken.

Elaris's scream rang through the camp. Colin pushed his way past the final obstacle and ripped open the tent to find Hatti lying dead on the floor and a very distraught Elaris kneeling next to her, her veil cast aside. He stood motionless—unable to breathe. Elaris looked up slowly, tears streaming from bright violet eyes. He had never seen anything like them.

"She's gone," Elaris sobbed, covering her face with her hands, her shoulders shaking in despair.

Colin dropped down next to her and, without thinking, folded her into his arms. She stiffened at first but quickly succumbed to his comfort. Her sobbing increased, her lungs fighting for air.

"My lady, breathe," Colin soothed.

She continued clinging to him, crying all the harder. Realizing the situation was only getting worse, Colin took her by the shoulders and held her at arm's length.

"My lady... *Elaris*," he pleaded.

Upon hearing her name, Elaris stopped crying and stared into his eyes. "You said my name," she said, wiping at her eyes.

"I apologize," Colin murmured. "I felt the situation called for it."

Elaris continued to collect herself but said nothing more.

"I need to go check on the situation outside. Will you be alright?" he asked gently.

She gave a barely noticeable nod of her head and turned back to Hatti. Colin regretted having to leave her, but comforting her would have to wait.

Stepping out of the tent, he was greeted by Bren. "We've finished most of them off. Some ran—cowards! And we have a prisoner," he growled.

Dawn had broken, and light had begun to spread across the campsite. Dozens of bodies littered the ground. All were still—except one, who moaned loudly.

Colin, followed by Bren, made their way to the man.

"Ah, if it isn't our friend from the road! I see you have yet to escape my sword. Let me help you with that!" Colin taunted, slowly removing the blade from the man's shoulder.

"You bastard!" the prisoner cried.

"What was that?" Colin asked, holding his hand to his ear.

Without hesitation, he drove his sword into the man's other shoulder. "Did you have something to say?" Colin asked calmly.

His prisoner's scream echoed across the camp, drawing the attention of the remaining Guard, who had started to gather.

Not receiving an answer to his question, Colin turned the blade slowly and deliberately. The man sobbed in agony.

"Where are my men?" Colin growled.

"I don't know," he cried.

Colin continued to twist the blade, pressing on it each time. "Where are my men?" he asked again.

By this time, the Guard had formed a circle around the prisoner, undisturbed by the torture he was enduring. Looking up at them, he screamed, "They're dead! All dead! We threw their bodies in the river!"

Colin stopped and looked down at him, hatred in his eyes. "Who are you? Who were they?" Colin asked, pointing to the dead.

"I am no one! They are no one! Most were hired mercenaries!"

"Hired by who?" he shouted.

The man struggled for freedom under the blade.

"The wizard Claudius!" he moaned.

"Why are you after Lady Vaelora?"

The man's face darkened. "She will end us all. She must die!"

"Explain!" Colin ordered.

"I will tell you no more—now release me!" the man begged.

Colin's eyes went cold and dark as he stood. Looking down at the man, he said calmly, "I believe you."

Turning to Bren, he ordered, "Release him."

A moment later, Bren sliced the man's neck from ear to ear.

Hours later, Colin stood quietly, surveying the aftermath of the battle. Far outside the edge of the camp, a pile of twenty-eight attackers burned, the two travelers among them. On the opposite side of the camp, laid out on funeral pyres constructed by the Guard, rested Corporal Whyte, Sergeant Downey, Sergeant Archer, Corporal Nurburg, and Hatti.

Briggs stood at the pyre of Corporal Nurburg, his hand resting on the man's chest. They would have a funeral at nightfall and take the time to honor their dead, including Sergeants Grayston, Whilthouse, and Pike, who would never return.

Eight gone.

Colin felt their loss deeply, struggling for the words he must say in their memory.

"How is Lady Vaelora?" Bren asked, returning from overseeing the packing of their gear. They would not be staying here tonight.

Colin considered telling him what he'd seen in the tent but believed the lady had the right to her secrets. He would not break her confidence.

"She seems to be holding it together, considering. She did ask who attacked us and why. I had no answers for her, but I swear I will."

"What's the plan? I have a feeling those that got away will be returning."

Bren was right, of course. Colin couldn't chance another encounter like they just survived.

"We will be changing our route."

"We were ordered not to take the direct route," Bren cautioned.

Colin looked at him with annoyance. "I don't intend to take us over the mountain. I mean to take us through Vale Forest."

This news made Bren's brows arch in surprise. "I thought the idea was to stay out of sight."

"They won't be looking for us there. It would never occur to them—that we would take her so close to civilization."

Bren nodded in agreement. "It's a good plan. Hell, it's even faster, if we don't linger."

"That's my hope," Colin sighed. Looking toward Elaris's tent, he wondered how she would handle the journey without her companion. Colin had taken personal responsibility for recovering Hatti's body and placing it on the pyre, opting to give Elaris as much privacy as she needed in the safety of her tent.

The sun was nearing the horizon, the smoke from the fire making the sunset's usual brilliance hazy.

"It's time," Bren said soberly, touching his friend's shoulder.

Colin straightened his uniform and made his way to Elaris's tent. Standing outside, he called, "Lady Vaelora, I am here to escort you."

Elaris emerged from the tent, head bent but veil secured, holding a small bouquet of flowers in her hand—the ones Colin had brought to her for Hatti. She made her way slowly to the funeral pyres, Colin following at a respectful distance. Once there, she laid her flowers on Hatti's body, stopping to touch her cloaked hand. Colin took his place in front of his thirteen remaining soldiers as Elaris stepped back, nodding to him in silent readiness.

Clearing his throat, Colin began. "Whyte. Downey. Archer. Pike. Whilthouse. Grayston. Nurburg. Hatti."

Colin paused for a moment—his voice rough. "Each stood their ground. Each did what they were trained to do—what they swore to do. We don't get to decide when or how the call comes. We choose how we answer it—they answered with everything they had."

Pausing, Colin took the time to look into the eyes of each of his men. "Their watch is over. Ours continues. We burn our fallen—we carry their fire."

With that, he took a torch from Bren and lit each of the pyres, one by one.

A time of deafening silence followed as each of them stood and watched the flames engulf the pyres.

Elaris stood alone, unable to seek comfort from anyone there. She cried quietly under the privacy of her veil, tears blurring her vision. Despair gripped her, and she felt her heart tighten.

Warmth rushed through her body, and streams of colors invaded her mind and sight.

In a panic, she looked toward the captain—but he was surrounded by rivers of gold, each one moving away from him in dozens of directions.

Not understanding what she was seeing, she closed her eyes and held them tightly shut, but the currents were there—in her mind.

Soon, other rivers and streams of red, blue, and green joined the gold, all coming from those around the captain.

The harder she tried to block the visions out, the more intense they became. She was seeing each of the soldiers, the captain included, in multiple places and times—an old man—a child—bodies lying in a heap.

As she grew more agitated, the images became more numerous and intense. She grabbed her head and collapsed to the ground as darkness took her.

CHAPTER 6

Colin ran toward Elaris as her body hit the ground. The men all circled her. Coming so soon after the ambush, most were on high alert, scanning the area for whatever enemy had attacked her. Colin knelt next to her and pulled her head into his lap. "My lady... my lady!" he pleaded as he gently shook her.

Elaris moaned softly and came to. "What... what happened?" she groaned.

"I believe you fainted."

Elaris sat up slowly, instantly embarrassed by the sight of the Guard surrounding her, all looking concerned. "I believe I'm alright now," she said.

Colin helped her to her feet and escorted her back to her tent. "We shall be leaving in a few hours. You have had a very strenuous day. Rest now, my lady. I will come get you when it's time."

Elaris walked carefully into her tent and lay down on her cot.

Her head was throbbing. She reflected on what she last remembered before she fainted. Water? Flowing water.

People. The soldiers. All different but the same. An image of Colin stood out, but it made no sense. He was older, gray— eyes clouded, enfolded in golden currents. She saw one of the sergeants as well, but younger—the water surrounding him had been blue.

As the visions came back to her, so did the pain in her head. She closed her eyes and breathed deeply, focusing on memories from her childhood. She thought of Hatti's smiling face and her laugh—the times when she would be scolded for breaking some rule but would see Hatti's frown crack into a grin when she didn't know she was looking.

Hatti... she would never see her again. The rest of this journey would be without her guidance or friendship. She had prepared all her life for this. Dozens of teachers, years of study—all to learn Lord Mordane's likes and dislikes, his hobbies, the history of Ashcar, her responsibilities as queen.

Her destiny.

Destiny. She had heard the word thousands of times. One of her earliest memories was of a monk telling her of her destiny. He explained how Lord Mordane had chosen her at birth, had arranged for her to live and study at the monastery in preparation for their union. She was told how fortunate she was to be chosen. She didn't feel very fortunate now.

She had asked once about her mother. Hatti explained that she had died in childbirth. Elaris had no memory of her, but knowledge of her death had always made her sad. Growing up, she often imagined what life with her mother would have been like. Would she have lived in a real home? Would she have had brothers and sisters to play with? She sometimes imagined her mother's face as Hatti's. The thought made her eyes well up with tears.

Rolling to her side and gathering her knees to her chest, Elaris tried to sleep. She had never had a night without Hatti visiting her and giving a blessing. She felt empty and alone. Darkness eventually overtook her, leading to nightmares of suffering and death. In the middle of all of it—*her groom*.

Colin marched from Elaris's tent with purpose. Now that the dead had been honored, it was time to get some answers. Approaching the campfire, he spotted just the man for the job.

"Briggs!"

Sergeant Briggs ran up to his side. "Sir?"

"I have a job for you."

Briggs stood tall, ready to receive his orders.

"This attack was planned and organized. I want to know by whom and why."

"Yes, Sir!" Briggs said, his voice full of enthusiasm.

"I want you to do some investigating. Visit the local villages. Ask about this 'wizard Claudius.' Find out why he is targeting Lady Vaelora."

"Happy to, Captain."

"You'll need to disguise yourself. No one is likely to talk to you as a Royal Guard. We plan to camp outside of Oakhaven in three days' time. Meet us there."

"Yes, Sir!"

Briggs jogged off to grab his pack and horse and quickly left. Colin had no doubts the man would succeed in his mission. He only hoped he found the information they needed quickly.

Bren walked up to his side and asked sarcastically, "Briggs deserting?"

Colin smirked. "I sent him to get some answers."

"Best man for the job."

"I thought so."

The two men watched as Briggs disappeared over the horizon, the last vestiges of light capturing his departure. Colin wanted to get out of there. The place reeked of death, and the dangers of another attack were all too real. "Are we almost ready?" he asked.

"Almost. We need to finish taking down the last of the tents and load the cart with the rest of the gear."

"The sooner, the better."

"Understood."

Bren hesitated, and Colin could tell his friend had something to say. "What's on your mind, Bren?"

"Lady Vaelora. She has brought unexpected complexity to this mission."

Colin understood where his friend was coming from, and he doubted he was the only one with misgivings. "Let's not forget that she *is* the mission."

"Understood. But I don't think any of us were expecting this level of... excitement."

"Agreed."

"And what happened to her earlier?"

"I believe she fainted. She was probably overwhelmed with losing her companion."

Bren seemed to accept that explanation.

"Let's hope the rest of the journey is uneventful," Bren said lightly.

Somehow, Colin feared it wouldn't be.

Elaris woke to the sound of the soldiers preparing the camp for departure. She quickly got out of her cot and donned her veil. Exiting the tent, she noticed one of the soldiers standing by, ready to take it down and pack up her bedding. "Thank you," she said quietly.

The captain waited for her at the road by her horse. Darkness had completely fallen, and the only light was from the moon, which showed itself only when the clouds parted. "It's so dark—is it safe to travel?" Elaris inquired as she took Colin's offered hand and mounted.

"It isn't preferred, but we should be fine. It's important we make it to the next stop by sunrise."

Elaris frowned. She imagined there were plenty of creatures that she didn't want to meet roaming at this time.

"If you're sure, Captain."

Colin chuckled, "We shall be fine, my lady."

The company set off, traveling more briskly than they had the day before.

She rode encircled by guards on each side. The men were tense and watchful, no conversation happening except the occasional order from the captain.

With every step, Elaris felt further and further away from home.

Pyete may not have been warm or cozy like she imagined a real home would be, but it was the one she had been given.

In it, she had made some happy memories.

About two hours later, the captain ordered them to stop so they could attend to nature's call. As Colin took her hand to help her down, Elaris was again consumed by visions of golden rivers enfolding him. She saw dozens of currents in the many rivers, all distinctive, each flowing in a different direction. She focused on the most prominent one and followed it.

She could see the captain. He was standing in a cornfield, sickle in hand. There was a small cottage on a hill behind him. Children played just outside.

The vision became so intense that Elaris shut her eyes and tried to slow her breathing. "My lady? Are you unwell?" Colin asked, concerned.

The vision suddenly stopped, and Elaris realized that she had yet to get down from her horse. She had been sitting, frozen, holding his hand.

"Yes, Captain," she stammered.

Dismounting, she took a step back from him and released him. Colin looked concerned and lowered his voice so no one else could overhear.

"Lady Vaelora, I regret we couldn't give you more time to rest."

"I am alright, Captain. I just need to walk a bit."

"Certainly," he murmured. "You should be safe to get a bit of exercise, just stay within sight of the Guard."

Elaris could see the captain watching her as she walked around a grassy area near the road. She considered telling him what she had seen but thought better of it. Visions? It was just the thing to make people think she had gone mad.

No, she was just tired and stressed. She was sure they would pass.

When the time came to resume their journey, Elaris approached her horse again but decided against physical contact with the captain, just in case. "Thank you, Captain. I believe I can manage on my own," she said as she mounted.

She thought he looked disappointed as he walked away.

The rest of the journey was uneventful aside from some wildlife sightings and Sergeant Keswick's horse being spooked by a snake in the road, causing it to bolt suddenly.

Elaris allowed herself to giggle a little at the poor sergeant, who was teased mercilessly by his comrades for his inability to control his animal.

Just before sunrise, they reached their next camp at Hilbrow Grove. Elaris was exhausted and sore from riding all night. The men got to work immediately, preparing food and setting up the sleeping accommodations.

Elaris took a seat by the fire and watched all the activity. Lieutenant Holt came over to offer her some stew, and she gratefully accepted.

"Thank you, Lieutenant," she sighed.

Bren smiled at her. "Your tent should be ready shortly, my lady."

Elaris looked up from her bowl, about to thank him, when streams of blue invaded her sight. She groaned and rubbed at her eyes through her veil.

Concerned, Bren came closer to her. "My lady?"

Elaris held up a hand. She tried to make the images go away, but the closer he came, the more intense they got. Blue rivers, flowing off left, right, up, and down.

She focused on one to his left and was immediately pulled into the current. It led to the lieutenant, but he was younger. Much younger. He stood over the body of his mother, crying. She was clearly dead, the mark of plague on her forehead.

"Lady Vaelora?" Bren asked again, this time more urgently.

Elaris focused on returning, breathing deeply and slowly until she could see just the lieutenant with no rivers or currents. Taking another breath, she held up her hand again.

"Just a bit of a headache, Lieutenant. Nothing to worry about."

Bren seemed unsure but began to move away slowly.

"Lieutenant?" she called.

"Yes, my lady?"

"Do you get to see your mother often?"

Bren thought this an unusual question but answered, "Not often, my lady. I do plan to visit her next month, however, for her birthday."

Elaris took a moment to respond, deep in her thoughts. "I'm sure she will love that."

Bren waited a few moments before determining that she was done speaking with him and walked away.

CHAPTER 7

Sergeant Briggs arrived in Glendale shortly after noon. It was the first village he came upon after taking the road the group had watched the two travelers take to the east of Lake Road. There was a good chance someone here had seen them.

Walking into the nearest inn, Briggs sat in a chair closest to the innkeeper—a bald, greasy, short man who looked like he badly needed a bath.

"What can I get ya?" the man croaked, wiping down a table.

The rancid smell rolling off the man nearly made Briggs gag. He decided breathing through his nose was no longer wise.

He coughed. "A pint and a room."

The innkeeper came back shortly with his order and a key to his "best" room—something Briggs seriously doubted.

As the man placed his drink on the table, Briggs leaned forward and asked, "I'm looking for a friend of mine. Short. Dark hair. Carries a bow. Often has his friend with him—

taller, with blond hair and pox scars. They may have come through here two days ago."

The innkeeper's eyes narrowed suspiciously. "What's his name, this friend of yours?"

Briggs pulled out his coin purse and dropped a few silvers on the table.

The innkeeper paused, licking his lips at the sight of the money.

Seeming to think better of it, he turned and walked away, grumbling, "Don't know anyone like that. I'd say you should move on. You won't find them in Glendale, no."

So that's how it was going to be.

But Briggs wasn't one to be deterred so easily—he wasn't leaving Glendale without answers.

After paying for his drink and room, he headed back out onto the street. Across the way, he spotted just what he was looking for—the local market.

Walking in casually, Briggs took his time perusing wares. The market bustled with people shopping and talking—many of them clearly locals. He carefully listened to their conversations, waiting for the right moment.

"My Phillip took down a ten-point buck yesterday," an older woman bragged to her friend.

The friend's eyes widened in approval. "Wonderful! You will be feasting this winter!"

The older woman smiled but leaned in as if to whisper, though her voice stayed just as loud. "Bri said *her* husband got himself a fourteen-pointer—but I don't believe her!" she hissed.

Briggs saw his opportunity and took it. "Fourteen points! Well, that *is* hard to believe!" he said with a grin.

Both ladies stopped and looked up at the giant man, stunned into silence. Briggs flashed them both his most devastating smile and continued, "I don't know many bowmen who could manage such a feat."

They both blushed under his intense gaze, the older woman stammering, "Do you do much hunting, Sir?"

"Me? Oh, a little, when the need arises. I've actually been looking for a hunter I met on the road—thought he might be able to teach me a thing or two. He was headed this way. Perhaps you've seen him?" he asked silkily, leaning in and intensifying his gaze.

The friend fanned herself, visibly gulping, unable to take her eyes off him. "Who is he?" she breathed.

Briggs got in closer, making his answer more intimate. "Now, I have forgotten his name! He was a short man with dark hair, about to his shoulders. He had a friend with him— blond, with pox scars."

"Oh! That's Mr. Taylor and Mr. Quinn!" The older woman sang proudly. "Mr. Taylor owns a farm with his wife on the north side of town. It's the first one you come to. Mr. Quinn recently moved to Glendale and has been lodging at the inn. He has no family, poor fellow."

Briggs smiled warmly at her, took her hand, and kissed it, all while keeping his most intense eye contact.

The friend let out a huff, barely concealing her jealousy.

Briggs bowed dramatically as he took his leave. "Ladies, you are a godsend. If only you weren't married!" he winked.

Both women giggled and blushed furiously as he turned to leave. It had been even easier than he expected.

As Mr. Quinn had conveniently died without a family, Briggs focused his efforts on Mr. Taylor, turning north and heading down the first road he came to.

It didn't take long before he happened upon the farm the women spoke of—a nice little house situated on a hill, surrounded by green fields.

He decided to do some reconnaissance before approaching, stepping back into a wooded area across the way. Several minutes later, the door to the house opened and a woman stepped out holding a bundled infant.

She walked out a few feet and scanned the horizon, her free hand shading her eyes from the sun. Apparently not finding what she was looking for, she hesitantly turned and went back into the house, closing the door.

Briggs had a suspicion he knew what she was searching for, and he wasn't coming home.

Stepping out of the woods, he made his way to the home. She answered after one knock, ripping the door open excitedly.

Seeing Briggs, her face fell.

"Can I help you?" she asked, a mix of annoyance and disappointment in her voice.

"Good afternoon, Ma'am. I was looking for Mr. Taylor," he said, bowing to her.

"What business have you with my husband?" she asked suspiciously, casting glances behind him.

"I met him on the road two days ago," Briggs began.

Her eyes lit up. "You saw John? Where? Was he alright?"

Briggs decided telling her that her husband had lost his head to the lieutenant—probably wasn't the best strategy.

"He was on the Lake Road, Ma'am. He and his friend—a Mr. Quinn, I believe—were traveling south."

Mrs. Taylor's face darkened. "South? Was it just the two of them?"

Briggs found this question curious. "Now that you mention it, there may have been a few more in their party."

The baby started crying, so Mrs. Taylor stepped back from the doorway to get him. She was quiet, rocking the baby in her arms. Briggs could see she was deep in thought, and those thoughts weren't good.

Without asking for an invitation, he stepped into the home, leaving the door open so he wouldn't startle her.

After a few minutes, she put the now-sleeping infant back in his cradle and turned to Briggs. "Why are you here? What did you need from John?" she asked soberly.

"I have a bit of a problem, Ma'am. A bit of a magical problem. Your husband said he knew of a wizard that may be able to help me."

Mrs. Taylor's face turned instantly red as she screamed, "Do not speak to me of that wizard! Because of him, my husband is likely dead!"

Sobbing, she fell to the floor.

Briggs bent down and, grasping her arms, pulled her back up.

"Mrs. Taylor! Calm yourself. I'm sure your husband is alive and well!" he lied.

Her crying slowed slightly, and she sobbed, "I told him not to go! I begged him not to go with them!"

"With whom?" Briggs gently shook her.

"The wizard's men. Some of them are hired killers!"

Briggs decided to change tactics. "Mrs. Taylor. I can help you. I can help you find John. But you need to tell me about this wizard and these men."

Her crying stopped and she looked at Briggs with suspicion. "I don't even know you."

"All you need to know is I can bring John home." Briggs felt a little guilty lying to the woman, but it had to be done.

She wiped the tears from her eyes and pulled away from him. After a long pause, she began, "John met him a year ago. He was traveling through Glendale, looking for information on a woman. He was convinced she lived in the area but couldn't find her."

Pausing, she took a seat at the kitchen table and signaled for Briggs to do the same.

"He searched for months to no avail. He began gathering men to search in other towns, telling them that she would bring an end to us all, that she had to be destroyed. Ridiculous, of course, but some believed him. John has always been too trusting of people. He and his friend Mr. Quinn became believers in this madness. They recruited even more followers. Soon, half the town was doing the wizard's bidding."

"Is that where he has gone? To do the wizard's bidding?" Briggs cautiously asked.

Nodding, she answered, "Word came that the girl had been found at a monastery in Pyete. One of the men reported he had seen her through the gate when he rode by."

"How did they know it was her?"

Mrs. Taylor smirked. "Apparently, she has violet eyes. Have you ever heard anything so absurd?" she laughed bitterly.

Briggs now understood why Lady Vaelora was always hiding behind that veil. She had evidently failed to wear it when it mattered most.

Starting to cry again, Mrs. Taylor continued, "They went to kill her. Some poor, innocent girl! The wizard said she would be heading south soon, so they have been scouting, waiting for the right moment. The fools left days ago. Most haven't returned—and those that have aren't saying anything."

Briggs gave her a moment to collect herself again before asking, "The men that returned—who are they?"

"I only know two of them—the rest weren't from here."

"Names?" he asked impatiently.

"Mr. Drake, the blacksmith, and Mr. Baker, the innkeeper."

Briggs was going to *enjoy* his next discussion with Mr. Baker.

"The wizard. You said he traveled here?"

Nodding, she answered, "Yes. He came from the south. A town north of the palace."

Briggs grew irritated but maintained his calm voice. "What town?"

"I'm unsure. John never told me."

"Is the wizard still here?"

"No," she replied. "He left with the men and never returned."

Briggs felt he had all the useful information he was going to get out of the woman. Standing, he made his way to the door, saying over his shoulder, "I'm sure John will be home soon, Ma'am." He stepped out and closed the door quietly behind him.

Making his way back to town, he went in search of the smithy. He found him easily, just down the road from the market. Briggs approached the man, who was standing outside polishing a sword.

"Good afternoon," he greeted.

The smithy grunted a reply but didn't look up from his work.

"I'm in need of your talents. Have a horse that threw a shoe."

Looking up at him, the man grumbled, "Busy today. Will have to be tomorrow."

"That's fine," Briggs said casually. "I didn't think I was going to make it back from Lake Rehl, limping as he was."

The smithy stood and gave him his full attention. "Lake Rehl?" he inquired cautiously.

"Yes. I believe you were there too. Got some nice shots off, if I remember correctly."

The man narrowed his eyes at Briggs. "I don't remember seeing you there."

Briggs laughed. "Oh, you wouldn't have. My mother always said the only thing I show up for on time is breakfast!"

This caused the smithy to chuckle.

"Did anyone else make it back? I've been looking for a few friends of mine," Briggs asked lightly.

The smithy's face grew angry, and he growled, "The only ones I know of are myself and the innkeeper! Those guards killed most of us!"

Briggs adopted a serious face. "Well, they are trained killers."

The man scoffed. "I got one of 'em! In fact, I got the first kill!"

Briggs's blood boiled but he maintained his calm. "Really?"

"Dropped him like a deer at thirty paces."

Briggs resisted the urge to snap the man's neck. He wanted to know more. "The wizard. Have you seen him?"

The smithy barked with laughter. "He ran away when the witch came out. Probably went home—wherever that is. Wish I knew where he was. He owes me money."

Briggs nodded. "Good to know. I'll be seeing you," he said as he turned to leave.

"Hey, what about your horse?" he yelled.

"Oh, I'll be back," Briggs growled.

Minutes later, Briggs entered the inn. The place had filled up with several dozen people, all drinking, laughing, and enjoying their evening.

He took a seat in the corner of the room and waited.

He could see the innkeeper at the bar serving customers. The man caught his eye and looked nervous. Slowly walking to his table, he kept his head down and asked for Briggs's order.

"I'll have a pint and some mutton stew."

The innkeeper returned shortly with his food and ale. He turned to leave, but Briggs grabbed his arm tightly.

"The wizard. Where is he?" he snarled.

The smelly man let out a whimper as his arm was squeezed tighter. Looking desperately at the people around him, he found no help—everyone too busy enjoying their revelry.

"The wizard!" Briggs snapped, twisting the arm hard.

"He left! I have no idea where he is!" he whimpered.

"Where did he come from?"

Briggs's grip increased with every syllable.

"I don't know! He never told us! Just somewhere south of here!" he cried.

Briggs released his arm, flinging it away. Mr. Baker stood where he was, as if asking for permission to leave.

Briggs glared at him and barked, "Go away."

The man scurried off without another word.

Briggs finished his stew and ale and left to go to his room. It wasn't the worst place he had slept, but he swore the pillows had the same sour stench as the innkeeper. The smell alone made him hate the man more.

Throwing the pillows to the floor, Briggs crawled onto the bed to get some rest. A few hours of sleep should be enough. He never got more than five hours anyway.

Around two in the morning, he woke up to a silent inn. The last of the patrons had left, probably passed out in their rooms.

He grabbed his gear and made his way quietly down the stairs. Earlier, he had noticed that there was a door to private living quarters on the main floor. He guessed that's where the innkeeper would be sleeping.

Quietly opening the door, he heard snoring. Creeping up to the bed, he pulled his knife and held the tip to the man's chest while covering his mouth.

"Don't move!" he hissed.

A whimper came from his captive.

"Tell me. How many soldiers did you kill?" Briggs growled.

The man shook his head violently, trying desperately to speak through Briggs's hand.

"Tell me!" Briggs demanded, pressing his blade harder into his chest.

The innkeeper's head flew back and forth, with an unmistakable "none" being yelled into the hand.

"Are you telling me you killed no one?"

Mr. Baker nodded urgently.

"You are not going to call out. Do I make myself clear?" he ordered.

The man nodded again—eyes desperate.

Briggs slowly released his mouth but moved the blade to his throat.

"I didn't kill any of them!" the innkeeper pleaded. "I only went along for the money—and I didn't even get paid!"

Briggs took a close look at the pathetic wretch. He believed him. He doubted the man even knew how to shoot a bow, and he was certainly no swordsman.

"If I were you, I would be more careful of the company you keep, Mr. Baker. You don't want me coming to see you again."

The innkeeper sighed in relief as the blade was removed from his throat. Briggs stood up to leave. Mr. Baker would be spared today. Briggs had other things to attend to.

Before closing the door on a wide-eyed innkeeper, he turned to him and ordered, "And take a damn bath!"

It only took him a few minutes to make his way to the blacksmith. Mr. Drake was fast asleep in his room up the stairs from the store. Briggs had considered many different methods for dealing with him but had decided on the tried and true.

In one swift movement, he drew his sword and had it at the ready.

70

He whistled softly until the smithy woke up, sitting up in shock and confusion at what he was seeing.

The man had no time to react.

Briggs simply said, "For Corporal Whyte," before plunging the blade into his chest.

He stood and watched as the man fought for breath, confusion and terror in his eyes. The struggle didn't last long.

Briggs wiped his blade on the man's bedsheets and made his way to his horse. It was time to leave.

CHAPTER 8

Hilbrow Grove was the perfect place to get some rest, Colin thought. Quiet and secluded, it offered plenty of trees for shade and a creek nearby—where he hoped they would be able to catch some fish.

Lady Vaelora had gone to her tent to sleep while the soldiers took shifts, some resting and others guarding or working on provisions. With seven of his men now gone, those who remained needed to fill the gap, including himself.

Colin picked up the axe next to him and lined up with his target. Letting the axe do the work, he brought it down with a clean, practiced arc. The log split easily in two.

Colin bent to pick up his reward and add another log when he heard a whistle. Turning to see who was producing the sound, he saw his friend approaching, a wide grin on his face.

"Look at you!" Bren laughed. "I am in awe at the sight of you!"

Colin looked down at himself, shirtless and covered in dirt and sweat. "Shut up, Bren."

Bren laughed all the harder. "I can't remember the last time I saw you chopping wood. I believe you were a scrawny corporal at the time."

Colin smirked. "I was at least a sergeant, and I was damn good at it!"

"I'm sure you were!" Bren teased.

Colin shook his head in exasperation and asked with annoyance, "Is there a reason you are bothering me, or did you just want an example of real manhood to follow?"

Bren roared with amusement. "I'll have you know I have slain at least three trout this afternoon."

Colin looked unimpressed. "Only three? You should have one of the corporals give you some lessons. One day, you might catch as many as they do."

Bren just grinned but couldn't disagree—the corporals were better at fishing.

Colin pulled his shirt over his head just as Bren's expression turned more serious.

"Lady Vaelora seemed to be unwell earlier."

"I'm not surprised. She's been through a lot."

"Yes," Bren responded quietly.

"Hopefully some rest will help. We could all use some."

As they walked back to the camp, Bren decided to address some concerns.

"Vale Forest," he began.

Colin nodded for him to continue.

"You remember the last time we traveled through there."

He did—and it didn't bring back happy memories.

"We have even fewer men this time, and a woman," Bren said with apprehension in his voice.

"It's still the best option," Colin noted.

"It is," Bren agreed.

Colin stopped walking to focus on Bren. "Suggestions?"

Bren contemplated for a moment. "Perhaps we could send a small detachment ahead?" he asked, sounding uncertain.

Colin hated that idea. Not only did it put those men at risk, but it would also shrink their already reduced company even more. Bren seemed to realize this immediately after suggesting it, shaking his head in frustration. Colin could see his friend's concern and placed a hand on his shoulder.

"We'll figure it out. We always do. I have some ideas—but first, we need to get to Oakhaven. Then we worry about Vale Forest."

Bren nodded in agreement and resumed walking.

"I want to give Lady Vaelora and the men time to rest after the events of the last few days. Let's plan to depart at sunrise," Colin ordered.

"Understood. I'll let the men know."

As Bren walked away, Colin turned to go to the creek and wash up. He would be waking Lady Vaelora a couple of hours before supper, as she had requested earlier. She had seemed distant. Before she went to her tent to get some rest, Colin had tried to talk with her to see if she was alright, but she had dismissed him. Perhaps some sleep and a warm meal would help, he hoped.

Cleaned up and presentable once again, Colin went to Elaris's tent and softly called her name. She apparently had been awake for a while already, because she emerged immediately.

Her head tilted up at him, and Colin wished he could remove that veil and see those magnificent violet eyes again.

74

"My lady—supper should be ready in a couple of hours. There is a creek just inside the trees over there. Let me know if you'd like to freshen up, and I can ensure your security while you're there."

Elaris replied, "Thank you, Captain. I will take you up on the offer. It would be nice to wash the dust off."

Colin guided her to the creek and stepped away to a respectful distance, turning his back. He could hear her boots hitting the ground and then water splashing. Short bursts of laughter occasionally rang out. He wondered what was bringing her such merriment.

"Are you alright, my lady?" he asked cautiously.

Elaris giggled and responded, "Quite alright, Captain. I've never walked in a creek barefoot before—the water is so cold!"

Colin smiled at the idea of her wading around in her bare feet. "Be careful—some of those fish will bite your toes off!" he joked.

Elaris laughed at the ridiculous idea. "I'm sure the fish have better things to eat, good Sir."

Colin couldn't contain a chuckle. He could hear Elaris emerging from the water and putting her boots back on.

"You can turn around now, Captain."

Colin turned to see her standing before him, still wearing that cumbersome black dress, but without the veil. She smiled at him, and Colin was shocked by her beauty. While he had seen her face before during the ambush, he hadn't really had time to process just how exquisite she was. Her eyes shone brightly like gemstones. Her hair, raven black, complemented her porcelain skin.

He was speechless.

"Captain?" Elaris said, sounding concerned.

Colin coughed once, regaining his bearing. "My lady—my apologies. You surprised me."

Elaris shrugged. "You have already seen my face. There is no point in concealing it if it's just the two of us. Besides, I hate it."

Concerned, Colin asked, "Why do you wear it then?"

"It is Lord Mordane's wish. Not for everyone—but for strangers or when I am out in the open."

"Ah," Colin responded simply. This sounded exactly like the type of control *he* would take over someone.

Elaris, seeming to recognize his annoyance, said quietly, "I'm sure he has his reasons."

Colin said nothing. Those reasons were never for anyone's benefit but *his* own.

"I've never met him, of course," she said softly, "but I have always been told he is wise—that he chose me because I am special. I'd like to believe that's true."

That she was special, Colin had no doubt. His jaw clenched at the thought of Lord Mordane possessing her.

"May we stay a bit longer? The sun and the air are so lovely, and I would prefer not to put this thing back on," she asked, as she waved the veil in the air.

"Of course, my lady," Colin bowed.

Elaris went back over to the creek and looked in. She dragged her foot back and forth through the mud, deep in thought. Finally, she spoke.

"You called me Elaris before."

"I did," he murmured.

"I liked it."

Colin could feel his pulse starting to increase. He had to be careful here.

"It would be inappropriate for me to call you by your given name, my lady."

Elaris nodded, seeming to understand, but her shoulders slumped in disappointment.

Colin then made a decision he knew he would probably regret. "At least in front of the men. I could always call you Elaris in private, if you'd prefer."

Elaris smiled up at him brightly, clearly pleased. "That would be wonderful, thank you."

Colin was about to say more but stopped short at the sound of branches cracking nearby. His men were all on strict orders to stay away from the area while Elaris was there, and no one would disobey one of his commands.

Signaling her to move to him quickly, he whispered low but sharp, "Put on your veil," as he took her hand and pulled her through the trees toward the camp. Emerging from the tree line, he yelled, "Guard!" while indicating where their focus should be. All thirteen of his men surged forward, some running from their tents in only their undergarments, but all brandishing their swords. Another branch crack had them all on high alert.

Colin pushed Elaris gently toward her tent, indicating he wanted her to go, but she stood her ground, eyes fixated on the trees.

Before long, another snap could be heard, this one closer. Colin stood in front of Elaris, sword drawn and at the ready. Bren grabbed Corporal Knoll and pointed forward, indicating an order to advance. The two crept silently into the trees, the rest of the Guard waiting for the enemy to arrive.

In seconds, they heard a scuffle, and then a laugh.

Bren emerged with a huge smile on his face—Corporal Knoll with him—dragging a hog.

"Gentlemen," he chuckled, "dinner has arrived."

Cheers and laughter erupted from the men, making Elaris giggle in relief.

Elaris sat in her chair by the fire, enjoying her meal. Someone had made a lovely stew out of fish, vegetables, and the hog that Lieutenant Holt and Corporal Knoll had captured.

The men, while still on alert, seemed more relaxed than they had been on the journey there. She sat and listened to their stories and occasional laughter, all while keeping her distance.

When she had awoken earlier in the day, she was thankful to discover that her headache was gone and there were no visions plaguing her. She had lain in bed thinking about the journey ahead, about Hatti, and about the captain.

She had regretted being distant from him but was hopeful that, now that she was feeling better, she wouldn't have to do so any longer. She felt she could trust him, perhaps even confide in him.

Earlier, at the creek, she had made the bold decision to let him see her again. She could almost hear Hatti scolding her. But Hatti wasn't there, and the captain was the closest thing to a friend she had.

She didn't want to hide from him anymore.

She thought back to the moment the captain had seen her—really seen her. He seemed pleased, she thought with a blush.

"Do you need anything, my lady?" he asked as he approached.

"Nothing, Captain. The stew was delicious!"

He smiled at her, and she could feel her face getting hot again. For the first time, she was thankful for the veil.

"May I?" he asked, indicating the chair next to her.

She nodded, and he sat.

She decided this was the perfect time to get to know him.

"How long have you been in the Royal Guard, Captain?" she asked.

"Fourteen years. I was conscripted when I was sixteen."

"So young."

Colin shrugged. "I was considered old for a recruit. Some in my company were much younger."

"You said conscripted. I had assumed you were all volunteers."

Colin let out a short bark of laughter. "No, my lady. All of us here were drafted. Most by force," he grumbled.

Shocked, Elaris replied, "But how can loyalty be assured this way?"

Colin was impressed that she had considered it. He didn't want to shock her, so he avoided any unnecessary details.

"For some, money is a great motivator. For others, the safety of their families."

Elaris was stunned. She had been taught that Lord Mordane's subjects served him because he was such a generous master. Granted, when her teachers had told her this, she always felt they weren't quite telling the whole truth. When she tried to challenge one of them with more questions, she would be sent off to do something else. Now she knew why.

"Conscripting children should be outlawed," she said angrily.

Multiple heads turned at her words, some looking at her in shock. Colin gave the men a warning glance, and they went back to their conversations.

"My lady," he began, "I would caution you to keep those thoughts to yourself."

Confused, Elaris continued, more softly, "But why?"

"It's unfortunate, my lady, but it's the way things are right now. Those who oppose the idea are often... corrected."

Elaris remained quiet. She turned to look at the faces of all the soldiers who had so bravely defended her. Some older, some so young—all apparently forced to be here.

Her eyes started welling with tears as she thought about them being pulled away from their homes and families as children.

Colors flashed all around her.

Oh no, not again, she thought.

The currents were more intense this time, all circling around the soldiers at the fire, some intertwining with each other. She rubbed at her veiled eyes frantically but to no avail.

The rivers stretched far and wide. This time, however, she noticed that each person had a distinctive current that was brighter, more powerful. She focused on one of these currents, belonging to Sergeant Keswick, who had rivers of green.

She was pulled into it, flashing to a wooded area she didn't recognize. There were people all around. The soldiers, and... creatures. Strange creatures that were like something out of ancient lore. She smelled something this time. Blood.

She looked down to see Sergeant Keswick, his body broken and limp, riddled with slashes across his chest.

She screamed in terror, clenching her fists and pressing them into her eyes.

"Elaris!" Colin yelled, shaking her.

Elaris sobbed and fell forward out of her chair, Colin just barely catching her before she hit the ground.

"Sergeant Keswick," she cried.

Colin looked up to the sergeant who, like the others, was now focused on the scene before them.

"What about him?" he asked urgently.

"He's dead," she choked.

Colin frowned in confusion, helping her to her feet. "The sergeant is alright, my lady. Look here," he said, pointing to Keswick.

Sergeant Keswick, looking confused, dipped his head at her. Elaris slowly let go of the captain's arm, smoothing her skirts.

"My apologies," she stammered. "I must be tired."

The concern on Colin's face was apparent as he led her to her tent.

"Are you quite certain you are well, Elaris?" he asked quietly.

"I'm not sure," she whispered—and disappeared into the tent.

CHAPTER 9

Colin woke early, anxious to get moving. He hadn't slept well at all, consumed with thoughts of Elaris—her eyes, her smile, her apparent distress.

He had returned to the campfire after seeing her to her tent, only to find his men quietly discussing her. Words like "madness" and "strange" floated through the air.

It hadn't taken much to remind them of whom they were speaking about—one disapproving glare, and they were back to their military bearing.

One man was not so easily silenced.

After many of the others had gone to their beds, Bren had pulled Colin aside with a knowing look. Colin had raised a hand in defense and sighed.

"I know what you're going to say, Bren."

Bren adopted the look of a man feigning innocence.

"No. No, you don't. All I was going to say is that Lady Vaelora may need some additional rest. I think the strain of it all has been too much for her. Perhaps we can find a healer to help her."

Colin rubbed his temples. He hadn't known exactly what had happened earlier, but it wasn't the first time he'd seen strange behavior from Elaris. Bren had every right to be concerned.

"Perhaps you're right," he'd conceded.

Bren looked genuinely surprised.

"I am?"

"Yes. You can see it wearing her down. We shall give her more chances to rest, and seek out a healer in Oakhaven if she still needs one."

"Good plan," Bren said, clearly appeased.

"In the meantime," Colin growled, "keep the men in line. I don't want to hear another word about this from them. She is their future queen, after all."

Bren nodded once and took his leave.

Now, preparing for another day on the road, Colin wondered what state Elaris would be in. How should he address what had happened the night before? He understood she was grieving—they all were—but this seemed like something deeper than sorrow.

Packing up the rest of his gear, he made his way to Elaris's tent and called her name. She was slow to respond, but eventually came out, head lowered and shoulders stooped.

He decided not to embarrass her by asking about the night before. There would be time for that, but for now, they needed to get moving.

After eating a quick breakfast, he helped her onto her horse and mounted his.

He had decided to ride closer to her today, just in case.

For the first few hours, he found himself just watching her—waiting. She was quiet, not wanting to converse except for the occasional pleasantry.

Colin noticed that his men also kept a close eye on her—some out of curiosity, and he was sure some out of concern.

Over the last few days, many of them had shared conversations with her, and he believed they had begun to feel a fondness for her.

She was easy to like, he thought.

With good weather and barring any surprises, they would reach Oakhaven tonight.

Colin wanted to make sure they were there when Briggs returned. He also wanted a bit more distance between them and Lake Rehl.

Colin hoped whoever was after her would not expect them to have gone this route. With a few days' distance, the chances of another encounter would diminish.

Coming upon a clearing by a river, Colin called for them to stop. Elaris dismounted and walked to the river's edge, dipping her head toward the water. Colin gave a few quick orders and then went to join her while food and refreshment were prepared by his men.

"Elaris," he said quietly as he approached.

Her head lifted and turned to him, but her shoulders remained slumped.

"I'm sorry about last night," she whispered.

Colin paused for a moment before responding. "Do you want to tell me what happened?" he asked gently.

Elaris sighed and looked down to the water. "You'll think I'm mad."

Colin drew closer, wanting to reach out to her. "Please, Elaris. You can trust me."

After a moment of hesitation, she spoke. "I saw Sergeant Keswick. He was dead."

"You *saw* him?"

"Yes. I saw him on the ground, covered in blood. His chest was ripped open," she said, her voice trembling.

Colin frowned. This wasn't good. It wasn't normal to be seeing visions of dead people—especially when they weren't even dead.

"Tell me more," he prodded.

"It was someplace strange. Trees all over. I think maybe it was daytime, but the trees made everything dark. There were peculiar creatures there, and the Guard."

Colin took a moment to process what she had said. "You have had a very strenuous couple of days. Are you certain it wasn't a dream?"

He knew the question was absurd, as she clearly had been awake when it happened, but he had no other ideas to explain it.

Elaris shook her head, saying, "No. It's not the first time."

Although Colin had suspected as much, the news still came as a surprise. "Have you always seen death?" he pried carefully.

"No, only once before. I saw Lieutenant Holt."

"You saw him dead?" Colin asked, concern in his voice.

"No, his mother. But it was strange. He was a child. His mother had died from the plague."

Relief poured through Colin. "Lieutenant Holt's mother is very much alive."

"Yes, I know. I asked him about her to make sure."

"Have you always had these... visions?"

Elaris kicked a rock with her toe. "They started at the funeral."

They fell into silence, both considering what all of this could mean. Colin had the feeling that Elaris wasn't telling him everything, but he knew that he would have to earn her trust first.

"We will be in Oakhaven tonight. We will be staying there until Sergeant Briggs returns, so there will be plenty of time for rest."

Colin decided against mentioning the healer. He sensed it would only cause hurt. One thing was for certain—she needed help, and he needed to get it for her.

Elaris rode next to the captain an hour later. She had noticed the looks shared between the soldiers when she was around. She understood, of course. There was no way to justify what they had witnessed the night before. Telling the captain what she had seen had not been her intention, but when he asked her so kindly and gently, it tumbled out.

She had held back about the colorful rivers and currents, as well as her vision of him.

That all sounded strange enough—no need to make him think she had gone completely mad.

Although, the idea had occurred to her.

She let herself reflect on the vision from the night before. The current she had followed for Sergeant Keswick had been brighter, bolder.

It seemed to accept her journey down it more readily than the others had. All the soldiers there had one of these distinctive currents. She wondered why they stood out.

Although she hated the idea of having another vision, she decided that she would follow one of these brighter streams when next given the opportunity.

Rounding a corner, she saw a signpost indicating a blacksmith as well as a trading post up ahead.

Turning to the captain, she asked excitedly, "Are we going to a town?"

Colin smiled at her obvious enthusiasm over a simple country village. "Well, not quite," he said. "But we will be camping outside of it. Oakhaven is a village."

Elaris was thrilled. "Will we be able to see this village?"

Colin thought about the wisdom of taking her to such a populated area and shook his head. "I'm afraid not, my lady. Some of the men will gather provisions there, however, so if there is something you might desire, they may be able to find it for you."

Elaris tried not to show her disappointment. She knew what she had asked was not possible, especially after the attack. "Thank you, Captain. I shall give that some consideration," she replied.

An hour later, they were setting up camp on a hill overlooking the village of Oakhaven. The area was wooded enough to keep them hidden from travelers on the road, while still allowing them access to everything the town had to offer.

Elaris wasted no time finding a good vantage point that would allow her to see the warm glow of the village below.

Houses dotted the perimeter of Oakhaven, while a multitude of larger buildings were clustered in the middle.

Smoke rose from chimneys, and she could hear music rising, accompanied by the occasional bark of a dog.

Elaris contemplated what the villagers were doing tonight. Were they having supper with their families, all gathered around a roaring fire? Were they sharing a pint in the tavern? She wished more than anything that she could experience it for herself, but it wasn't meant to be.

"My lady, your tent is ready," Sergeant Keswick said, carefully approaching her.

Surprised to hear his voice, Elaris turned and was immediately haunted by the vision of him. "Sergeant Keswick," she choked out.

He hesitated before continuing. "My lady... I just wanted to say... I hope you are well."

"I am, thank you," she lied.

"And I wanted to assure you, my lady, that I plan to live a very long time, so there is no need for you to worry," he said with concern.

Elaris did something she was sure Hatti would disagree with. She took the sergeant's hand and squeezed it. "Thank you, Sergeant. I am so glad to hear it."

Keswick's ears turned a fantastic shade of pink as he turned to leave. Just then, Colin appeared, looking confused as the sergeant walked past. "Is all well?" he asked her.

Confirming that they were alone, Elaris peeled off her veil and breathed a sigh of relief. "Yes, the sergeant was just telling me my tent was ready," she replied.

Looking at the veil in her hand, Colin remarked, "You need not wear that thing any longer, Elaris—at least not around the Guard."

Elaris looked down at the dreaded thing. "But what about Lord Mordane? He was insistent."

Colin looked intently at her and shrugged. "We are the Royal Guard. If you can't trust us, who can you trust?" he asked, completely discounting anything concerning *him*.

"You're absolutely right, Captain," she laughed as she threw the veil to the ground.

Colin laughed with her and guided her back to the center of camp, where the soldiers waited. Upon seeing her, they all stopped in their tracks. The wonderment on their faces was unmistakable—and Colin was sure every man there had just fallen in love with her.

CHAPTER 10

E laris woke early, anxious to see everyone and find a
good spot to observe the comings and goings of
Oakhaven. Supper the night before had been
wonderful, with good food and conversation. The Guard
seemed to have warmed up to her more, likely because they
could actually see her now. They had all sat around the fire
telling stories of adventure and tales of romance.

She had never laughed so hard in all her life, especially at
what some of them considered romance. She had gone the
whole day without a vision. That left her hopeful that the
issue had passed.

She stepped out of her tent and was surprised to find
young Corporal Rowan posted outside. She smiled hesitantly
at him and said, "Good morning."

The corporal snapped to attention and returned the
greeting eagerly. "Good morning, Lady Vaelora!"

She smiled at him again and started her journey to the
center of the camp, where they had built a large fire and
served the meals. She had almost reached it when another
soldier, whom she believed was Sergeant Fenlow, came

running up to her, excitedly declaring, "Breakfast is ready, my lady! Let me escort you to your chair."

Elaris was confused by all the attention she was now getting but assumed the men were just relaxing around her. On the other side of camp, she could see the captain talking to the lieutenant and Sergeant Briggs. She breathed a sigh of relief upon seeing that he had made it back safely.

He must have arrived in the middle of the night. Though nothing had been said and she didn't know why he'd left, she had sensed the captain's worry.

Sitting down in the chair that was offered to her, she thanked Sergeant Fenlow for a plate of food and turned her attention back to the captain. He kept glancing at her, concern written across his face.

Briggs looked equally serious, and the lieutenant stood with his arms folded, listening intently. She very much wanted to know what they were discussing.

"Can I get you anything, Lady Vaelora? Perhaps a blanket?" Sergeant Darrow asked her.

Smiling up at him, she replied, "No, thank you. I am quite warm enough."

The sergeant bowed to her and walked off, looking somewhat disappointed.

Elaris glanced back at Colin to see him still talking to Sergeant Briggs, once again looking intently at her. She really needed to find out what the sergeant was telling them.

She focused on Briggs and noticed for the first time just how large he really was. He stood much taller than the rest of the men and looked like he could rip a tree out by its roots.

In the little time they'd spoken before he left, she'd found him a calm presence, but sensed that underestimating him could be a deadly mistake.

Gazing at him, rivers of green flowed out all around him, extending to the horizon, twisting and intertwining at times.

She breathed deeply and decided to focus this time. She looked for the most prominent, most intense current.

Stretching both in front of him and behind him was the brightest one—the current she was looking for.

She intensified her attention on that one, but chose to look upstream, traveling behind him.

She was swallowed by the current and blinked to find herself in a room with Sergeant Briggs. There was a small, bald man on a bed. Elaris immediately became aware of a wretched smell emanating from the man, like spoiled milk and manure.

She grasped her nose in an attempt to block it out. Briggs had a knife to his throat and was asking him about how many men he had killed. Elaris feared what Briggs might do, but he surprised her by letting the man go.

She closed her eyes and was immediately back by the fire. Her head ached a bit, but for the first time during one of these visions, she appeared to be mostly composed. She wondered what she had seen. Why had Sergeant Briggs been interrogating this man?

Colin stood with Bren, listening to Briggs finish his report. The sergeant had managed to find information concerning the attack at Lake Rehl, but there were still a lot of pieces missing—namely, this wizard Claudius.

"Rumor is, he lives north of the palace. That doesn't exactly narrow it down for us," Briggs said, frowning.

"I'm assuming they wouldn't have used the palace as a reference unless it was close to it. Once we clear Vale Forest, we'll start asking around at the local villages," Colin mumbled.

He looked over to see one of his men escorting Elaris to her chair. When had that started?

"Sir," Bren said, calling his attention back to the discussion.

Colin cleared his throat. "Anything else, Sergeant?"

Briggs stifled a yawn. "No, Sir. I think that covers it."

Colin turned to see yet another of his men hovering around Elaris. What was going on, exactly?

"Excellent work, Sergeant. Now let's go get you something to eat. You must be tired and hungry."

Briggs yawned again and nodded in reply.

As they walked to the center of camp, Colin held Bren back a step and asked in an annoyed voice, "Why am I seeing so many of my guards around a certain lady this morning?"

"I know that, as a man who spends entirely too much time with his horse, you aren't going to understand this, but..." Bren began, chuckling and rolling his eyes.

"Shut up, you bastard," Colin muttered.

As the three men approached the fire, Bren gave a warning look to the soldiers surrounding Lady Vaelora, and they scattered. Colin scowled.

"Sergeant Briggs! So glad to see you have safely returned," Elaris said with a smile.

Briggs took a moment to adjust to her new look but, to his credit, he didn't let his surprise show. "Thank you, my lady. I am happy to be back."

"Did you travel far?" she prodded.

He knew the captain had probably not shared the details of his mission with her, so he kept his reply vague. "I fortunately found what I was looking for without having to travel too far, my lady."

Elaris pouted a bit at this evasion of an answer. "Did you get to go to a village?" she pried harder.

Briggs turned to Colin with a questioning look. Colin sighed but decided no harm could come from her knowing. "Sergeant Briggs visited Glendale on his journey."

"Glendale! But they have a library there!" she cried.

Library or not—after what Briggs had shared—Colin was glad they hadn't taken her to Glendale like she'd wanted.

"I remember you telling me that, my lady," Colin noted.

Elaris's disappointment was apparent, and Colin felt he knew the best way to appease her. "You know the palace has a grand library, full of ancient tomes. I doubt you could read everything there in a lifetime."

Elaris's face brightened a bit at this.

Briggs, seeing what the captain was trying to do, decided to add, "Glendale was quite dull, my lady. The only inn in town is a dirty, dingy place run by a short, balding man who smells like spoiled milk."

Elaris laughed—too quickly, as if something had just clicked for her. "He did smell awful!"

Briggs and Bren looked at her in confusion, Colin with concern.

"My apologies, my lady," Briggs began, "I didn't know you had met the man before."

Laughing nervously, she replied, "I misspoke, Sergeant. What I meant to say is, I'm sure he did smell awful."

Briggs smiled at her and turned back to Colin. "With your permission, Sir, I will turn in."

Colin nodded at him, and he spun to leave.

After Elaris had finished her meal, Colin walked with her to the overlook. She was quiet as they strolled, and he wondered what was on her mind. Her slip-up with Briggs may have been exactly what she had claimed—a mistake— but somehow, he suspected it was more.

"Do you want to tell me what that was about?" he asked.

Elaris didn't ask what he meant. Colin could tell by the wary look in her eyes that she already knew. She hesitated, then let out a slow breath, clearly weighing her response.

"I had another vision... this one about Sergeant Briggs."

Colin immediately looked concerned. "Did he die in this vision?"

Elaris laid her hand on his arm to assure him. "No," she replied softly. "In fact, there was no death. He was in a room with a bald man—he smelled awful! The sergeant was holding a knife to his throat and was asking him if he had killed any soldiers. The man was very upset but claimed he hadn't... and then the sergeant let him go."

Colin felt a mixture of shock and confusion. There was no way she could have known that. "Sergeant Briggs just got done briefing me about such an encounter he had while in Glendale."

"But I thought my visions were false? The lieutenant's mother..."

Colin shook his head. "I thought so as well, but that no longer appears to be the case."

Elaris stood in silence, letting him think in peace.

After a few moments, Colin's expression changed from confusion to determination. "I have a friend—a wizard—about a day's ride away. I believe we should go ask for his help."

"A wizard?" Elaris hesitated.

"I promise you, he is a good man."

Elaris looked unsure, furrowing her brow in worry.

"He may be able to help us discover why you are having these visions and what they all mean," he explained.

"Won't that delay us?"

"We are a few days ahead of schedule due to the route change. We still have well over a week of travel, and your visions seem to be getting worse."

Nodding, Elaris conceded, "I trust you. If he is a friend of yours, then I will go."

"This is a bad idea," Bren declared.

"We need answers, Bren, and this is the only way I can think to get them," Colin insisted.

Colin had spent the last hour filling him in on Elaris and her visions. Bren had gone from intrigued to horrified to confused within minutes, and then Colin told him his plan. That's when Bren had become cross.

"Tell me again why you need to go without the Guard?" Bren asked, a mix of concern and belligerence in his voice.

Colin understood his friend's misgivings. He wasn't sure it was the best idea either, but it was the best one he had come up with.

"She will be much less noticeable without a company of giants surrounding her," he argued.

"See, I may agree with you there, but you are bringing Briggs with you, and he is the most giant of all," Bren countered.

Colin shrugged. "Well, I may be crazy, but I'm not stupid. I recognize bringing some additional muscle is a good idea."

Bren folded his arms over his chest in defiance and glared at his captain.

Colin slapped his shoulder in response and grinned at him. "Don't worry, Bren. You weren't exactly my first choice for commanding the men in my absence, but you'll do fine, I'm sure."

Bren let out a low growl. "Let's just see if we are still here when you return."

Colin laughed and walked away in search of Sergeant Briggs.

Briggs was found next to his tent, polishing his sword. He snapped to attention when Colin approached.

"Captain," Briggs said, dipping his head slightly.

"Sergeant Briggs. I have another job for you."

Briggs looked intrigued. "Certainly, Sir," he replied.

"You and I will be leaving at first light with Lady Vaelora. We travel east to Millcross."

Briggs, ever the military man, kept his features neutral. "Alone, Sir?"

"The Guard will be staying behind. We will rejoin them when our business is complete."

"Of course, Sir."

Colin turned to leave, but paused and added, "It should be a quiet trip, Briggs."

Colin could almost hear him groaning inwardly.

The rest of the day was spent preparing for their trip. Colin had sent a few soldiers into Oakhaven to purchase some provisions they might need, including one he wasn't sure would be well received.

Walking up to Elaris's tent, he called to her.

"Come in," she replied.

Colin entered and let his eyes adjust to the low light.

"Hello, Captain. What can I help you with?" Elaris asked.

"I have a gift, of sorts, my lady."

He handed her the parcel his men had returned with.

She looked delighted and opened it excitedly. Inside, she found a light blue country dress. She blinked in surprise and stammered, "Thank you."

Colin rushed to explain. "While your black dresses are perfectly... serviceable, my lady, they aren't exactly what you would see the common woman wearing in town. This dress should make you less conspicuous."

"I see," she said, holding it up in front of her with a quizzical eye.

Colin coughed, suddenly uncomfortable, then adopted a commanding tone. "We leave at first light."

Elaris didn't have time to respond before he was gone.

CHAPTER 11

Colin rode quietly next to Elaris, who was deep in conversation with Sergeant Briggs. He was having trouble keeping his eyes off her. She had opted for the blue dress instead of the black one this morning, and the change in her was significant. She not only looked less pale and sad, but she also seemed happier.

"Sergeant Briggs, how old were you when you were conscripted into the Royal Guard?" she asked.

"I was ten when I was taken from my home, my lady, but I didn't lay hands on my first sword until I was fourteen."

Elaris looked horrified. "I don't understand. Why did they take you so young?"

"Plenty of work for a young lad to do in a camp. I spent the first years mucking out stalls, and then, when I was twelve, I was moved up to squire and assisted the officers."

"And a soldier at fourteen?"

"Not quite, my lady. I started training at fourteen but was officially inducted into the Royal Guard at seventeen."

"I can't imagine leaving home so young," she murmured.

"I was one of eight boys in my village who were taken. I was lucky. Being chosen for the Royal Guard is an honor. The rest of the boys… well, they weren't so lucky."

"What happened to them?" she asked, wide-eyed.

Briggs answered carefully. "Well, my lady, some are still serving as stable hands. Some… well, they weren't cut out for it."

Elaris looked confused at first, and then her expression changed to realization. "Oh, I see."

They rode on in silence, Elaris looking lost in thought. Colin wondered how this impacted her view of *him*.

After several minutes, she asked, "You talked of boys working in camps. Do they normally travel with the soldiers as well when they are off on a mission?"

Briggs nodded. "Yes, my lady."

"Then why are there none with us?"

"Captain wouldn't allow it," he beamed, "said children belonged at home with their families, not out doing the work of grown men."

Elaris turned to Colin and looked intently at him, as if trying to solve a puzzle. After a moment, she asked him, "You said that loyalty to the Guard is sometimes assured through money or a desire to keep your family safe."

Colin nodded. "Yes."

"What is your reason… for staying loyal?"

Colin was surprised by the question and didn't immediately know how to respond. "Well, I have no need for more money, and my family is gone. I suppose I do it because I want to serve the people of Ashcar. I want to ensure their protection from our enemies."

She didn't respond except to smile lightly at him, turn back and remain silent.

The next hour was spent mostly silent, with the occasional remark about the weather or the road. Around noon, they stopped by a small lake and ate lunch. Briggs excused himself to go "explore the trees", leaving Colin and Elaris alone. She watched him as he ate, once again like she was trying to figure something out.

"Is there something on your mind, Elaris?" he asked.

She paused a moment before answering. "Your men admire you."

"The feeling is mutual."

"I've noticed that you and Lieutenant Holt are especially close."

Colin nodded. "Yes. We have a long history together. And he saved my life."

Elaris leaned forward, completely focused on whatever he was going to say next. Colin laughed lightly at her apparent excitement.

"Several years ago, we were on a mission in the south. We were ambushed. I was injured. Bren got me to safety and found a healer. I would have died without him."

Elaris was stunned. "Your life is very dangerous, Captain."

"It is indeed," Colin said with a laugh.

Hours later, as they neared Millcross, Colin could see Elaris's anticipation growing. She had spent the afternoon asking questions about the town, the people, and their accommodations. What was mundane for Colin and Briggs was an adventure to her.

"Is that it?" she asked excitedly as they rounded the last corner.

"That's it, my lady," answered Briggs.

They crossed under the gate and entered a busy village, with shops on every corner and people populating the street. Colin guided them to the local stable, where they left their horses before continuing on foot to the inn.

"I think it would be a good idea for you to keep your head lowered when we are talking to people, my lady," Colin whispered as they entered the door to the inn.

She looked disappointed but complied. The inn was clean, and the rooms were comfortable. Colin made sure all their rooms were next to each other.

"I have a view of the marketplace from my room!" Elaris announced happily when she rejoined them in the hallway after putting away her things.

"We should get supper and then get some rest. We go to see my friend tomorrow," Colin said.

Elaris looked disappointed. "I was hoping to see a bit more of the town."

Colin looked at Briggs, who gave a warning glance.

"We can go across the street to the market. But then we must come back," Colin said sternly.

Elaris beamed with happiness and followed them down the stairs.

Both men were tense, looking around every corner and down every hallway. Once outside, they crossed with her cautiously across the street to the market.

It wasn't very busy at this time of day and many of the vendors were packing up their wares. It was the perfect time to let her look around and then get her back to safety.

Elaris kept her head lowered as Colin had asked her, but that didn't stop her from smelling all the delicious food and seeing the interesting textiles, jewelry, tools, and artwork that people were selling.

She was immediately drawn to a table full of silk scarves being sold by what appeared to be a sweet old lady. Elaris picked one up in her hands and smoothed the fabric over her arms, appearing mesmerized by the feel. "I've never felt anything like it!" she exclaimed.

Colin stepped forward and asked the old woman, "How much?"

She smiled sweetly up at him and answered, "Ten silvers."

Colin, shocked by the exorbitant price, asked again, "*How* much?"

The old woman adopted a tight smile and knowing eyes. Colin was sure he had seen those eyes on thieves before.

"Ten. Silvers," she enunciated.

Colin was sure that, had he been wearing his uniform, the price would have been far more reasonable. Keeping a low profile, unfortunately, meant leaving it at the camp. He was beginning to regret that decision now.

He turned to Briggs and rolled his eyes before starting to pull out his change purse—only for Briggs to step forward instead.

Flashing his best smile, he leaned in and mumbled to the old lady, "Are you sure you can't do better? The young lady is very fond of it."

The woman pulled back from him and cackled, making a shiver go down Colin's spine. "You are right, my dear. The lady is quite fond of it. Ten silvers. And your handsome face won't make it lower!"

Elaris remained unaware of the exchange, having moved further down the table to look at some jewelry. Colin grumbled in defeat as he paid the old woman. "You drive a hard bargain."

The woman flashed another smile at him and handed over the scarf which, on closer inspection, he began to question the quality of.

She immediately packed up her stall, putting all her wares in a cart, and moved off, leaving no time to argue. Colin and Briggs shared a knowing look as they refocused on Elaris. They had just been taken.

Colin walked up to Elaris and handed her the scarf. "For you, my lady."

Elaris took it carefully from him, as if she were afraid it would disappear. "Captain... thank you!" she exclaimed, beaming at him.

Colin smiled warmly at her as she wrapped the scarf around her shoulders. It went perfectly with the dress and her lovely smile. Perhaps ten silvers were a bargain after all.

With the shops closing, they made their way back to the tavern and entered the dining hall. Briggs found a table in a darkened corner, where they sat until a maid came to take their order.

Elaris sat in between the two men, like a dove positioned between two gargoyles.

Their meal came, and, with the room quickly filling up with patrons, they ate in silence.

Although Elaris kept her head down, she still managed to attract attention—unfortunately, from the wrong person.

A large man in dirty clothing, who had been drinking at the counter when they arrived, made his way drunkenly to their table, bumping into several people and chairs on the journey.

"Wot we got here?" he slurred. "Pretty little thing."

Colin gave him a warning glare, and Briggs kept one hand on the table and the other on his knife. "Move along," Colin growled.

The man managed to stumble over his own feet while standing in one place, nearly falling on their table. Belching loudly, he slurred, "Who are ye? Her brother?"

The drunk reached his hand out toward Elaris who, in shock, looked up at him.

Colin had the man's wrist in a vice grip in under a second, twisting his arm in an unnatural direction. "I said. Move. Along," Colin ordered.

The man yelled out in pain and stumbled away, but not before looking again at Elaris. "Those eyes," he murmured.

Colin and Briggs decided they had attracted enough attention and that supper was over. Guiding Elaris through the crowded hall, they led her to her room.

"Don't open your door for anyone but Briggs or myself," Colin demanded.

Elaris nodded.

"And yell if you encounter any trouble. We are in the rooms just next door to you. We will wake you in the morning in time for breakfast."

Elaris remained quiet, causing Colin to ask if she was alright.

"That man…" she began.

"He is no one. Just a drunk," Colin said softly. "But we need to be more careful from now on."

She nodded again and went to her room. Crawling into her bed, she quickly fell asleep but was plagued by dreams—her groom standing next to her—his hands closing around her neck.

Lord Mordane opened the door to Kaz's rooms and was hit with the distinctive smell of death. He could see something cooking in a large cauldron in the corner and wondered if that was producing the offensive odor. In the opposite corner manacles hung, with one end affixed to the wall and the other lying in a pool of blood on the floor.

"My lord!" Kaz squeaked.

"Your messenger said you have an update on Lady Vaelora," he grumbled, gazing into a large vessel filled with a mysterious liquid.

"Yes, my lord," Kaz replied.

Draegor waited a moment and then looked at his Royal Sorcerer in annoyance. "Out with it!" he snapped.

Kaz jumped in surprise and quickly responded, "They are in Oakhaven. At least, most of them are."

"Oakhaven? What are they doing in Oakhaven? That is days away from the Lake Road."

"I am unsure, my lord. My tracking spell shows all but two are there."

"Which two are gone?"

"Captain Aedric and Sergeant Briggs."

"Well, where are they?" he snapped.

Kaz jumped again and stammered, "Oh—on the road to Millcross, my lord."

Draegor's face went cold, and he turned his back. Walking around the perimeter of the room slowly, he stopped by the cauldron to smell it, confirming it was, indeed, the source of the wretched stench.

"My lord?" asked Kaz.

"Captain Aedric is heading to the wizard," he growled, his words like venom.

"What wizard?"

"Alec."

Recognition fell on Kaz's face. "For what purpose, my lord?"

Draegor clenched his jaw, lowering his voice to a hiss. "Because of her. She must have revealed herself in some way."

He turned sharply. "I assume she is still in Oakhaven?"

Kaz shook his head. "Unclear, my lord. I only sense her when she is using her powers."

Draegor was across the room in a heartbeat. "What do you mean, 'when she is using her powers?'" he barked.

"Well, I can feel her power emerging. Every day she has had one or two magical... outbursts."

Draegor reached out his hand and grasped the man's throat, squeezing tightly. "Did you not think that you should have told me this from the start?"

Kaz looked panicked as he fought for breath, clawing at his master's grip. Draegor waited until he turned blue, and then released him, causing him to fall to the floor.

After recovering enough breath to speak, Kaz choked, "My apologies, my lord."

Draegor ignored his apology, focused instead on this new problem. Captain Aedric had disobeyed orders. Worse, he was involving someone who might unravel everything.

"How strong is she?" he snapped.

Kaz coughed, rubbing at his neck. "Hard to tell. I will say that, for one who has just started awakening, she emanates more energy than one would expect. I believe she will be quite powerful when she is at full strength."

Draegor was silent for a long moment.

Kaz coughed again. "There's something else, my lord."

Draegor turned and glared at him impatiently. Before he had a chance to yell at him, Kaz finally spoke up. "Claudius has been following them."

Draegor growled.

CHAPTER 12

After last night's encounter with the drunkard, Colin opted to bring breakfast to Elaris's room. Colin and Briggs stood in the hall while she finished eating, and then escorted her to the stables for their horses. Within an hour of waking, they were on their way.

It was still too early for vendors to be out, and the market stood empty. They traveled through the town, observing shopkeepers opening their stores, with the smell of fresh bread emanating from the local bakery. The sun had barely burned through the morning mist as they turned from the stone road onto a narrow forest path. As they traveled, the tree line moved closer and closer to the path, slowing their progress. The air thickened in a haze that made everything hard to focus on. Speech became difficult, and their eyes became heavy. Colin stopped them as they came to the top of a small hill and yelled, "Alec!"

A few moments later, a tall man with dark hair, wearing long blue robes, emerged from the trees. "Colin!" he laughed. "Whatever are you doing here?"

The haze that had addled their minds dissipated. Colin rode over to Alec and dismounted. They greeted each other with a warm embrace. "We need your help, old friend. May we go inside?"

"Of course! Follow me."

The three followed Alec to the bottom of the hill, where a small cottage was located. He looked over Elaris as they entered the home, but she kept her head lowered. Alec immediately went to the sink to start preparing tea, while Colin, Elaris, and Briggs took seats next to the fire.

"Tell me, friend, how can I help you and your companions?" Alec asked warmly, his eyes focusing on Elaris.

Colin knew his friend wanted to know who these strangers were and didn't keep him waiting. "Alec, this is Sergeant Briggs and Lady Elaris Vaelora, future Queen of Ashcar. The Royal Guard is charged with escorting her to the palace."

Alec's eyes snapped to Colin, a tiny flash of fear passing over them. He focused on his friend and gritted his teeth. "And why have you honored me with a visit from Lord Mordane's future bride?" he hissed.

Colin understood his anger. His friend wanted absolutely nothing to do with Lord Mordane—let alone the woman he was planning on marrying.

"Alec," Colin urged, "there is more to this."

"I should hope so," his friend snapped.

Colin turned to Elaris and moved his hand under her lowered chin, pushing it up. Her violet eyes rose to gaze at Alec, who collapsed into his chair. "Could it be?" he breathed.

"What? What is it?" Colin asked, concerned.

Alec ignored his friend, continuing to examine Elaris. As he stared at her, she grew unsettled, looking at Colin for reassurance.

"My dear lady, where have you been?" he asked.

Elaris looked to Colin and received a warm smile. "If you are asking where I grew up, I have been at Pyete Monastery since I was an infant."

Alec frowned. "I suppose there are worse places to train you. Who was your teacher?"

"I had several teachers, but Hatti was the one who arranged my instruction." Elaris sniffled at the memory of her.

Seeing her emotion, Alec turned to Colin. "Who is this 'Hatti'?"

"Her companion. She practically raised her at the monastery. She was killed on the first night of our journey to the palace," he whispered.

"What happened?" Alec inquired.

"A wizard named Claudius enlisted several dozen men and two wizards to attack our camp in an attempt to assassinate Lady Vaelora," Colin answered.

Alec frowned. "I have heard the name, but do not know him personally."

Colin tried to hide his disappointment. "I was hoping you would know where I might find him."

"I'm sorry, my friend, I do not," he said apologetically.

Alec waited a moment before turning to Elaris. "How can I help you, my lady?"

Elaris was still unsure, but trusted Colin's judgement. "I have been... seeing things."

Briggs, to his credit, only raised a single eyebrow.

Alec looked confused. "Well, of course you have."

This was not the answer she was expecting. "You don't understand," she cried, "I see things—people. Some dead."

"Yes?" Alec prodded, expecting more.

Elaris looked to Colin for help.

"Alec. She has been having visions. She saw one of my men dead, killed in an apparent attack. Another, she saw as a child by his dead mother. His mother is not deceased. And then two days ago, she had a vision of Sergeant Briggs."

Briggs's other eyebrow went up.

"She saw him on a mission I had sent him on. She gave me details of the mission that Briggs had only told to me."

Briggs shifted uncomfortably in his chair, his normal stoic demeanor slipping.

Alec looked back and forth from Elaris to Colin in puzzlement. "Has she not been trained?" he blurted.

"I have had much instruction," she replied.

"I don't refer to instruction, my lady. Mathematics and literature will not help you now. I speak of training. For your powers."

"Powers?" Colin choked.

Alec didn't respond, turning back to Elaris. "Tell me. When did these visions start?"

"At the funeral for Hatti and the soldiers," Elaris stammered.

Alec sat back in his chair and frowned again.

"Hatti. Was she a witch, by chance?" he inquired.

"No," Elaris insisted.

"Perhaps," Colin interjected.

Elaris turned to him, confused.

112

"She used some sort of magic to kill the wizard who was after you," he explained.

"Well, that explains things," Alec mused.

Colin was growing frustrated. "Explains what?"

Once again, his friend ignored him and turned to Elaris. "It appears your companion had a shielding spell on you, my dear. She would have had to perform the spell quite often to block a power such as yours. It takes direct contact. I'm surprised you didn't notice."

Elaris frowned. "Hatti would give me a blessing every night."

"Ah. There we have it."

"Have what?" Colin snapped.

"Patience, my friend," Alec grumbled.

Turning back to Elaris, he smiled warmly and asked, "Have you seen the currents?"

"Yes," she murmured.

Colin's head snapped to her in confusion.

"Tell me," Alec urged.

Elaris took a deep breath, preparing for the worst. "I see... rivers... currents. A different color for everyone, although some are similar. When my visions began, I would see flashes of them, with several images. Now, I can choose which current to follow. They take me to my visions. Recently, they have become more vivid. I hear sounds and can smell what's there."

"These more vivid visions, did they come when you followed the brighter current?"

"Yes!" she blurted, surprised.

Alec nodded. "My dear, I think that you are owed an explanation."

"I think we all are," Colin grumbled.

Alec gave him an agitated glare before continuing, "What you have been experiencing is the Embercurrent. Every thousand years, someone is born with this power—the power to see and control a person's current—their fate."

"Control it?" Elaris asked.

"Yes. The power allows the wielder to not only see past, present, and future of a soul, but all the possible fates of that soul."

Elaris's brow furrowed in confusion. Alec smiled at her patiently. "For example, you are here with me, Colin, and Sergeant Briggs. But what if, instead of Sergeant Briggs, Colin had chosen another soldier to accompany you? That was a possibility, yes?"

She nodded slowly.

"And let's say that Colin had never been born."

"Thanks," Colin grumbled.

Throwing a warning scowl at his friend, Alec continued, "Like I said, let's say Colin was never born. What would your trip, so far, have looked like? You see, my dear, our fate is made up of the choices we make, the people we encounter, the places we go. Some things, like the possibility of never being born, are out of our hands, while others, like the choice you made to wear that lovely scarf, are completely in our control. But those choices—every one of them—determine the current we are on. We call those the *chosen* current. The other currents are possibilities, such as the choice to go left instead of right. These are called *alternate* currents. You wouldn't think something so minor would make that much of a difference, but what if an attacker was on that left path, while a chest full of riches were at the right?"

"Why is this starting to make sense?" Colin quipped.

"But what did you mean by controlling it?" Elaris asked.

"The Fatewaker has the ability to move a soul from one current to another, changing their fate."

"Fatewaker?"

"You, my dear. That's who you are."

Alec smiled at her and let her have a moment to process what she had just heard.

"So, you are saying a Fatewaker is born every thousand years?" she quietly asked.

"Yes, so it's a particularly rare power to have."

"And you believe that Hatti was blocking this power in me?"

"Oh, most assuredly," he said confidently.

"But why?" she murmured.

"I know why," Colin interjected.

Alec turned to him and nodded. "My thoughts, exactly, my friend."

Colin's face had turned hard. "He wants your power," he bit out.

Elaris took a moment before realizing who Colin was referring to—Lord Mordane, the man she was supposed to marry.

She shook her head to clear her mind. Tears welled in her eyes. "Was this the plan? Is that why he wants to marry me?"

Alec spoke to her gently. "We may never know what his plan was, or why he has chosen to marry you. One thing is for certain—he knows who you are. He wouldn't have gone through so much effort to keep you from the truth otherwise."

Colin, trying to give Elaris a moment of reflection, asked, "How do we help her? She loses herself in these visions. She sees disturbing images and seems unable to control when they appear."

"With training, she will learn to wield the Embercurrent so that she controls it, instead of the other way around. Unfortunately, she has awakened very late in life. She will struggle until she learns control."

"Can you teach her?" Colin pleaded.

"I can help her to come into her power more fully, even learn how to control it. But even my abilities are limited. Much knowledge was lost after the death of the last Fatewaker. I won't be able to guide her to her full awakening, but I can certainly get her started."

Colin placed his hand on Alec's shoulder and said, "Thank you, my friend."

Alec smiled and nodded at him, then focused back on Elaris. "If you come back tomorrow, we can get started."

Elaris looked at him with tears in her eyes. "Can you take it away?" she pleaded.

Alec gave her a look of pity. "I'm afraid not, my dear. Please try not to fret. I will help you, and all will be well."

Colin only hoped his friend was right.

CHAPTER 13

The next day, Elaris was greeted by rain, hammering down on the inn's roof. She found it fitting, as it matched her mood. She had spent most of the night considering all she had learned from Alec. There was her magic, her role as the Fatewaker, Hatti's betrayal, and her future groom's questionable motives. It was all too much.

The thing that bothered her most was Hatti. She had always considered Hatti not only her companion, but a mother figure and her closest—her only—friend. Now, she questioned everything. She wondered if Hatti knew about her powers, if that's why she used the protection spell on her every night, or if she was just blindly following orders from Lord Mordane.

Lord Mordane. She was never foolish enough to think that he loved her—how could he? She just knew that he had chosen her, that she was special in some way and should be honored to be his bride.

Now she knew there was another reason why he had selected her. He clearly knew about her powers and had arranged for her to be taken away and kept from any contact with the outside world. Did he want her to use her powers for his own gain? Why not have her spend her life training in their use so that she could be valuable when the time came to marry? Why keep her in the dark?

A knock sounded at her door, and she could hear the captain calling her name. She opened it to find him alone in the hall, a plate laden with biscuits, honey, and fruit for her breakfast.

"Where is Sergeant Briggs?" she asked as she looked past him to an empty hallway.

"He has gone to fetch the horses. It's a downpour out there," he explained.

Elaris took the offered plate and motioned for him to come in, but he kept his feet firmly planted in her doorway.

"I'll just wait out here," he mumbled.

She smiled at his propriety and went to a small chair in the corner of her room to eat. She finished quickly, threw on her cloak, and went to join him in the hall.

They found Briggs waiting outside, soaking wet, holding all three horses' reins, and looking decidedly unamused.

Colin let out a bark of laughter when he saw him, earning a deadly stare from the sergeant. This only served to make Colin laugh again.

"Don't worry, Briggs. There's a nice warm fire waiting for us at Alec's house."

Briggs didn't say anything, instead grunting and mounting his horse as Colin helped Elaris get on hers.

They found Alec happily shielded from the rain in the warmth of his home. Briggs cheerfully hung up his coat, accepted a warm cup of tea from Alec, and took a seat in an oversized chair by the fire. Colin sat down at the same table

118

he had used yesterday, as it gave him the best vantage point in the room.

Alec greeted Elaris with a warm grin, clapped his hands together, and asked, "Ready to get started, my dear?"

Elaris nodded and answered quietly, "Yes, I think so."

Alec seemed to understand her trepidation.

"You are going to do wonderfully—you shall see," he reassured her.

Turning to Colin, he pointed to a stack of books on the table, some of which looked like they would turn to dust if he touched them.

"Colin, as you will be waiting for Lady Vaelora for quite a while, I suggest you spend your time looking through those manuscripts. I haven't had time to look through them yet, but I suspect some may make mention of the Fatewaker or the Embercurrent, and I believe one speaks of the last Fatewaker."

Colin picked one up in disgust as clumps of dust fell to the table.

"I see this one is often read," he said sarcastically.

Alec waved him away and turned back to Elaris.

"Let's get started," he chimed.

Alec guided her to the other side of the room where he had cleared most of the furniture.

"Now, I want you to close your eyes. Take a deep breath. Feel the breath going in and out of your lungs. Feel the presence of others in the room. Feel their energy. Feel their very souls."

"Their souls?" she interrupted, keeping her eyes closed but scrunching her face in confusion. "How does one feel a soul?"

Alec stopped for a moment to think and then waved his hand again.

"You just do, my dear."

Elaris frowned and focused harder.

"Do you feel the energy of Colin and of Sergeant Briggs?" he inquired.

"I believe so," she stammered. She could feel them somehow in the room—their strength and goodness.

"Now I want you to focus on the energy coming from Sergeant Briggs. What does it look like?"

Elaris concentrated on the sergeant until the currents appeared in her mind.

"It's green," she breathed. "Currents of green flowing out from him in all directions."

Briggs, who up until now looked perfectly content, appeared concerned.

"Good!" Alec cheered. "Now take a deep breath and slowly open your eyes and look around you."

Elaris breathed deeply, peeking her eyes open.

"The currents are gone."

"As they should be," he praised.

"I don't understand," she whispered, confused.

"The first step in wielding the Embercurrent is learning how to not wield the Embercurrent. Right now, you are uncontrolled. You see them with your eyes open, without summoning them. In time, you will be able to see them with your eyes open again, but for now, we learn how to summon the currents with them closed."

Elaris glanced over at the captain, who, although busy looking through the texts, kept a watchful eye on her. She found that she appreciated his protectiveness.

"What's next?" she asked.

"We shall now try to manifest the Embercurrent," Alec announced.

"Excuse me?" Colin blurted.

With another wave of his hand, Alec dismissed his friend's concerns.

"You will be fine, my dear," he declared. "I will guide you."

Elaris gave a half smile, unsure of what he meant by *manifest*.

"Now, same process as before. Close your eyes. Take a deep breath. Feel the breath moving through your body. Sense the energy in the room. Feel the energy of Sergeant Briggs."

"I see it," she whispered.

"Good. Now I am going to join my magic with yours to guide you," Alec said gently as he placed his hand on her back.

Elaris could feel the warmth of his hand and could sense what she could only describe as power flowing through her. Her pulse began racing, and her breathing became rapid.

"Breathe deeply. Breathe slowly. Focus on the energy from Sergeant Briggs. Focus on the brightest current—his chosen current. You've seen it before. Go back to it."

Elaris focused intently on slowing her breathing and doing what the wizard was telling her. She found the rivers and streams even more pronounced, with the brightest one giving off sparkles of light.

"Very good, my dear. Keep breathing. Feel the energy in your body. Now slowly open your eyes."

Elaris took a deep breath and cracked her eyes open. She still felt the warmth and power flowing through her veins.

"Focus on Sergeant Briggs. Feel the energy. Sense his soul. See his fate," Alec commanded.

A wave of power hit Elaris and flooded through her body, down her arms, and to her hands. Rivers of green energy flowed out from her fingertips, snaking their way to Sergeant Briggs.

Briggs jumped from his seat and landed on his feet, poised for action. Ever the soldier, he stood his ground, ready to battle the green streams that were consuming him. Unsheathing his knife, he sliced at his foe, only for the blade to pass right through as if nothing was there.

Colin had taken up position closer to Elaris, watching her intently and ready to grab her at a moment's notice.

Elaris faltered, her breathing increasing rapidly. She covered her eyes as fear gripped her. Falling to the ground, she cried, "I'm sorry! I'm so sorry!"

Colin ran to her, pulling her hands away from her face.

"Elaris! Are you alright?"

Tears ran down her face as she sobbed, "I didn't mean to!"

Alec knelt next to her, placing a hand on her arm.

"My dear, do not fret. You manifested the Embercurrent flawlessly. I couldn't have wished for a more perfect result!" he murmured.

Elaris wiped her tears and gazed up at him, unsure of what he had just said. "That was supposed to happen?" she choked.

"Well, yes," Alec smiled proudly.

"You could have given her some warning," Colin growled.

"Yes, a warning would have been appreciated," Briggs scowled.

Alec smiled meekly at them.

"My apologies, friends. I honestly didn't think it would work the first time. Lady Vaelora is quite talented. Yes, quite talented and powerful."

Briggs grumbled as he took his seat again, this time less comfortably.

Elaris gathered herself and, taking Colin's offered hand, stood, brushing off her skirts.

Alec took one look at her exhausted face and declared that it was time they took a break.

Elaris and Colin sat at the table, Briggs joining them, as Alec served tea and biscuits. Elaris ate happily while sipping her tea.

Turning to Colin, Alec inquired about his research.

"Have you found anything useful yet?" he coaxed.

Colin shook his head. "Not yet. I am only on the first volume, however."

Alec looked discouraged but quickly recovered, turning to Elaris.

"My lady, do you feel better now?"

She smiled sweetly and replied, "Yes, quite."

"I'm so glad to hear it. We can continue after you have finished."

"You mean there is more?" Colin choked.

"My friend, we have just begun," Alec grinned.

The rest of the afternoon was spent with Elaris repeatedly manifesting the Embercurrent until Alec no longer needed to aid her. When Briggs grew impatient with the exercise, they turned to Colin, who became equally annoyed at the constant streams of gold encircling him.

Seeing Elaris grow weary, Colin called a halt to the training for the day, leaving Alec disappointed. Agreeing to meet the next morning to continue, the party gathered their things to leave.

"You are doing exceptionally well, my lady. Please rest tonight. You have earned it," Alec praised as they departed.

The rain had finally stopped, the sun was setting, and they were rewarded with beautiful shades of pink and blue on the horizon as they made their way back to the inn. Upon arrival, Briggs took the reins and led the horses back to the stables.

"I will bring a plate to your room," Colin offered as he guided her up the stairs to her room.

"Thank you," she yawned.

Colin stopped her as they came to her door.

"I know that Alec asked a lot of you today," he began.

Elaris yawned again in response.

"But you really did perform exceptionally well. I was quite impressed."

Elaris blushed. His words made her feel warm and... loved.

"I'll be back in an hour with your supper," he called as he moved down the hall.

Closing her door, she considered the captain... Colin. She had noticed the growing friendship between them, their affection for each other deepening. She believed that he liked her. He clearly felt protective of her. Of course, that was his duty. He also had the duty to deliver her to Lord Mordane. The thought caused a vice to squeeze around her heart.

She had a duty as well—to be the queen. It was what everyone wanted, what everyone had worked for—what she had worked for her whole life. Despite now knowing why she had been chosen for the role, she still felt an obligation to fulfill what she had been told was her destiny.

Elaris sat on her bed, pulling off her shoes and stretching her feet. Thinking back to her conversations with Colin and even Sergeant Briggs, her view of Lord Mordane was now quite different than it had been just a week ago.

She couldn't imagine being pulled from her home as a small child, forced to work for the Royal Guard. The whole idea made her sick. She couldn't believe that the man who had been described to her as a generous ruler was the same man who would support such a thing.

If there was one thing she would do as Queen, it would be to abolish that abhorrent practice.

Stifling a yawn, she decided to lie down and take a nap while she waited for Colin to return. She closed her eyes and quickly fell asleep—dreams of a red Embercurrent carrying her to a palace on a hill, where pools of blood littered the ground.

CHAPTER 14

Elaris woke the next morning feeling unsettled from the dreams that had haunted her all night. Colin had woken her for supper last night, but she had been unable to eat, choosing instead to go back to bed. She quickly dressed and opened her door to find Colin and Briggs sitting at a table at the far end of the hallway, enjoying a hot cup of tea.

The men both stood upon seeing her, Colin stepping forward to welcome her to join them. "Would you like something to eat before we depart?" he asked.

Elaris's stomach growled in response, and she laughed.

"I believe that would be a good idea."

"I will go get the horses," Briggs said, bowing.

When he was gone, Elaris leaned forward and whispered, "I'm sure Sergeant Briggs is horribly bored."

"I'm sure you are right," Colin chuckled, "but I will be putting him to work today. He will be joining me in my studies of all those dusty books Alec gave us."

Elaris suddenly felt very sorry for Sergeant Briggs.

An hour later, the three arrived at Alec's home, Colin and Briggs taking their places at the table and Elaris taking hers in the cleared space next to them. Alec had managed to find even more books for Colin to research, making him grumble at the sight of them.

"Are you ready to get started, my dear?" Alec inquired.

Elaris forced a smile and nodded, earning a large grin from Alec.

"Good! Today's lesson will build on yesterday's, but this time you will be learning how to wield the Embercurrent. We will be taking it slow, as we now enter dangerous territory."

"Dangerous?" Elaris frowned.

"Well, yes. What you have been doing so far is just learning how to see the Embercurrent in your mind and then manifest it. Today you will expand that skill to manipulate the Embercurrent to change fate."

"I'm not sure I understand."

Alec smiled patiently at her.

"You will soon enough. First, let's practice what we learned yesterday as a warm-up. Then, we will move outside for the next lesson."

Elaris spent the next hour practicing her control of her power. Colin and Briggs continued researching but were often distracted by rivers of gold or green twisting around them. Each time Elaris manifested the Embercurrent, it became easier, and she didn't have to focus so much on every step. The process became more natural, and her own power took the place of the power she had "borrowed" from Alec the day before.

"I believe you are ready for lesson two!" Alec boasted.

Elaris followed him outside to a small clearing. The sun was shining, and she appreciated the warmth of it on her face.

"Alright. We are going to take a step back and focus on viewing the different currents."

"But Sergeant Briggs and Captain Aedric are inside," she noted, confused.

"We will not be needing them. You will be working with creatures far simpler to influence."

Elaris, still unsure what to expect, stood in the spot he indicated and waited for her next instruction.

"Alright, now close your eyes. Breathe deeply and slowly. Feel the breath enter you and sense how it travels through you. Focus now on the energy around you. Birds, rabbits, mice. Their energy is different, but somehow the same, yes?"

Elaris did as he instructed and was surprised that she was able to feel so much around her. She wanted to spend more time exploring the sensation, but Alec continued, "Choose something close—perhaps the blackbird in the tree above. He seems to be missing part of his beak, poor fellow."

Elaris focused on the energy from the creature and could see multiple currents forming in her mind, all coming from the small bird. Tiny rivers of silver stretched out and entwined around trees and bushes, many stretching into the sky.

"Unlike the last lesson, we will be exploring the blackbird's currents. We shall see what other fates are out there. Choose one of the alternate currents—not the brightest one, that's his chosen current—and follow it downstream a bit."

Elaris found one that wove through a bush and then went sunward. She let herself be pulled in, traveling rapidly down the stream. She was suddenly transported to a nest, the blackbird perched on the edge. His beak was perfect and unbroken. Inside the nest was a smaller blackbird, resting on three tiny eggs.

"What do you see?" Alec whispered close to her ear.

"The blackbird," she mumbled, "but his beak is not broken, and he has a family."

"How lovely—that sounds perfect," Alec smiled. "I want you to come back now to the blackbird on the branch above. To do this, focus on him again."

Elaris focused on the energy of the blackbird and was brought back to him above her, with his currents flowing out.

"Look at the bright chosen current. Now look to the alternate current you were just in. Focus. Breathe slowly and deeply. Open your eyes and manifest both currents."

Elaris did as he instructed, the Embercurrents flowing out of her fingertips.

"Wonderful!" Alec shouted. "Excellent!"

The blackbird looked down at the Embercurrents swirling around him—one bright and shiny silver, the other duller. He twisted his head left and right, fascinated by them.

"Alright, last step," Alec said excitedly. "You must pull the bird away from the chosen current and place it on the new one. Focus and breathe. Let it happen naturally."

Breathing deeply, Elaris focused on the bird's chosen current and, without knowing how, managed to move it slowly to the new current. In a flash, the bird disappeared, and Elaris shrieked in surprise.

Alec clapped his hands, howling in elation.

"Wonderful! Incredible! You did it, my dear!"

Horrified, Elaris croaked, "Where did he go?"

"I assume to his nest, or perhaps he is flying. Shall we look for him?" he offered excitedly.

Elaris started walking around, looking up into the trees. She heard a laugh from the wizard.

"No, my dear. Not that way. Find his energy. Just like you did before."

Realizing what he wanted her to do, Elaris closed her eyes and began the process she had practiced so many times the day before. She had difficulty at first weeding out the energy of all the creatures that surrounded her, but eventually found the blackbird.

"I found him!" she declared with relief.

"Where might he be?" asked Alec.

"He is in a tree, not far from here."

"Let's go find him!" he declared.

Elaris led him to the tree she had seen in her mind and looked up to find the blackbird. He appeared to be working on building a nest, and his beak was unharmed.

Stunned, Elaris grabbed hold of the tree to steady herself.

"Did I... what did I... what did I do?" she shuddered.

"You changed his fate. He will soon have a lovely family in that nest, and he doesn't have to worry about that broken beak," Alec said matter-of-factly.

The realization of what she had just done slammed into Elaris's chest. She had changed its *fate*? Her power didn't just let her see a creature's past and present and all the other possibilities, but it let her manipulate that creature's destiny.

The possible implications of this were amazing—yet horrifying.

While she may have improved the fate of the blackbird, Elaris recognized that she could have, just as easily, chosen an Embercurrent that wasn't so pleasant to move it to.

"I need to sit down," she breathed.

Alec immediately looked concerned and guided her into the house, where Colin and Briggs jumped up to help her.

"What did you do to her?" Colin yelled.

"I only taught her how to use her power to change the fate of a bird," Alec argued.

Elaris took the seat she was offered. Briggs brought her a cup of tea and placed it in her hands. She sipped it slowly, a look of panic still lingering in her eyes.

"My lady?" Colin pleaded.

"I'm alright," Elaris replied quietly.

Colin hovered next to her, concern overtaking his face. He turned back to Alec and glared at him. "Explain!" he barked.

"He did nothing wrong," Elaris interrupted before Alec could reply.

Colin looked into her eyes and waited for her to continue, giving his full attention.

"My powers. I didn't realize what I could do. I didn't realize the potential harm I could cause."

"My dear, you helped that bird," Alec interjected.

Elaris nodded.

"Yes. But I could have just as easily brought it to harm, couldn't I?"

Alec started to say something but stopped, lowering his head in acknowledgment.

"I could hurt someone," she said sadly.

"Yes. Your powers allow you to do incredible things to help others or, if you chose to, you could unleash destruction on lives everywhere. However, I don't believe for a moment that you would ever harm someone deliberately, and I know that you have it in you to learn the control necessary to ensure that only good comes when you use your abilities," Alec soothed.

Elaris gave him a small smile.

"Thank you, Alec. I'm glad I have you to guide me through all this."

"It is truly my pleasure, my lady," he grinned.

Walking over to the table, Alec looked at the mess Colin and Briggs had made of his books. "What do we have here?" he asked accusingly.

Colin ripped his gaze from Elaris and met Alec's. "Well," he mumbled, "we have been busy."

"I see," Alec chided. "I hope that you have something to justify this disorder you have wrought?"

"Yes!" Colin announced proudly. "We have. We found writings about the last Fatewaker from almost a thousand years ago."

Colin got up and moved over to the books, picking one up.

"This one speaks of the Fatewaker, a man with unmistakable violet eyes. He came from the south, traveling to these lands before they were known as Ashcar."

Colin stopped there, suddenly looking to Elaris with concern.

"What is it?" she pressed.

Colin hesitated before continuing.

"He apparently chose to use his powers to destroy those that stood in his way. He killed thousands and was rumored to be a follower of dark magic."

Elaris turned pale.

"What happened to him?" she murmured.

"He disappeared suddenly and was presumed dead. There is no mention of him after that. Ashcar went on to be settled and the kingdom established."

"Intriguing," Alec mumbled as he took the book from Colin, flipping through the pages.

Briggs sat in his chair examining a book that was covered in a thick layer of dust. As he flipped through the pages, he stopped at one and gasped.

"Captain. You need to see this," he urged.

Colin walked over and took the book from Briggs, examining the page he was on, a look of shock forming on his face.

"It can't be."

Alec's attention grabbed, he joined the two and examined the same page.

"Intriguing. He must be a descendant."

The three men stared in wonder at the ancient sketch of the last Fatewaker. The resemblance to Lord Mordane was uncanny.

CHAPTER 15

The next morning, Elaris, Colin, and Briggs met Alec at his home early. They had agreed the day before that this would be the last day of training, as they needed to get back to the camp. Alec was confident that Elaris had learned enough to control her powers—or, at the very least, to prevent unprovoked visions.

The topic on everyone's mind was Lord Mordane and his possible relationship to the last Fatewaker. They had continued looking through Alec's books last night but couldn't find any other information.

"I just don't have the correct texts!" Alec grumbled in frustration. "I suspect, as I'm sure we all do, that Lord Mordane is some sort of ancestor to the last Fatewaker. The only way we can know for sure is to find the Mordane lineage text. The only copy is kept in the palace library."

"Well, that's convenient, as we are due to arrive there in a couple of weeks," Colin mumbled.

The thought of reaching the palace had grown increasingly unpleasant to Elaris. She'd kept her feelings to herself, knowing Colin had a duty to fulfill and not wanting to complicate his role. The nightmares of Lord Mordane had worsened. This, coupled with the uncertainty about his intentions—and now, his possible relationship to a Fatewaker—had given her thoughts of running away. Only the sense of duty that had been instilled in her since she was a child kept her moving forward.

"I will keep looking, of course," Alec said, the sorrow in his voice apparent.

Elaris stepped forward, anxious to change the subject.

"What will I be learning today, Alec?" she asked, grinning hopefully.

Instantly distracted by her smile, Alec forgot Colin and turned his attention to her.

"After yesterday, I believe we shall take a step back and practice following the Embercurrent of creatures to see their past and future."

"Birds again?" she asked.

"Or whatever animal you would like. The choice is up to you. Shall we go see what the rabbits have been up to and what sort of trouble they may be plotting for my garden?" he asked, winking.

Laughing, Elaris led the way outside into the sunshine. Closing her eyes, she went through the process of choosing her first creature—a small mouse.

Although she had done it many times before, Alec guided her through following the Embercurrent in a more controlled manner. She went upstream on the bright green chosen current, emerging a few days in the mouse's past. She could see it running through the fields, then entering Alec's cottage via a small hole in the back wall. It made its way to the kitchen, where it stole a crust of bread Alec had left lying on the table.

"I'm afraid Mr. Mouse has been visiting your kitchen, Alec. You may want to patch that hole in your wall," she laughed.

"That explains a lot," Alec chuckled.

She then explored the future of a small bluebird, delightfully watching as it soared through the trees.

"What would you like to do next?" Alec asked her.

"The bird was wonderful. I sensed an owl nearby earlier. I'd love to see what he's been up to."

Elaris went through the motions of sensing the owl and finding its chosen current. But this time, she saw something strange. The owl's current was a copper color, but it was twisted with a thick black stream. She felt cold instantly and sensed something was wrong.

She followed it upstream to a few days' earlier, finding herself in a tree—the owl perched on a branch, looking down below. She heard familiar voices and, following the owl's gaze, saw herself, the captain, and Briggs, traveling on the road to Millcross.

"How strange," she mumbled.

Going back to the current, she followed it forward from the last vision. She emerged to find the owl perched again, sitting in a tree next to a very familiar cottage—Alec's cottage. Once more, it looked down, this time on her and Alec training.

"This doesn't seem right," she said in alarm, opening her eyes to find Alec looking at her with concern.

"What is it, my dear?"

"The owl. It's been following us."

"What do you mean?"

"I saw it four days ago, watching us on our journey to Millcross, and then again just yesterday, watching you and me training."

"That is odd," Alec frowned.

"His Embercurrent is also strange. It's tangled with another one—a black one."

Alec's face changed from contemplation to alarm. "Where is this owl?" he whispered, looking frantically up to the treetops.

"He is in that tree over there," she pointed, indicating a large oak to the right of the cottage.

Alec walked slowly toward the tree, spotting the owl perched on a high branch. Raising his hands, he murmured ancient words Elaris did not understand. In a flash, the owl fell from the tree, wings limp, and Alec caught him before he hit the ground.

"Is he dead?" Elaris cried loudly.

"Not dead. Merely stunned," Alec explained.

Hearing her cry, Colin and Briggs came racing from the cottage, where they had been going over the texts again.

"What happened?" Colin yelled, confusion on his face at the sight of the owl.

Alec rested his hands on the bird, mumbling something unintelligible under his breath. Once he was finished, the owl woke up. Alec released it in just enough time to avoid its massive wings hitting him as it made its escape.

"It seems, my friend, that the owl was a spy." He glowered.

"A spy? Sent by whom?" Colin demanded.

"I am guessing your friend Claudius. You said he was after Lady Vaelora."

Elaris shivered. The idea that someone had been watching her—possibly hunting her—made her chest tighten.

"Where is he? Is he nearby?" Colin asked while touching his sword.

Briggs was also on alert, scanning the trees, ready to fight.

"He would be a fool to come here. I would have sensed another wizard in the area. It was a clever maneuver to use the owl. We would have never known except Lady Vaelora could see his control of the animal on its Embercurrent. I doubt he will try the same method again."

Turning to Briggs, Colin ordered, "We need to leave."

Briggs nodded once and ran into the home to gather their things.

"We're leaving?" Elaris asked, clearly disappointed.

"I can't chance another attack like the last one. Not with just Briggs and me here to protect you," Colin murmured.

"What about me?" Alec brooded, hurt about being forgotten.

"I'm sure you would be very useful in a fight, my friend. But I would rather avoid one altogether. We will regretfully be leaving immediately for Oakhaven."

Approaching Elaris, Alec took her hands in his and smiled.

"It has been a genuine pleasure meeting you, my lady. I have full confidence in your ability to control your powers enough now to avoid unwanted visions. There is so much more I wished to teach you—you have barely scratched the surface of your abilities. I don't know what the future holds for you, my dear, but I beg you to please be safe. Trust in Colin. He will always do what he must to protect you."

Elaris had tears running down her face as she kissed the wizard on the cheek and thanked him.

"I shall never forget you or what you've done for me."

Seeing Briggs had returned with their things, Colin guided Elaris to her horse and helped her into the saddle. Colin and Alec shared a somber embrace and said their goodbyes. The three waved farewell as they quickly made their way down the path toward Millcross and the inn, Elaris looking back until the cottage and her new friend were out of view.

After hastily gathering their sacks and settling the bill with the innkeeper, they started their journey back to Oakhaven. All the while, Colin and Briggs kept a sharp eye on the trees above.

Sitting on a patch of grass by a creek, legs crossed, Claudius watched. Eyes closed but mind focused, he observed the Fatewaker and the wizard. The girl was talented, he could see. She was much more powerful than he had thought possible. The wizard had taught her much in just a few days. With more time, she could be a truly formidable foe.

But time was not on her side. He planned to take care of her personally this time. Hiring those fools to kill her at the lake had been a mistake. Taking his apprentices was equally unwise. They were not up to the challenge. This time, he would face her alone—no companion to stand in his way.

As he watched her and considered his plan, he felt her presence. She had discovered the owl. Would she sense him?

A few moments later and his question was answered as the wizard captured the creature and removed his spell, immediately eliminating his ability to see and hear them.

His eyes shot open, and he growled in frustration. He had underestimated her. She was able to see his control over the owl. He would have to be more careful next time.

Standing and walking to the creek to take a drink of water, he thought of the girl. She reminded him, in a way, of his daughter, Sophie. She had been very talented as well—just not talented enough.

Images of Sophie playing in the fields as a child flashed through his mind. He smiled as he remembered her laugh and the mischief she used to cause. He would give anything to hear that lovely sound again.

His face turned dark suddenly, thinking of how quickly they had lost her. She had been a pretty child and had only become more beautiful as she grew into a woman. She had inherited her father's skill, practicing magic at a young age—something they had kept secret for fear of her being taken and used by Lord Mordane.

But, as it turned out, he didn't want her magic.

Needing a mistress to give him a son, Lord Mordane had gone on the hunt. In Sophie, he had found the perfect breeding stock, young and beautiful. Sophie didn't want to go with him. She had tried her best to fight, but her magic just wasn't strong enough against Kaz's spells.

Claudius sobbed, recalling the moment she had died in his arms. She had looked up to him and apologized. *Apologized.* She had thought she had done something wrong. He would never forgive that bastard for what he had done to his sweet Sophie.

The Fatewaker would be used to give Mordane more control—of that Claudius was sure. He didn't know exactly what he had planned, but no good would come of their union. He knew he probably wasn't powerful enough to face Kaz on his own, but he could certainly eliminate the threat of the girl.

It was a shame she would have to die, but it couldn't be helped. Sacrifices must be made for the greater good. Now, all that stood in his way was the Royal Guard. A little planning, and they would no longer be a problem.

Wiping the tears from his eyes and adopting a look of determination, Claudius declared, "I'm sorry, my dear, but you must die."

CHAPTER 16

Draegor strode down the hallway swiftly, jar in hand. Kaz had become increasingly frustrating in his communications and needed a reminder of what was at stake. Opening the door to the sorcerer's rooms, Draegor walked in and slammed the jar down on a table, its contents vibrating with the impact.

Kaz stood and watched the jar, terror etched on his face, stunned into silence.

"I hear you have an update—and let me make this clear, Kaz: I want the whole update, up front. No messing about," Draegor hissed.

Kaz, pale and shaking, quickly jumped forward and began rapidly speaking. "Yes, my lord, I do have an update. Captain Aedric and Sergeant Briggs are still in Millcross and have been at the wizard's home multiple times. The rest of the Royal Guard remains in Oakhaven."

Draegor raised an eyebrow.

Kaz quickly continued, "Lady Vaelora has grown more powerful every day. I sensed complex magic from her. She has more than likely learned to manifest the Embercurrent."

Seeing his master's face turning red, Kaz frantically tried to remember what he had forgotten to say.

"And where is she?" Draegor growled.

"Oh, yes, my lord. She is with the captain and sergeant," Kaz replied, happy for the prompt.

Draegor picked up the jar and tilted it slowly from side to side, causing its contents to swirl madly. He kept his eyes trained on Kaz the whole time, glaring at him. Kaz, on the other hand, had dropped to the floor in supplication. "My lord," he begged.

Draegor kept tilting the jar from side to side. "What have ⌐d you about priorities?"

⌐z looked up in confusion. "You said I should tell you ⌐t pressing priority first."

⌐ct, my worthless friend. But you seem to have ⌐hat Lady Vaelora *IS* THE TOP PRIORITY," he

⌐what he had done, Kaz trembled and bowed his ⌐"Forgive me, my lord."

⌐wirled the contents of the jar around once more ⌐ it back down.

⌐t of Claudius?"

⌐ollows, my lord."

⌐ate," he muttered.

⌐nodded in response.

⌐o a shelf littered with various animal parts and ⌐or picked up a small bird beak and examined it. ⌐dric has disobeyed me, Kaz," he sighed deeply. ⌐cerned about his presence at the wizard's house ⌐aelora. I can only assume that he is helping her ⌐wers."

143

Kaz looked up hopefully, happy that the subject had moved away from him. "Yes, my lord," he agreed readily.

"Lieutenant Holt—he is loyal to the captain, is he not?"

"Most assuredly. From what I have seen and heard, the two are like brothers."

"And one can assume that the captain's men are also loyal to him?"

"Oh yes, my lord. Captain Aedric has a reputation for earning the loyalty of his men. They would die for him."

"Convenient," he murmured.

Draegor took his time examining more objects on the shelf, taking random samples, and rolling them between his fingers or smelling them.

Finally, after what felt like hours, he announced, "I believe it is time for Captain Aedric to be relieved of his command. I have given him time to correct his course, and instead, he takes her to the wizard. Send for Captain Karr."

Kaz left quickly to carry out his master's wishes. Draego opened a book of spells and began rifling through the page randomly, his thoughts on Lady Vaelora.

She was growing more dangerous by the day. absolutely had to get her to the palace before she gained much power.

Captain Aedric taking her to Alec had been an unexp move. He had been ordered to stay on the Lake Disobedience was out of character for him. Befo mission, Draegor had considered him the most trus of all his Guard—a favorite of his.

Now, he was just a weed to be plucked out.

An hour later, Captain Thorne Karr and his company of twenty men entered the main hall of the palace, where Draegor was waiting, with Kaz cowering behind him.

"My lord, you sent for me?" Karr inquired, lowering himself to one knee and bowing.

"Captain Karr. You and Captain Aedric have a long history, yes?"

Karr's head shot up and his deep brown eyes filled with darkness. "We do," he answered tightly.

"Good," he purred. "Captain Aedric has, unfortunately, gone astray. He had orders to escort my bride down the Lake Road but seems to have found himself lost in Millcross, leaving the rest of his men abandoned in Oakhaven."

"I see, my lord... and you wish me to... fetch him?" Karr sneered. He knew Colin was a favorite of Lord Mordane's.

Draegor managed a believable look of sadness. "Regretfully, the captain is no longer able to handle the burdens of command."

"And his men, my lord?" Karr asked hopefully.

"Also astray, I fear."

Karr's lip curled up in a derisive grin. "I understand, my lord."

"Understand *this*, Captain—you will return with Lady Vaelora as soon as possible. No delays. No failures. Or you will share the fate of Captain Aedric," he snarled.

Karr bowed low in acknowledgment.

Waving to Kaz behind him, Draegor ordered, "Kaz here will be giving you and your men a blessing."

Karr and his men stood, going through the same ritual as Colin and his men had gone through a few weeks prior. Afterward, Draegor went to Karr and, lowering his voice, said, "Be careful with my bride, Captain. You will notice she possesses certain… abilities. You may need to… protect her from herself. But she is not to be harmed."

"I will see she is brought to you safely, my lord."

"There is something else. A wizard named Claudius. He may cause trouble. If you see him, make sure he is dealt with swiftly."

Karr nodded, "Of course, my lord."

"Good! Now leave without delay."

Karr bowed and made his way out of the hall with his men, leaving Draegor and Kaz alone.

"He will kill Captain Aedric, my lord. They hate each other," Kaz said cautiously.

"Do they? What a shame," his master drawled.

Captain Thorne Karr marched his men out of the gates of the palace, on their way to the barracks to collect their gear and leave in the direction of Oakhaven. Karr knew that, despite Colin being in Millcross, he would never leave his men for long in Oakhaven. He would find him there.

This mission was everything Karr could have hoped for. He had been waiting years for an opportunity to kill that self-righteous bastard, and now he had it. He thought back to the day when Colin had brought embarrassment and shame to him and his men.

It was spring and Karr and his company had been ordered to the nearby village of Houck to investigate a potential thief in the area who had been stealing from the tax collector. It was a crime punishable by hanging to steal from Lord Mordane's treasury.

Entering the town, Karr and his men had started the investigation by pulling families from their homes and searching through their belongings. Some of the villagers resisted, earning them a whipping. Others—all women—were suspected of other potential crimes, and were rounded up and placed in the custody of his men, who were anxious to interrogate them.

Reaching the last home, Karr had found a sack of money in a farmer's home—far too much money for the farmer to have. He declared the man a thief and dragged him out to the courtyard.

Karr glowered as he thought back to the moment. He had been stringing a rope around the man's neck, ready to enact his punishment, when Colin showed up with his men. Apparently, they were in the area and had heard the commotion.

Colin, who had outranked him at the time, had ordered the immediate release of the farmer and the other prisoners. This would have been bad enough, but he then berated Karr in the public square with all his men and the villagers looking on.

Later, it was discovered that the tax collector himself had been the one stealing the money.

He had lost the respect of his men that day, appearing weak. Word had also gotten back to their commander, who demoted him for a year.

It was a humiliation he swore he would one day repay, and now was his opportunity.

He smiled menacingly as he considered the many ways of killing a man, imagining Colin in every scenario.

CHAPTER 17

The day had mercifully stayed sunny as Colin, Elaris, and Briggs made their way down the road back to Oakhaven. They had been traveling for a few hours and had stopped to rest the horses and eat something. Briggs had scouted the area to make sure it was safe, and now the three sat in a small clearing, partaking of some bread and cheese they had packed from the inn.

"I wish we didn't have to go back," Elaris sighed.

"Missing Alec already?" Colin teased.

"I wish we could have taken him with us," she laughed.

"I'm afraid Alec would not be welcome at the palace, my lady."

Elaris frowned. "Whyever not?"

Colin shared a knowing glance with Briggs. "Alec used to be one of the Royal Wizards, but he left due to... differences of opinion with Lord Mordane and his Royal Sorcerer."

"What do you mean?" Elaris pressed.

Briggs shifted uncomfortably and directed his gaze at a tree on the horizon, doing his best to ignore the conversation.

Colin felt he had already said too much. He had taken her to Alec and had diverted from the route they were to take. If Lord Mordane found out that Colin had filled her mind with stories about his schemes, he would find his head on a chopping block.

Colin smiled at her and began packing up their things. "I'm sorry to cut our picnic short, but we need to get moving. Our late start today means we won't be arriving until after dark."

It didn't escape Elaris's notice that Colin had ignored her question. She didn't understand why he hadn't answered it. She couldn't imagine why a sweet man like Alec wouldn't be welcome at the palace. What possible conflict could he have had with Lord Mordane? From what she had been told, he was understanding of those with differences of opinion. Perhaps Alec had misunderstood and left prematurely?

Elaris kept a watchful eye on Colin for the next few hours. He seemed more distant since lunch, riding ahead to scout and leaving Briggs to guard her. She was confused and hurt by his avoidance. She felt they had been growing closer, and she valued his friendship. She had hoped they would remain friends after she became Queen.

Frowning, Elaris realized how naive that hope was.

Colin was a captain in the Royal Guard. She would be Queen. A friendship would be inappropriate. Perhaps that's why Colin was avoiding her. Maybe he had already considered this and was preparing her for the inevitable.

Thinking back on the last few days, she pondered her future. She had discovered much about herself—that she was the Fatewaker and had power, that she had been kept in the dark, with her powers suppressed her whole life.

She had to believe there was a reason for it. Perhaps Lord Mordane was trying to protect her in some way. She was anxious to learn what he had planned for her. Would she be using her gifts to help Ashcar somehow?

"My lady, are you well?" Briggs asked, concern lacing his voice.

She smiled at him, replying, "Yes, Sergeant, why do you ask?"

"You looked like a person with a heavy burden."

"Perhaps I am a bit overwhelmed by everything," she conceded.

Briggs looked at her with something akin to affection. "I hope you remain safe, my lady," he said sadly.

Elaris, confused, was about to ask him what he meant when Colin returned from scouting the road ahead. "Our path is clear," he reported.

"Sir, will we be staying in Oakhaven long?" Briggs asked hopefully.

"I'm afraid not, Sergeant. We are already behind schedule. We will be leaving tomorrow."

Briggs tried to hide his disappointment but failed. Elaris wondered if he had a girl in Oakhaven, or perhaps he was looking forward to some time off.

A few hours later, just before nightfall, they arrived at the camp. Half a dozen soldiers rushed to help Elaris down from her horse, causing Colin to frown in annoyance.

"Welcome back!" Bren yelled as he approached.

"Thank you, Lieutenant. I hope you and the men have been well," Elaris said as she navigated out of the crowd of soldiers.

"We have, my lady! I hope that your trip was enjoyable," he replied.

"It was productive, at least," Colin interjected.

"I'm looking forward to hearing about it. My lady, would you like some time to rest before supper?"

Elaris smiled at him gratefully and replied, "Oh yes, thank you."

Corporal Knoll jumped forward to escort her to her tent, annoying Colin further.

Once the soldiers and Elaris were out of earshot, Colin snapped, "Really, have they nothing else to do?"

Bren ignored his friend's question and immediately started interrogating him. "Where have you been? It's been five days—I was about to pack up and come find you."

"We were with Alec. Much has happened. I'll explain later. For now, I need to wash up and get some food."

An hour later, orders had been given to prepare the camp for an early morning departure, and Colin was back in uniform, feeling at home in command again. From what he could tell, Bren had kept the men busy training and gathering provisions for their upcoming journey into Vale Forest. He was proud of the work his friend had done. Now, he just needed to fill him in on everything they had discovered.

He found Bren by the campfire, giving final orders to Sergeants Renshaw and Bryant, who would be standing guard that night.

After sending them off, Bren approached and sighed, "It will be hard to leave the tranquility of this place for Vale Forest."

"Agreed. I wish we could avoid it. Unfortunately, our delay in Millcross has put us behind schedule, and we now have no choice but to go that route."

"Are you ready to tell me what happened?" Bren asked.

"Let's go for a walk," Colin said, indicating a path nearby that led to the bluff overlooking Oakhaven.

Once they were away from the camp, Colin launched into the story of the last few days. He filled Bren in on the discovery that Elaris was the Fatewaker, her subsequent training to hone her newfound powers, and her uncovering of Claudius's spy.

Bren was speechless, fighting to find the right words in response.

Colin laughed at his struggle. "I know. And I haven't told you all of it yet."

"What more could there possibly be?" Bren cried.

"We found an old text about the last Fatewaker. He used his powers to take control, and it's believed he turned to dark magic. Eventually, he disappeared. There was an old sketch... Lord Mordane and he could be brothers. We can only assume he's a descendant."

"He's descended from one of these Fatewakers? But what does that mean?"

"I don't know. But it worries me what he has planned for Elaris."

"We are calling her Elaris now?" Bren teased.

Colin rolled his eyes. "She asked me to... when we are alone."

"Just how often have you been alone with her?" Bren questioned—eyebrows raised.

Colin scowled at him. "Everything has been completely innocent."

"I should hope so, my friend. You're in enough trouble as it is. If he finds out you were spending private time with his lady, you're a dead man."

Colin couldn't deny his friend was right. "I know," he conceded quietly.

"Let's hope he doesn't discover where you've been the last few days. Explaining the diversion is one thing, explaining going to Alec's is another."

Colin shrugged. "Let me worry about that. I've talked my way out of worse."

"Yes, you have," Bren laughed.

Colin chuckled, remembering all the times he and Bren had escaped being caught in some mischief when they were younger.

"In all seriousness, you need to be careful, Colin," Bren implored, using his friend's first name for impact. "I can see you have feelings for her."

He sometimes hated how observant Bren was. It had come as a shock to Colin when he realized that his protectiveness of Elaris had turned into something more. She ruled his thoughts, and more than anything, he wanted to tell her not to go to Lord Mordane.

Doing so would be unfair to her, however. With *him*, she had a future as a Queen. With Colin, she would spend her life on the run, being hunted by Lord Mordane's soldiers. It was too much to ask.

"My feelings are nothing to be concerned about, Bren," he said with conviction.

Bren looked at him intently. "Whatever happens, you know I have your back."

Colin merely nodded.

Morning light stretched across the horizon as Elaris rode silently with the Guard, nerves twisting tighter with each step her horse took.

The men had spoken of Vale Forest the night before—of dark creatures and dangers that waited beneath its trees. Their voices had gone quiet when they realized she was listening.

Sergeant Briggs now rode beside her, where Colin usually would. But today, he'd chosen to ride point. She hadn't spoken to him yet, and his quiet avoidance stung more than she wanted to admit.

Turning to the sergeant, she said, "I have heard the men talking about the dangers of the forest. What might we expect to encounter there?"

Looking displeased, Briggs answered, "The men shouldn't be discussing such things in your presence, my lady."

Elaris pursed her lips impatiently at this response, waiting for him to continue. Briggs adjusted in his seat and spoke cautiously. "The forest is ancient. In it, many creatures, both light and dark, live."

"Light and dark?"

"Some may call them good and evil, my lady, but it's not that simple. Some of the creatures serve dark powers or were created with dark magic, while others use the forest to hide from being captured and destroyed. These light creatures are harmless and only seek asylum."

"Who would destroy them?" she asked, distress coloring her voice.

Briggs hesitated, looking around as if searching for an escape, but found none. "Not everyone is accepting of these creatures, my lady. The important thing to remember is that if you leave them alone, they will generally leave you alone."

"What of the dark creatures? Will they also leave us alone?"

Briggs didn't answer right away, his gaze drifting to the tree line with something unreadable in his eyes. Elaris sensed there was more he wasn't saying—perhaps memories from the last time they'd traveled that path. Whatever had happened, it hadn't gone well.

"You shall be safe with us, my lady," Briggs said with a confidence he didn't necessarily feel.

Elaris remained unsure, her nerves on edge. They had two days of travel before reaching the forest. She thought of her vision of Sergeant Keswick. He had been in the woods, slashes all over his body. Could she possibly have been seeing Vale Forest? She now understood that the Embercurrent she had followed for him had been his chosen current, not a possible alternate. She worried that she had seen his death, but she didn't know how she was to prevent it.

She considered her powers and the short amount of training she had done in moving someone to an alternate fate. She had only done it once, with the blackbird, and that had terrified her.

Could she do the same to save Sergeant Keswick? What if she chose the wrong fate? What if she caused a catastrophic change? The possible outcomes were endless, and she feared the damage she might do.

She needed to train more, to gain more knowledge of her powers. She wished Alec were here. Without him, she felt lost. What good was seeing someone's possible fates if she was incapable of helping them?

Watching Sergeant Keswick riding ahead of her, she made a promise to herself that she would do everything possible to save him. She would start by picking up where she and Alec had left off.

Elaris spent the rest of the morning finding the energy of various animals around her and exploring their Embercurrents. Many of the men looked confused, as she still needed to close her eyes to concentrate and often looked like she was sleeping on her horse.

"Do you need some rest, my lady?" Briggs asked, concern in his voice.

Smiling at him, she leaned over and whispered, "I'm just practicing, Sergeant."

Realization hit him, and he nodded in understanding. As long as she wasn't shooting colorful rivers of light out of her hands again, he would remain content.

CHAPTER 18

Colin wasn't pleased. They were all too exposed. The stretch of road was lined with high walls of rock, the perfect vantage point for an ambush. He kept his eyes upward, scanning.

"I'll be happy when we get clear of this section of road," Bren grumbled, reading his mind.

Colin didn't take his eyes off the rock walls. "We need to pick up speed. I *swear* we're being watched."

Bren didn't need to be told twice. He signaled the rest of the company, and their pace quickened.

"What's happening?" Elaris asked.

"Nothing to be concerned about," Briggs assured her. "Captain probably just wants to get to camp."

An hour later, they cleared the mountainous area and entered a stretch of road lightly lined with trees. Colin relaxed a little, as they were now able to see clearly around them, and the area didn't give many opportunities for someone to stay hidden.

"We'll go an hour longer and then make camp for the night," he ordered Bren.

"Sounds good. Hopefully we can find a good location next to a stream. Some of these guys could use a bath," Bren joked, earning several protests from the men.

The site they found for camp did, in fact, have a stream. Despite Colin's silent agreement that some of the men could use a wash, he made sure that Elaris had access first, offering to escort her.

"Thank you, Captain," she said with a smile as she gathered a few things and walked down a wooded path next to the camp to the stream.

Colin stood a respectful distance away, turning his back as he had before. He heard her drop her things, then the splash as she entered the water—followed by her sharp intake of breath when the cold hit her feet.

Clearing his throat, he said, "Sergeant Briggs tells me you were practicing today."

"Yes. I want to ensure that I can help if the need arises."

"Help?" he asked, sounding confused.

"Should we be attacked again, I want to be able to assist in any way I can."

Colin became instantly anxious. "Should we be attacked again, you need to stay hidden. You certainly shouldn't be helping with the fight," he said, perhaps too harshly.

He was answered with silence. He could still hear her splashes in the water, but after a few minutes of still not getting a reply, he grew concerned. "Elaris?" he asked hesitantly.

"What about Sergeant Keswick?" she murmured.

"What of him?"

"You know I had a vision of his death."

Colin frowned. "I thought that you also had a vision of Lieutenant Holt's mother being dead?"

Frustrated, she replied, "I did. But that was different."

Colin could hear her emerging from the water and shuffling about behind him. After a few moments, she walked in front of him wearing her blue dress, her dark wet hair hanging down her back. His breath caught in his throat.

"I... I mean... how was it different?" he stammered.

"I learned so much those few days with Alec. I now understand that what I was seeing with Sergeant Keswick was quite different from what I saw with Lieutenant Holt. With Lieutenant Holt, I was seeing an alternate current, a possible fate. With Sergeant Keswick, I was viewing his chosen current—his actual future, unless something changes."

"And you hope that, with enough practice, you can change his future?"

She shrugged. "I honestly don't know. So far, I've only practiced on animals. Viewing a person's Embercurrent can be... disturbing. I've been avoiding doing it. And changing someone's fate—I've only ever done it once with the blackbird. I have no idea if I can do it with a person, and the possibilities of making things worse terrify me."

"I'm not sure there could be many things worse for Sergeant Keswick than his death."

"Perhaps. But everyone's Embercurrents are intertwined in a way. Changing his fate could also change the fate of others. I just don't have the knowledge to control it yet."

Colin considered this. He wished he could help her, give her more time. But he couldn't.

"I promise I will keep an eye out for Sergeant Keswick. If you feel you need to practice your skill, please do. But promise me that, should we come under attack, you will stay hidden and safe," he pleaded.

Elaris could hear the panic in his voice, and it made her want to reach out to him. Instead, she nodded and whispered, "I promise."

Feeling only mildly appeased, Colin led her down the path and back to the camp.

After supper, Elaris sat at the campfire with Colin, Bren, and several of the soldiers, including Sergeant Keswick. She listened intently as they entertained her with their tales of conquests—most of which had been significantly exaggerated, she was sure.

As Sergeant Linwood began telling them about a particularly large bear he had slain, she turned her concentration to Sergeant Keswick. She knew what she needed to do, but feared it just the same.

Closing her eyes, she focused on him and found his Embercurrent. She saw his chosen current but opted to ignore it, moving instead to one of his alternate currents. Following it downstream, she found herself in a dark room with stone walls, moss growing between the cracks. The sergeant was in the corner on the floor, shackles on his wrists and feet. Whip marks riddled his back. The look in his eyes was vacant, all happiness gone.

Pulling away from the current, Elaris opened her eyes and refocused on the conversation. *No, not that one*, she thought.

As the evening continued, Elaris dove into the sergeant's Embercurrent again and again, trying to find the right one. She found one that gave her hope—the sergeant had a lovely family and a cozy home—but when she went a bit further, she saw him killed again, this time by a fall from a horse.

Discouraged, she excused herself and went to her tent. She went to sleep and dreamt of the red Embercurrent again, stretching far and wide, rivers of blood flowing around her. A palace on a hill.

The next morning, Elaris woke, exhausted. She was beginning to hate going to sleep, as nightmares came more and more frequently. She splashed water on her face from a basin and got dressed, donning one of her black dresses. Looking in a mirror, she could see dark circles around her violet eyes.

Leaving the tent, she was greeted by Colin, who was walking to the horses. "Good morning," she said with forced cheerfulness.

Colin instantly looked concerned, stopping and examining her face. "Are you well, my lady?"

"Oh yes," she lied. "I just had a bit of trouble sleeping. I shall be fine."

"I noticed you left for your tent quite early last night."

"I was tired from the journey."

Unconvinced, Colin pressed further. "I also noticed you were practicing again."

Elaris knew there was no use trying to hide it from him. "Yes. I was trying to find a good alternate current for Sergeant Keswick, just in case."

"I thought it was too dangerous," he said, confused.

"It is... but isn't letting him die worse?" she choked.

162

"Elaris," he sighed, "you must try not to worry. Didn't Alec say that these currents are made from the choices we make?"

"Yes," she mumbled.

"Well, we will just make sure Sergeant Keswick makes the right choice."

Seeing she still looked unsure, he murmured softly, "Trust me."

She did trust him. In fact, she was sure he would do anything to protect her. But, on this, she needed to follow her heart.

Seeing that Colin was waiting for a response, she nodded in agreement, earning a warm smile from him.

An hour later, they were back on the road traveling south, expecting to be at Vale Forest by nightfall. Sergeant Briggs had, once again, taken position next to her.

"Will we be camping in the forest tonight, Sergeant?" she inquired.

"No, my lady. The forest is too dangerous to enter at night. We shall camp a bit away and enter it in the morning."

"But won't it take us several days to get through? Won't we be sleeping there at night?"

"Yes—but we won't be traveling at night. We will make sure to have the camp set up before sunset, with guards posted. A much safer plan."

"I see," she replied.

Elaris turned her attention to Colin, riding up ahead. He seemed excessively focused on the road. He and the lieutenant took turns riding ahead or investigating side roads. She thought about Claudius and wondered if they were looking for him.

Colin returned from one of his excursions and joined her, inviting Briggs to fall back. "Have you felt anything... strange... during your practicing?" he asked, still scanning the roadway.

"Strange?"

"Yes—like the owl."

"Oh—no. I haven't sensed Claudius again."

Colin seemed to relax a bit.

"You think he is following?" she asked quietly.

"Absolutely," he grumbled.

"Will he attack?"

"He would be a fool to attack us now. I doubt he has had time to gather help like he did last time, so he would be on his own. No, he will watch and wait."

"Wait for what?"

"For us to have our guard down."

Elaris thought about the wizard who was most likely still spying on them and wondered why he was trying to kill her. As she had never met the man and, to her knowledge, had never done anything to harm him, she assumed that his attack on her was due to some conflict with her future husband.

Although no one had said anything negative about Lord Mordane directly, she had sensed that he was not well liked. She also found many things about him troubling, such as his practice of conscripting children, his apparent conflict with Alec, and, of course, his choice to keep her in the dark about her powers.

The dreams of what she could only assume was the palace—and of him choking her—didn't help either.

As the days passed, her anxiety grew. She only hoped she was wrong—that he really was the honorable, generous man she'd heard about all her life—but something inside whispered otherwise.

Seeing Sergeant Keswick riding off to the side of her, she decided to refocus her efforts on finding a good alternate current, should the need arise. She closed her eyes again and found his chosen current, bright and green.

She was about to disregard it and move to an alternate current, but noticed something she had missed before—a tiny stream that shot off from the chosen current downstream, and then continued, running parallel to it.

Curious, she followed this alternate current until she emerged, finding herself in a forest. The same forest she had seen the sergeant's death in. There was fighting all around, with strange creatures amongst the soldiers.

Fighting alongside the captain was Sergeant Keswick— very much alive. She saw a large, winged creature, not unlike a gargoyle, fly at him, talons raised. Instead of getting hit, the sergeant was pushed out of the way by the captain, causing the creature to fly headfirst into a tree. She saw Sergeant Keswick smile at the captain and continue fighting.

Pulling herself back to her horse and the path they were traveling, Elaris smiled happily. She had found it.

Later that afternoon, as they drew closer to Vale Forest, the trees along the road grew denser, hanging over the company like a dome. Colin called for them to step up their pace as, the clouds had darkened and the wind had picked up, indicating rain was coming.

Another hour later, they arrived at a clearing about a mile outside the entrance to the forest. The soldiers hurried to make camp as the first drops of rain began to fall, the last vestiges of light diminishing. Colin ensured Elaris's tent was ready first and then went to talk to Bren. He prepared himself for a fight as he approached his friend.

"All of the tents should be up soon, and supper is cooking," Bren reported.

"Good work. Make sure the horses are well secured. It looks like we are in for a hell of a storm."

"Will do. Anything else?"

Colin shifted, straightening his back and standing at his full height. "Yes. I will be departing soon for the forest. I will rejoin you before morning."

"The hell you are!" Bren bellowed.

If any other soldier had spoken to him in such a way, he would be severely punished. But this was Bren, and Colin knew he was doing so out of fear and friendship.

"Bren…"

"No. You, of all people, know the dangers ahead—and you want to go in alone. At night. What possible reason could you have for such a foolhardy trip?"

Colin sighed. "I have a plan to avoid a repeat of our last visit. I need you to trust me."

"At least take someone with you. Take Briggs. He would scare off the biggest monster just by looking at them."

"You may be right about Briggs," Colin said with a smirk, "but I need to do this alone."

Bren glared at him for a solid minute, unbudging. "If you aren't here by sunrise, we are coming in after you."

"I wouldn't expect anything less," he said fondly.

Bren grasped him by the shoulders and pulled him in for a quick, firm embrace. "Be safe, my friend."

Colin nodded once and turned to leave, grabbing his gear and heading for his horse. Bren stood by until he was out of sight.

"Was that Captain Aedric leaving?" Elaris asked, approaching him from her tent.

"It was, my lady," Bren murmured, his voice tight with worry.

"But where is he going?" she asked, clearly concerned.

"He will be back. Please try not to worry. There's a storm coming. I'll have someone bring your supper to your tent. Best to stay inside until the storm passes."

Elaris frowned and reluctantly went to her tent.

CHAPTER 19

Standing at the edge of the forest, Colin considered what he was about to do. The forest had nearly claimed his life once, and now he was walking back into it alone. He had been going over his options for the last few days and had concluded that this was the only way. He drew a deep breath, gave his horse a gentle nudge, and proceeded in.

Almost immediately, the air changed. The storm that had begun to rage outside was no more, replaced by stillness and a thick fog, coupled with the smell of damp forest floor. As he moved further, his eyes adjusted, and he became aware of luminescent plants all around him. Strange sounds in the distance hinted at dangers lurking just beyond his line of sight.

Colin was tempted to ride with his sword drawn, knowing from experience just how quickly the calm could be broken by chaos here.

He resisted the urge and rode slowly but confidently, keeping a watchful eye on his surroundings.

After a few hours, he came to a waterfall that supplied a small lake below. He followed the path downward, stopping at the lake to let his horse drink. A cracking sound to his right had him spinning on his heel, his hand instinctively moving to draw his sword. He froze when he felt a cool blade at his throat.

"I believe we have found ourselves a lost human, Tretch," the owner of the blade purred.

Colin turned his head slowly to see a tall, beautiful woman with waist-length red hair standing next to him and a small goblin-like creature at her side. She had wings that fell down her back and skimmed the backs of her feet. She wore silver armor on her torso that marked her as a warrior.

"We should kill him, mistress," the man named Tretch croaked.

"I would agree with you, but that is not her way," the beautiful woman sighed, clearly disappointed.

"I need to speak to your queen," Colin whispered, the blade pressing harder into his throat.

"What business do you have with her?" the woman demanded.

"I need a favor," Colin replied.

The woman burst out laughing, Tretch joining in with her.

"This, I have to hear," she chuckled, grabbing him by the hair and pulling him off the road and into the trees.

They walked for what seemed like an hour, going deeper into the trees. The darkness was only broken by the illumination of the plants on the forest floor, lighting their way. Neither Tretch nor the woman spoke to him. He gave no resistance as she kept the knife at his back and pushed him along.

The trees started to thin, and they emerged into a clearing filled with small huts. The huts all stood quiet—their occupants probably fast asleep. Fruit trees and berry bushes lined the pathway leading to a centralized building made of clay and mud. Colin's captor forced him down the path to the building, following close behind as he entered.

Inside what looked to be a meeting hall, he was greeted by the soft glow of lights suspended beneath a domed ceiling, its surface covered in colored stones.

Statues of various creatures lined the walls, all of them turned to judge those that entered. Seated on a dais, placed high above the main floor, was another beautiful woman— tall and radiant, with long golden hair. Like the redhead, she had wings cascading down her back. Instead of armor, she wore a dark blue gown that caressed her feet.

Colin was shoved forward and fell to his knees in front of her. The redhead went to stand next to the golden-haired woman and whispered something to her, while Tretch kept the knife at his back. After their private exchange, the woman in the chair stared at him intently, as if trying to analyze him.

"I am Lumirien, Queen of the Alari. Who are you, and what do you want with us?" she ordered.

Colin bowed his head respectfully. "I am Captain Colin Aedric of the Royal Guard. I come to ask for your help."

Upon hearing he was from the Royal Guard, both Tretch and the red-haired woman hissed. Lumirien held up her hand to silence them.

"We do not help those who serve the Butcher of Ashcar," she said with force.

Colin didn't argue. He couldn't blame her.

"My lady, I do not ask for myself, but for the one I protect."

Lumirien waved him away, saying, "I am aware you escort his bride. She is of no significance to us."

Colin tried to hide his surprise that they knew of his mission.

"Please... my lady... she is different. Special," he pleaded.

Something in his voice made her stop and consider him again. "How? What is so special about this girl?"

"She is the Fatewaker," he breathed.

"He lies!" the redhead hissed, jumping forward, poised to attack.

Lumirien stood abruptly, walking to Colin and waving Tretch away. Colin stood at her prompting and brushed himself off.

"How do you know it is she?" Lumirien asked.

"She has eyes the color of amethysts, sees visions of the past and future, and controls the Embercurrent."

Lumirien turned to the redhead and gasped, "Thistwyn, could it be?"

Colin was happy to finally know his captor's name.

Thistwyn looked shaken and replied, "My Queen... the human describes the Fatewaker... and it's been a thousand years."

Lumirien turned back to Colin slowly, considering her words. "I am almost as old as the forest, Captain, and can remember the time of the last Fatewaker. Tell me, is she here to destroy us?"

Colin smiled at her reassuringly and answered, "Lady Vaelora's heart is pure. You have nothing to fear from her."

Lumirien reflected for a moment, finally deciding to believe him, and smiled back. "How can we help the guardian of the Fatewaker?"

Colin breathed a sigh of relief. "We need safe passage through the forest—not just from dark creatures, but from a wizard that follows us."

Lumirien frowned. "I unfortunately cannot promise safe passage, Captain. I can only promise our aid should the need arise."

"Thank you, my lady. I am grateful."

He bowed.

"Please understand, Captain—this is a limited alliance. We will not involve ourselves in human battles. But we will defend the Fatewaker and her protectors."

"I understand."

"Thistwyn will take you to your horse and guide you out of the forest. Safe journey, Captain."

Colin bowed again and followed Thistwyn out of the building. She was silent for their walk back, looking contemplative. When the lake came into view, he saw that someone had secured his horse to a tree.

"I believe I can find my way back," Colin said while mounting his horse.

"What is she like?" Thistwyn blurted.

Colin paused before answering, smiling as he thought of Elaris. "Lady Vaelora is compassionate, kind, and intelligent. Her beauty is only matched by the strength of her heart."

Thistwyn looked thoughtful and, turning to leave, said, "We shall be watching you, human."

Colin wasted no time making his way back to the entrance of the forest. He counted himself lucky that his plan had worked, and he had managed to meet the right creatures. He didn't want to chance meeting the wrong ones on the way out.

The sky had just started to turn pink with the coming sunrise when Colin left the forest. He had felt like he was being watched on his journey back, hoping the whole way it was by friend and not foe. He gave his horse a nudge to encourage a faster pace, the mud left over from the storm the night before slowing it down.

As the camp came into sight, he felt his shoulders relax and let out a breath he didn't know he had been holding.

Bren was already up when he arrived, looking relieved when he saw him.

"You're lucky. Briggs was just about to go in and find you," Bren laughed as Colin dismounted.

"Well, you can tell him to stand down. The only thing I am in danger of right now is starving. Is breakfast ready?" Colin chuckled.

As the two men made their way to the campfire, Colin filled Bren in on his encounter with Lumirien.

"Do you trust they will actually help us?" Bren asked.

"I believe so—but time will tell."

"I have to admit, it's a good plan," Bren sighed.

"I do have them occasionally," Colin said with an eye roll.

Walking to his tent for a quick nap, Colin saw Elaris approaching, her face a mixture of relief and annoyance.

"Why did you leave?" she asked abruptly.

"I had business in the forest," he answered, stifling a yawn.

"Alone?" she snapped.

Colin smiled at her. "Yes. And now I am off to sleep. We shall be leaving in a few hours. I suggest you get some breakfast—the biscuits are particularly good this morning," he said as he left her.

Elaris stood in disbelief. "I don't care about biscuits!" she yelled behind him, making him smile.

CHAPTER 20

The forest did not want them there. Of that, Elaris was sure. As their horses entered the wooded area, she could feel the trees closing in on them—and sensed eyes watching. She wasn't the only one apprehensive. The soldiers also seemed to be on edge, instinctively resting a hand on their hilts as they watched the trees.

The captain rode to her right, while Sergeant Briggs was on her left. The remaining soldiers kept position in front and behind her. Unlike the days prior, she felt they were preparing for an impending attack.

"I don't like it," Briggs grumbled.

"What is it, Briggs?" Colin asked.

"We're being watched."

Elaris saw Colin give the sergeant a nod. He knew.

An hour into the journey, the forest had grown dark, despite it being around ten in the morning.

The canopy of trees above them blocked out most of the sun's rays, leaving only the luminescent plants to light their way.

Lieutenant Holt fell back from riding point and dropped into line with the captain. "This seems like as good a place as any for a rest, Captain," he said quietly.

"Agreed. Have a few scouts check the area, and we will make a brief stop," he murmured.

Elaris noticed that everyone, if they spoke at all, did so softly, as if they were afraid of being overheard.

Once the scouts returned, Colin helped her down from her horse. "Stay close," he whispered.

Elaris took a seat on a rock nearby. Sergeant Rowan brought her a light meal of apples, cheese, and bread.

She ate quickly while Colin stood watch.

A loud shriek echoed suddenly through the trees, causing the Guard to draw their swords.

They formed a circle around her without being told. Another shriek sounded—closer this time.

"Steady," Colin ordered.

Movement in the trees to the left drew everyone's eye. Branches cracked and treetops swayed as something moved toward them. Another shriek—this one loud enough to force Elaris to muffle her ears.

The Guard all stood poised, ready to fight. Elaris hunched down behind them, shaking with terror at what was coming.

A shriek, then a cry.

The trees groaned as they were impacted. Then, silence.

Elaris strained to hear any noise but heard nothing except her own rapid breathing. After a few moments, the Guard relaxed but maintained their posts around her.

"Is it gone?" she whispered.

"I believe so," Colin answered.

"What was it? Where did it go?" she cried softly.

"A creature of some sort. It appears it changed its mind."

Elaris raised an eyebrow at him. *"Changed its mind?"*

Colin shrugged and guided her back to her horse. "We're leaving," he ordered the lieutenant.

The men seemed happy to hear it and quickly mounted their horses, falling back into formation.

The darkness, coupled with damp earth and obstacles in their path, made the journey over the next few hours a slow one. It was after three in the afternoon by the time they reached the lake where Colin had met Thistwyn and Tretch.

"We'll camp here," he ordered.

Elaris dismounted and walked over to the lake, admiring the waterfall nearby. Colin kept a watchful eye on her, never letting her out of his sight. She noticed he seemed more relaxed here and wondered why.

"Are we safe here?" she asked him as he approached.

"No harm will come to you here, Elaris," he murmured.

"What was that thing earlier?" she pressed.

Colin sat down, tugging off a boot to remove a rock, and explained, "The forest is full of creatures. That was one of them."

"But what happened to it?"

He smiled and chose his words carefully. "We have friends here. Friends who want to protect us."

"But I thought the forest was dangerous?" she asked, growing more frustrated.

"It is. But for this journey, we have friends."

She frowned and was about to ask another question when he said, "It looks like your tent is prepared. I'll let you know when supper is ready."

She walked away slowly, looking back at him in frustration, and went to her tent.

Two hours later, several members of the Guard stood watch as everyone else ate their supper around a campfire. No one spoke. The mood was more somber, the men staying alert. Colin sat next to Elaris as she finished her plate.

Sergeant Linwood was the one to break the silence, calling, "Captain!" while pointing into the woods.

All eyes focused on the tree line. Soldiers jumped up from their seats, drawing their swords.

Emerging from the trees was a tall redhead.

"Thistwyn," Colin said, exhaling.

Elaris's eyes snapped to him in confusion. "You know her?"

Colin stepped forward, signaling his men to stand down. "Thistwyn, to what do we owe the pleasure?"

Thistwyn glanced over the Guard, looking unimpressed. "I come with a message from Lumirien. She wishes to meet the Fatewaker."

Colin glanced at Elaris, and Thistwyn caught sight of her—her expression a mix of curiosity and reverence.

Keeping her eyes on Elaris but still talking to Colin, she continued, "She desires to visit you here tonight."

Colin bowed and replied, "We would be honored to welcome the Queen of the Alari."

Thistwyn nodded once in acknowledgement. "Expect her at moonrise."

Taking one last look at Elaris, she spun and disappeared into the trees.

Colin turned to find Bren approaching. Pulling him away from the others, he asked, "Is that the redhead you told me about?"

"Yes," Colin replied simply, anticipating where this was going.

"I think I'm in love," Bren sighed.

"I'm sure she'd just as soon kill you as endure a conversation with you," Colin said with a roll of his eyes.

Bren grinned in response, undeterred.

Seeing Elaris looking at him intently, Colin waved Bren off and went to her.

"Who was that?" she asked anxiously.

"That was Thistwyn. She is the right-hand of Lumirien, Queen of the Alari."

"And is she a... light creature?"

"Yes."

"And Queen... Lumirien?... She wants to meet me?" she hesitated.

Colin smiled at her. "She does. I told her of you, and she is curious. She poses no danger."

"And she is a queen?"

"Yes—of the Alari. They are a people of light creatures—but not all light creatures are Alari," he explained.

"This is where you came last night, isn't it?"

"Yes. I came to ask for their help, and they have agreed."

Elaris considered this for a moment and nodded. "I look forward to meeting her," she said with a small smile.

Later that night, just as the moon began to peek over the horizon above the lake, Lumirien arrived.

She was accompanied by Thistwyn and several other creatures, all different species. They entered the camp slowly and cautiously, keeping their eyes on the soldiers. Colin had already given orders for the Guard to welcome the Queen when she arrived, so they stood respectfully to the side to let her pass.

Elaris waited for her down by the lake, her hands twisting with nervous energy. Colin stood by her side. Lumirien left the rest of her entourage behind at the campfire and approached them slowly. Elaris was immediately captivated by her wings. Her eyes became large and curious.

"Hello. I am Lumirien," she said, looking intently at Elaris's violet eyes.

"And I am Elaris. I was told you wanted to meet me, but I am unsure why."

Lumirien smiled at her like a mother to a small child. "My dear, because you are the Fatewaker. We have waited a millennium for you."

Elaris looked up to Colin, confused.

"But how do you know about me?" she asked.

"We creatures are ancient. We were here when the last Fatewaker walked these lands. It is said that the next Fatewaker would bring peace to us."

Elaris didn't know what to say. She had just learned of her powers a week ago. Bringing peace to an entire people seemed impossibly beyond her reach.

"I... I'm not sure I'm who you think I am."

Lumirien smiled again, soft and knowing. "Give yourself time, Fatewaker. It will come."

Her expression darkened as she turned to Colin. "Your enemies are numerous here, human. It was close today. Be careful of where you rest."

Colin bowed in acknowledgement. "Thank you, Lumirien."

As she walked away, she turned suddenly to Elaris and said quietly, "Not all your enemies carry swords, Fatewaker. Some carry lies."

Elaris watched as the Queen and her people departed into the woods.

"What do you think she meant by that?" she asked Colin.

Colin had a feeling he knew, but didn't know how to tell her. "I think she is just cautioning you to be careful who you trust."

Elaris was quiet for a moment before looking up to him shyly. "I trust you."

Colin's breath caught. If only she knew the man he was bringing her to, she wouldn't trust him at all.

Claudius couldn't believe what he was seeing. The girl was speaking with Lumirien. He had no idea how the queen had found out about the Fatewaker, but it was a dangerous development for his plan.

He had been following the girl for days, keeping his distance but never letting her out of his sight. Entering Vale Forest this morning had complicated things.

Earlier, while she ate her midday meal, he had nearly been caught—trapped between one of the Alari and a dark creature he hadn't sensed in time.

He couldn't watch any longer. He needed to enact his plan.

Leaving the area of the lake, he walked up a hill and traveled a path through the wood for several hours, eventually making his way into a darker, damp area of the forest. The smell of rot permeated the air, evidence of decay all around. This part of Vale Forest was different—its inhabitants equally singular.

It didn't take long for Claudius to be noticed—he didn't exactly try to hide himself. A gargoyle-like creature lunged at him from the trees, black wings spread wide, talons piercing into his arms as it seized him. More gathered nearby, watching in eerie silence. Claudius recognized them immediately: the Shriven, a race of dark creatures known for their bloodthirsty appetites.

With a simple charm, Claudius forced the Shriven to release him, causing it to screech wildly, its fellow creatures flying madly in circles all around.

"Wizard!" it bellowed, flapping its wings in distress.

"I have come with a proposition," he said calmly, brushing off his robes.

The Shriven screeched again. "What do you want from us?" it growled.

Claudius swept his gaze over the gathered Shriven, his voice low and deliberate. "I ask only for your assistance. In return, I will help you destroy Lumirien."

Laughter rang through the forest, mocking him. "Fool! Lumirien is too powerful!"

"I am more powerful," he replied flatly.

The first Shriven settled on a branch, its wings folded in. The others followed, circling down to perch among the shadows.

They were listening.

CHAPTER 21

Elaris didn't sleep a wink. Strange sounds from the forest kept her alert and anxious. She decided that if she wasn't going to sleep, she could at least practice her powers, especially now that a whole people were apparently depending on her to bring peace. Memories of her conversation with Lumirien only served to make her more unsure of who she was.

She lay quietly on her cot, focusing on the people and creatures all around. There were many to choose from, the forest around her filled with hundreds of inhabitants.

She decided to concentrate her efforts on the soldiers. She found their Embercurrents—all different colors, going in all directions and intertwining at multiple points. Everyone had a distinctive color, but some were similar, such as a dark green for one soldier and a light green for another. The only person with a unique color was the captain. His gold Embercurrent shone brightly and distinctly. It felt warm and comforting.

Elaris let her mind rest with him. She wondered what his chosen current would show. Did he have a future in the

Royal Guard? Would he marry and have a family? The idea made her stomach tighten.

She shouldn't know. She didn't want to know. In that moment, she made the decision not to invade his privacy.

She turned away from his Embercurrent, the pain from the idea of him with someone else still lingering. The captain... Colin... was everything that she had hoped Lord Mordane would be—honorable, compassionate, courageous, loyal, and inspiring loyalty from others—and he cared for her.

The more she learned of her betrothed, the more she realized he was not that man.

Of one thing she was certain: Colin took his role seriously. As much as she had started to wish she could run away, he had a duty to fulfill—as did she.

Pushing away the thought, she focused again on her powers. She wanted to be able to see the currents without taking so much time and having to close her eyes. Alec had told her during one of their sessions that it was possible—but would take practice. Well, she thought, no better time than now.

The image of Sergeant Keswick dying and the battle in the woods haunted her. She knew it was coming. She just needed to be prepared for it.

She went back to viewing the Embercurrents, but instead of focusing on one, she concentrated on her breathing and being calm in the moment.

She let herself grow comfortable around them, letting them flow all around her. When she thought she was ready, she opened her eyes. For just a flash, she saw all of them around her—and then they were gone.

It wasn't much, but it was progress. For the rest of the night, she worked, gaining more and more time seeing the currents with her eyes open.

Colin woke early. He wanted to get moving and make better progress today. As it was, they had at least two, maybe three, days left before they exited the forest—then another two to three days for the final road to the palace.

With any luck, they would make it there earlier than expected, and he wouldn't have to explain the diversion and their visit to Alec.

He exited his tent to find that Elaris was already awake and eating with the men, who surrounded her and seemed to be transfixed by her every word. Colin growled under his breath as he approached.

She looked tired. He couldn't blame her. The forest wasn't exactly peaceful at night. He had somehow managed to get some sleep, but only because of years of having to listen to the snoring of dozens of other men. It certainly made it easier to adapt to noisy accommodations.

"Good morning, my lady," he said, eyeing Corporal Knoll and Sergeants Colburn, Darrow, and Bower, who were seated next to her.

"Good morning, Captain," she said with a smile.

The soldiers quickly finished their plates and scattered, causing a look of confusion on Elaris's face. Colin smiled with satisfaction.

Sitting down next to her, he grabbed a plate and ate quietly.

"I was wondering, Captain, how long we would be in the forest," she said.

"I am hoping two more days, but it's more likely to be three. The journey gets more difficult up ahead."

"Difficult? Do you mean more creatures or the road?" she asked, concerned.

"Both. But all will be well, I promise," he said softly.

They left an hour later, following the lake until they came to another thickly wooded area. They rode in the same configuration as the day before, Colin on one side of Elaris and Briggs on the other, the remaining soldiers all around.

Colin kept his eyes scanning the trees. Occasionally, they would hear a sudden screech or cry from an animal, followed almost immediately by silence.

The company pressed forward—Colin increasingly grateful for Lumirien's assistance. He had confidence in the skill of his men but doubted they would have made it this far, uninjured, without her intervention.

"The air… it smells of rot," Elaris said, covering her nose.

Colin remembered the smell. Acrid, earthy, and tinged with something metallic—it had clung to his uniform long after they'd escaped. The last time they'd passed through Vale Forest, the Shriven had come without warning, lunging from the trees like shadows given form. Dozens of them had tried to drag the men from their saddles, their talons tearing through armor like parchment. They had barely escaped with their lives.

"We are entering the darker wood," he murmured.

Before Elaris could respond, the trees next to them began creaking and swaying, and a low rumble rose from the forest floor.

A loud cry sounded, followed by multiple screeches, coming from different directions.

Colin gave the order to pick up the pace, but it was too late. Whatever was coming for them gave another loud cry, causing Sergeant Briggs's horse to buck wildly, tossing him to the ground.

It bolted down the road but got caught in a vine just ahead, falling to the ground in a heap.

Another set of cries, and then the wood was silent. The only sound was the distressed horse fighting to get back up.

Briggs ran forward to his horse, kneeling next to it. The rest of the party followed, careful not to get too close.

"Are they gone?" Elaris asked, panic in her eyes.

"Yes—but we need to get moving," Colin replied, his eyes scanning the trees.

Elaris jumped down from the saddle, prompting Colin to shout, "Elaris! Get back on your horse!"

Moving toward Briggs and his animal, she looked back at Colin and said, "I can help."

Colin saw the look in her eye and recognized it—because he had seen it in the mirror too many times. Determination.

"Do what you can—but move quickly," he grumbled.

Elaris bent down and focused on the injured horse. Its leg was clearly broken, and there was no way it would be able to continue.

"Please help her—please help Sunshine," Briggs pleaded softly.

The soldiers all looked at her with anticipation. Colin had briefed everyone on her powers—but they had yet to see them.

Elaris closed her eyes. In moments, a white Embercurrent appeared, emanating from her hands to the animal. Gasps sounded from the men, all of them mesmerized at what they were seeing.

Another moment later, another current appeared. Elaris moved her hands slightly—and the horse vanished.

Briggs stood up with a start and yelled, "Where is she?"

Elaris closed her eyes, sensing the animal, and smiled. "She is right over there," she replied, pointing to where they had been when the horse bolted.

There stood Sunshine, mere feet from them, grazing in the grass.

Briggs ran over to her, checking her leg. "She's alright!" he cried.

The soldiers all whispered amongst each other, some looking at her in wonder, while others in reverence.

"Thank you, my lady," Briggs murmured as he bowed to her.

It took a moment for the men to collect themselves. Bren had to give them a warning look to get them back in order.

Colin helped Elaris up to her seat and called for everyone to get into formation. He had never seen Briggs so happy, his grin reached from ear to ear.

The man would be her devoted servant for life.

Elaris leaned over to Briggs and smiled, murmuring, "Sunshine is such a pretty name."

Colin barked out a laugh.

The rest of the day was spent moving quickly but carefully. They only stopped once to rest the horses, giving them a chance to drink at a small stream.

Numerous times, they heard the cries of creatures in the trees, causing them to keep their eyes and ears open for a possible attack.

By the afternoon, they were on the lookout for a good place to stop for the night, wanting to get the camp secured as soon as possible. They didn't have to look for the perfect place because one was pointed out to them.

Coming around a bend on the path, Bren, who was riding point, spotted Thistwyn. She was standing and waiting for them next to a clearing, spear in hand.

Colin broke from Elaris and rode ahead. "Thistwyn," Colin said, nodding his head.

"You shall stay here tonight, human. You will be safe here," she said brusquely.

Bren grinned at her. "Will you be guarding us?" he asked smoothly.

Thistwyn turned her head, looked him up and down, rolled her eyes, and turned back to Colin.

Colin stifled a laugh at the disappointment on his lieutenant's face. "Thank you," he replied. "it is most appreciated."

She merely nodded and turned to leave, but not before giving Elaris a smile.

Colin didn't even know she was capable of smiling.

After making camp, they prepared supper and ate. Some of the men who had previously surrounded Elaris at meals had backed away a bit tonight.

"They are unsure about her," Bren murmured.

The two men had stepped away from the others to talk about the road ahead.

"They will adapt. They always do," Colin said with a shrug.

Bren considered Elaris for a moment, still sitting by the fire enjoying a conversation with Briggs. "She is powerful, Captain. We may need to utilize that if the need arises."

"No," Colin said firmly. "If the need arises, she shall be safely hidden away, out of danger."

Bren was about to protest but saw there was no use. His friend had feelings for the girl. He may not understand that yet, but the rest of them did.

Changing the subject, Bren grinned at Colin. "Did you see the way Thistwyn looked at me?"

"You mean with disgust? Yes, we all witnessed your shame."

"There was something there…" he said wistfully.

"You smelled that too? I thought it was Briggs."

Bren groaned. "And here I thought we were bonding."

CHAPTER 22

The rain was relentless, coming down in sheets. Everywhere they walked, they were greeted by thick mud. Karr's men pulled desperately at their horses, trying to coax them forward—but got stuck with every step.

"Get moving!" Karr bellowed.

The men attempted to pick up their pace, but the ground wasn't cooperating. Some of them exchanged looks of frustration.

For several days, they had traveled, covering the land at breakneck speeds. The men were tired and hungry. Karr had chosen the forest route to intercept Captain Aedric, betting he would take the path from Oakhaven to Vale Forest to reach the palace faster. He didn't want to chance Aedric getting there before he had the opportunity to kill him.

This decision added another layer of misery to his men, who now had to contend with the creatures of the forest and the brutal landscape.

"I said get moving!" Karr yelled again, this time pulling a whip from his belt as a first and only warning.

The noise he was creating woke the forest, and soon the sounds of creatures echoed through the wood.

The men grew tense, knowing that providing an adequate defense while knee-deep in mud would be nearly impossible.

The sounds increased, moving closer. Branches cracked loudly as something neared.

In an explosion of tree branches, several large creatures emerged. Their faces were deformed and dirty, and they wore armor made of wood and stone. Standing at least seven feet tall, they towered over the men. In seconds, they were lunging at the soldiers, wooden clubs swinging. The men pulled their swords and began slashing at the attackers, but they were unable to maneuver adequately.

Corporal Yarr was the first to fall, bludgeoned in the head by one of the creatures. Next was Sergeant Garner, who had no way to escape the brutal beating he received.

The rest of the company slugged through, creating a formation meant to defend. Moments later, they had regained control, hacking away at the beasts, killing two and scaring off the rest.

Once they were sure the enemy had left, Karr surveyed the aftermath. Two of his soldiers were dead. That left him only eighteen to fight Aedric. They still had the advantage of the element of surprise. He wasn't going to let the death of two deter him.

"Get moving!" he bellowed.

Looking confused, his lieutenant stepped forward, murmuring, "But Sir—the fallen."

"Leave them where they fell," Karr barked.

This statement earned him grumbles of discontent from his men.

"Does anyone have something to say?" he hissed, pulling the whip from his belt again.

The men quieted and began the process of pulling their horses forward again as the rain continued to beat down on them.

An hour later, the rain slowed, and the ground transitioned to rock, so Karr's men were able to mount their horses and start making faster progress. Many had been injured in the fight but kept it quiet for fear of punishment.

Karr rode quietly at the front of the company, setting a fast pace. Behind him, his men talked softly. Overhearing a discussion from the back regarding their mission, he called for the company to stop. He rode slowly to the back of the line, carefully looking into the eyes of every man. Reaching his target, he stopped, glaring at the two men who had been talking.

"You admire traitors?" he asked with deadly calm.

Corporal Hewitt spoke first, stammering in fear, "No, Sir—I mean, what I was saying is that Captain Aedric is known for being a good leader."

The other soldier, Sergeant Hill, quickly interrupted, knowing his captain far better than the corporal. "What the corporal and I were discussing, Sir, is that our information was clearly wrong, and Captain Aedric is not the man everyone thinks he is."

Karr eyed the two intently. "Let me make something very clear," he yelled. "Loyalty to anyone other than Lord Mordane or myself will be rewarded with my sword through your gullet!"

The men all remained silent, no one wanting to draw attention. Turning back to the two soldiers, he eyed them intently one more time before returning to the front of the company.

As they continued their march, Karr reflected on the incident with Aedric at the village of Houck. The humiliation still grated on him. He had been perfectly in his right to interrogate those villagers, and Aedric's interference only served to endanger them all. Those villagers could have easily turned on them. He had the situation under control. The problem was, Aedric didn't have the stomach for what needed to be done. He was weak.

This mission would finally bring a little justice. Aedric didn't deserve to wear the uniform. He never should have been in the Guard to begin with. In fact, his death would be an act of mercy.

For the next few hours, Karr refined his plan of attack. They would find Aedric's company and ambush them as they slept. They would grab the girl and get back to the palace, reaping the rewards of a job well done.

"Branson!" Karr barked.

Sergeant Branson quickly rode from the middle of the company, falling in next to his captain.

"Sir?"

"I want you to ride ahead and scout for our target. He and his company may have left Oakhaven. If they have, they may be within a few days of us."

"Yes, Sir," the sergeant replied, turning to leave.

"And Sergeant—do so quietly. Don't engage. The kill is mine."

Colin woke to the sound of laughter. It was a nice thing to hear, especially since it was coming from Elaris. He left his tent to find her surrounded by six of his men, her face lit with a smile. He attempted to keep his growl to himself but failed.

Sergeants Bryant and Linwood were the first to hear him coming, giving their goodbyes quickly and departing. Corporals Finwick and Rowan had their backs turned, and were surprised when he appeared suddenly to their left.

Finishing out the group was Briggs and Bren, whom he gave a stern look to, but they remained where they stood, flashing a grin at him.

Briggs seemed to have taken on the role of her personal guardian.

"Good morning, Captain!" Elaris said brightly.

Bowing, he replied, "Good morning, my lady."

"Isn't it a beautiful day?" she sang, as the two corporals made their escape.

The sun was shining in the clearing where they had made camp, and Colin couldn't deny that the forest was beautiful when it wasn't dark and miserable. Seeing Elaris made the day perfect.

"It is indeed," he said with a smile.

"Can I speak with you?" Bren asked quietly.

Colin dipped his head at Elaris and reluctantly followed Bren to the other side of the camp.

"What's on your mind?" Colin asked.

"Today's journey. We go through the darkest part of the forest."

Colin sighed. He had been thinking of the same problem. "We will need to move quickly and quietly."

"Any chance we can make it out today?"

"Believe me, I wish that were possible, but those clouds I see on the horizon tell me we are in for rain."

Bren groaned. "I guess it was too much to ask to keep the sun going."

"Let's just hope I'm wrong," Colin replied, though he doubted it.

The company packed up quickly and departed. They had all been instructed to keep their voices low and move swiftly.

The area they were going through had a dense population of dark creatures. While the Alari would be watching over them, there was a real chance they could be outnumbered. The best defense, in this case, was stealth.

The day passed slowly, each sound that came from the trees causing them to pause and listen. They were like robbers trying to make an escape. Several times, they could hear what they assumed to be the Alari removing an enemy. Colin only hoped they could find a safe place to camp for the night.

They stopped for their midday meal by a river, one of the Alari standing downstream. Colin took Elaris her plate of food and sat down next to her.

"Are you doing well, my lady?" he asked.

"Quite well, Captain, considering," she said with a smile.

"We should be out of this section of the forest tonight."

"I can sense them. The dark creatures," she whispered.

"Have you tried to look at their Embercurrents?" he asked.

"No. Honestly, I fear what I may see."

Colin shifted uncomfortably. "Have you tried to... look at anyone else's Embercurrents?"

Elaris smiled at him and laughed softly. "Only those I have told you about, Captain."

Colin laughed with her nervously and breathed a sigh of relief. He wasn't sure he wanted her seeing some of his decisions from the past.

As he had predicted, the rain began that afternoon, soaking them to the bone. He kept a watchful eye on Elaris, who tried to keep a smile on her face despite the fact that she was obviously cold and miserable. Once they hit the mud, Colin made the decision that they needed to stop for the day. He wasn't going to chance the horses getting injured or his people freezing to death.

The Alari seemed to anticipate this decision and had a safe spot picked out for them down a path to the east. A goblin-like man pointed the way to a small pond and assured them that they would be safe for the night.

"I wonder where Thistwyn is," Bren murmured as they approached their camp for the night.

"I'm sure she made the difficult decision to stay away for fear of losing control and ravishing you," Colin drawled.

"You really think so?" Bren grinned.

Colin rolled his eyes. His friend obviously needed some rest.

Once they arrived, the Guard got busy getting the tents up and a fire started, a difficult task with rain still pouring down on them. Elaris took cover in her tent as soon as it was up, thankful to finally be dry. Colin spent time discussing the next day's travel with Bren, hopeful that they would be able to clear Vale Forest.

After that, it would be a smooth ride to the palace, and Elaris would be delivered to her groom. The thought made him sick.

Just before nightfall, the rain slowed, and Colin was told by one of the Guard that he had a visitor. Going to the edge of the camp, he saw Thistwyn waiting, her expression dark and serious.

"Thistwyn?" he asked carefully.

"Human. I need to speak to you."

CHAPTER 23

They had lost precious time. Karr growled as he thought about the delay. His men had been weak, moving slowly through the mud and getting bogged down by a little rain. When they got back to the palace, he would replace the lot of them.

As they neared the top of a hill, he could see the forest below and wondered where his target was. He closed his eyes and thought of how it would feel to slice Aedric's head off... slowly. The idea made him tremble with anticipation. When the attack came, he wanted to savor the kill... to see the life drain from the man's eyes.

His musings were interrupted by someone approaching fast on horseback. His men drew their swords but quickly stood down when they saw who it was.

"Branson!" Karr yelled as the sergeant approached.

"Captain—I return with good news," he said, panting from the exertion of the ride.

"Out with it!" Karr barked.

"Sir—they're just four hours away. They have made camp by a pond to the east."

Karr's expression went from annoyance to pure glee.

"Men! We strike at dawn!" he called.

Four hours later, Karr and his men looked down on their target's camp. The fire from the night before had been extinguished but still smoked, sending a cloud up to the heavens. The tents surrounded the fire neatly, their inhabitants apparently sleeping soundly.

Karr's heart raced with the anticipation of the kill. "Find Aedric. Secure him. Do not kill him. He is *mine*," he growled low.

After receiving his signal to proceed, his men crept quietly into the camp, swords drawn, each man selecting a tent to attack. Karr gave one last signal, and they all pushed forward in one coordinated move. Slashing and grunting erupted from the camp, and then—silence.

Karr stormed out of the tent he was sure was Aedric's and roared, "Where are they?"

His men exited the tents, confusion on their faces as they looked at one another.

In a heartbeat, Karr received his answer as a battle cry was heard from the trees.

Colin watched from the safety of the trees as Karr entered the camp. Bren and Briggs stood at opposite points with the remainder of the men filling in between, creating a broken circle around the camp that only allowed enough room for their attackers to enter.

Thanks to a warning from Thistwyn, they had seen Karr coming from miles away and had prepared. Although Thistwyn and the Alari were willing to help should creatures attack them, she made it clear that they would not get involved in a human conflict—leaving Colin and the Guard to handle this one alone.

The first move Colin had made was securing Elaris in a nearby cave.

Colin was no fool. Somehow, Lord Mordane had found out about their diversion to Millcross, and Karr had been sent to destroy them. He guessed that Karr had been told to bring Elaris back to the palace safe, but he didn't want to chance it. Her home, until the battle was over, was the cave.

Watching Karr and his men enter the tents, his suspicions were confirmed as the sound of swords slicing through sleep sacks reached his ears. He signaled his men to be ready. Karr came out, and Colin gave the call to battle.

His men wasted no time, running full speed at Karr and his soldiers. Several of Karr's men saw the Guard coming and dropped their swords immediately, falling to the ground on their knees in surrender. Others fought, swords swinging in a desperate attempt to hit their target.

Karr stood, stunned.

"I want Aedric! Find me Aedric!" he screamed, his expression one of pure rage.

Colin made his way through the battle, fighting one soldier at a time. One or two gave up upon seeing him, running away into the woods. Other—more seasoned soldiers—stood firm.

Colin respected their resolve—but not enough to let them live. He cut them down one by one, moving forward in a deliberate, deadly dance.

Though outnumbered at first, the Guard now faced only the few loyalists still willing to fight. Karr shoved past his own men, focused solely on finding his quarry.

He spotted Colin fighting Sergeant Branson, one of his more dedicated men. Seeing an opportunity to strike, he pushed forward—when the trees above erupted.

Shriven flew down from all directions. Deafening, shrill cries sounded all around as they soared in for the attack. Talons raised, they went for the men, indiscriminate of what leader they served.

Soldiers who had surrendered ran for shelter, unable to outrun the onslaught. Talons ripped into flesh, men carried away and dropped to the ground from above. Bloodied bodies littered the camp.

Soldiers who had been fighting each other turned their swords toward this new enemy, fighting together. Karr's pursuit of Colin was interrupted by one of these creatures. Grasping his arm, it attempted to take off but was stopped when Karr drove his sword into its side.

"Aedric!" Karr bellowed.

Colin turned to look at him, just in time to see Sergeant Keswick coming his way.

Elaris was not happy. When Thistwyn had come to tell Colin about the approaching attackers, she had wanted to help. She had explained to Colin that she could be of use to them—perhaps by using her newfound powers. He had given her a resounding "no" and sent her to this dark cave.

Outside, she could hear the battle beginning. She paced nervously as she thought about her new friends dying. Colin dying. The thought of him lying out there, hurting, without her able to help caused her heart to tighten. She felt absolutely useless hiding here doing nothing.

Determined to be involved in some way, she closed her eyes and sensed the people in the camp. She could see the familiar colors of the soldiers and the golden Embercurrent belonging to Colin. She also saw foreign currents—those that belonged to the ones trying to kill her friends.

As she watched the currents, she was startled when dark currents of grey and black appeared above them, intertwining with the others. Elaris didn't recognize these currents but suspected they weren't good. Letting herself fall into one, she was taken to the sky, soaring above the trees in the forest. Winged creatures with taloned feet flew with her, circling the camp below.

Dark creatures.

Looking at the talons, Elaris's thoughts immediately went to Sergeant Keswick. In a panic, she opened her eyes and ran out of the cave, stopping at the crest of a hill that overlooked the fighting below. There, fighting an enemy soldier, was Keswick. Elaris could sense the dark creatures closing in. She looked up to see them approaching, starting their attack.

Powerless to stop it, she watched as the winged creatures attacked. They seemed to be focused on the enemy soldiers, avoiding the lethal sword slashes of Colin's Guard. She took a deep breath and prepared herself for what she must do next.

Seeing Keswick running toward Colin, she closed her eyes to sense him and find his chosen current. There, next to it, was his alternate current—the one she had chosen.

Opening her eyes, she manifested the chosen current. Rivers of green extended from her hands down the hill and into the battlefield. Swirls enveloped Sergeant Keswick, causing him to pause in confusion.

Quickly, she manifested his alternate current. Taking a deep breath, she considered what she was about to do. Just then, a winged creature gave a cry from above and descended toward Keswick. Elaris made the decision then.

With a thought, she moved Sergeant Keswick from his chosen current to his alternate current. She blinked—and Colin was suddenly there, pushing Keswick out of the way, the winged creature flying into a nearby tree. Keswick smiled at the captain and went to fight another enemy, just like in her vision.

Elaris breathed a sigh of relief, happy she had been there to help. Just then, she saw the captain turn from his new position and stop suddenly—a sword protruding from his back. A man with a twisted grin was standing in front of him, laughing, still gripping the hilt. The world slowed for her as Colin fell.

Elaris screamed—just as she felt something hard strike her head. A ringing sounded in her ears, and the world went dark.

CHAPTER 24

Claudius observed the captain with his soldiers approaching Elaris's camp. He had seen them in the forest the day prior and had overheard their plans for attacking Elaris's guardians. Deciding that there was no better time to kill the girl than during a battle, when attention would be diverted, he had waited.

He was impressed by the captain whose task it was to guard Elaris. He had a good strategy—letting the enemy soldiers come into the camp and then ambush them. He laughed to himself as the expression on the enemy soldiers' faces went from determination to confusion and then to shock.

While the battle was entertaining, it was not what he was here for. There was a girl to kill. Claudius moved silently up a hill and toward the cave he had seen her enter. He paused just within sight of it, not wanting to alert the Alari who surely guarded her. He controlled his breathing and tried to slow the thumping of his heart.

The time would come. Patience.

Turning his attention back to the battle, he saw that Elaris's captain was winning. He couldn't think of a better time to introduce another element to the chaos. Closing his eyes and murmuring an ancient dialect, he called them—dozens of Shriven, all there for one purpose: destruction.

They flew down in droves, pulling men from the ground and breaking their bodies on the damp earth. If anything would draw the Alari's attention, it was this.

Creeping further up the hill, he froze at the sight of Elaris exiting the cave. Green currents suddenly moved from her hands down to the battlefield—specifically to a young soldier. A moment later, there were two currents. Claudius was stunned when, in the blink of an eye, the soldier was saved from an attack by one of the Shriven by a captain who had suddenly appeared beside him.

The girl had used the Embercurrent to save the man's life.

Her powers were greater than he had imagined. In a few days, she had learned to wield the currents and manipulate fate. Suddenly, the image of his Sophie flashed in his mind.

He had tried every spell, every potion, to bring her back and had failed. This girl could change fate. She could bring back his Sophie. And if she didn't want to, he would make her.

Running up the hill, he quickly picked up a rock and smashed it into her head just as she let out a scream.

"You, my girl, will do what I could not. You will bring back my Sophie," he rasped, grief clinging to every word.

Claudius looked to the heavens, spotted one of his new winged allies, and signaled it. The Shriven flew down and, at Claudius's command, seized Elaris by the arms and flew her away—keeping low in the trees to avoid being seen.

Colin didn't immediately feel the sword pierce through him. In fact, he was surprised to see that blood was forming where the blade had sunk deep into his side. Karr stood before him, laughing. Colin sank to his knees and fell over, oddly weak.

Then, a scream.

"Elaris," he moaned.

"Ah yes, the girl. Where is she, Aedric?" Karr mocked, pulling his sword from Colin's body. "You were a fool to go against Lord Mordane's orders. He wants you dead now, and I've been given the pleasure of doing it."

Colin could see his soldiers battling all around him, fighting off the winged creatures. Most of Karr's men were either dead, hiding, or were running into the woods. But... Elaris. Why did he hear her scream? What was she doing out of the cave? He must get to her, he thought, giving no consideration to the killer hovering above him.

Making a first attempt at standing, he was immediately knocked down by a rush of wind coming from above, the light from the sunrise blocked out by several creatures—light creatures. Thistwyn and several Alari like her flew in, slicing through the Shriven with their swords. The other, non-winged Alari came on foot, surrounding the camp and taking out the invaders one by one. In moments, they had extinguished them all.

Karr turned as his attention was momentarily drawn to the spectacle, but Colin was focused on his objective—getting to Elaris. Pushing himself up to his knees, he picked up his sword that had fallen next to him and used it to push himself up, warm blood running from his side. He steadied himself, and in one swift movement, he plunged his sword into Karr's back—straight through his heart.

Karr stood motionless and stunned. He twisted just in time to see a look of satisfaction on his executioner's face before he took his final breath and collapsed.

Colin looked up to find Bren running towards him, panic in his eyes.

"Colin!" he gasped, grabbing his friend just as he was about to fall again.

"Elaris. Where is Elaris?" Colin choked out.

"She's in the cave, where we left her," Bren replied, unconcerned.

"No. I heard her scream."

Bren looked up and toward the area of the cave, but saw no one. "Briggs!" he yelled, seeing the large man walking away from his last victim—a Shriven that no longer possessed its head.

Briggs ran over immediately and, seeing the captain bleeding on the ground, knelt next to him. "Captain! What did that bastard do to you?"

"I'm fine, Briggs," Colin lied. "But I heard Lady Vaelora scream. Please… go find her."

Briggs ran off quickly, determined to locate Elaris.

Bren looked around the carnage, desperate to find help for his friend. Spotting Thistwyn, he called to her. "Help, please! I can't stop the bleeding!" he begged.

Thistwyn glided over, using her wings to speed her way. Landing next to Colin, she knelt and examined his wound.

"Human. You are dying," she said simply, a frown on her face.

"You don't say!" Colin half-laughed, half-cried.

Thistwyn scowled at him. "I will never understand the human need for humor."

Pulling out a vial from a hidden pocket, Thistwyn put it to his lips and ordered, "Drink."

Colin did so, coughing down the sour liquid.

"What was that?" he choked.

"That, human, was me saving your life."

It didn't take long for Colin to discover just how powerful the concoction she had given him was. Immediately, he felt warmth at the wound site, then tingling all through his body. His vision momentarily became exceptionally vivid, allowing him to see colors he didn't know existed. His wounds started healing over, and he could feel his strength returning.

"Will he be alright?" Bren asked quietly.

"No... he will still be human," she sighed.

Bren blinked, then let out a surprised laugh, leaving Thistwyn very confused.

Elaris was woken by the ringing in her ears and the smell of blood. She lay where she was, eyes closed, assessing the sensations in her body.

The headache was the first thing she noticed, followed by pain in her arms. The ground beneath her felt cold and damp.

Slowly, she opened her eyes, to find strange, glowing eyes looking back at her, the forest as their backdrop.

She had seen the eyes before, in a book perhaps. She had also seen them at the camp, attacking the soldiers. With a start, she sat up—instantly regretting the swift movement. Grasping her head, she moaned.

"It's going to hurt for a while," a man's voice said.

Elaris turned her head, slowly this time, toward the voice and saw a man with white hair in a black cloak. He was standing next to one of the creatures. She soon realized that there were a dozen or so more surrounding her in a circle.

"Who are you?" she swallowed, her throat parched and burning.

The man considered her for a moment before speaking. "I am Claudius."

Elaris instantly jumped to her feet, swaying unsteadily. Realizing that she had nowhere to escape to, she croaked, "You... you are trying to kill me."

"Yes," he said simply. "Or at least I was. Everything has changed now."

Her head started to clear—images from the attack at the camp flooded back to her. "Colin!" she cried, tears welling in her eyes.

"I'm afraid your guardian was struck down by Captain Karr. Grisly fellow, that one."

Elaris's breath caught in her throat, and she felt the world spinning around her.

"He's... he's dead?" she whimpered.

"I'm afraid so," he answered unapologetically.

Elaris fell to her knees and sobbed. Colin was dead. It was her fault. She had caused him to move with the Embercurrent and had put him in harm's way. If she had just stayed in the cave like he had asked her to, he might still be alive.

Claudius watched her cry, no emotion in his expression. "While I would love to give you time to mourn your friend, we must be moving," he said coldly.

"Where are you taking me?" she choked out.

"As far away from the Alari as possible. They will surely have started a search for you by now. I don't plan on them finding you."

In that moment, Elaris felt something that she had never experienced before—pure rage. This man was trying to kill her, and she wasn't going to let him.

Standing slowly, she closed her eyes to sense those around her and... sensed nothing. Breathing deeply, she tried again—and still nothing.

She felt... nothing.

Her heart started to race in panic.

Opening her eyes, she found Claudius looking back at her, amused. "I'm afraid your powers are not needed now. I have ensured you cannot use them," he said with a laugh.

Elaris glared at him. "You used your magic on me?"

"Of course." He shrugged.

Signaling to one of the dark creatures, Claudius stepped closer and grabbed her by the wrist. "Time to leave," he ordered as he pulled her forward.

"Wizard!" screeched the creature angrily, "Lumirien!"

"I will deal with her later," he said as he tried to push past them.

"Now!" they growled.

In one swift motion, Claudius turned on them and sent ribbons of fire in their direction. Those creatures who couldn't escape the flames burned, screaming in agony.

Elaris covered her ears, trying to block out the sound, but it was no use.

Claudius grasped her wrist again, sending one final burst of fire toward the horde.

"Now, my dear—we are leaving!" he declared, and pulled her swiftly into darkness.

CHAPTER 25

Bodies littered the ground of the camp. Thistwyn, once done tending to Colin, had moved on to help those who could be saved.

Colin stood up slowly, grasping his still painful side, to survey the grounds. By his count, five of the enemy soldiers had surrendered and survived the attack by the dark creatures.

Eight more were dead. The rest had fled to the trees to try their luck with the forest.

As for Colin's men, Sergeant Fenlow and Corporal Rowan were dead. It was difficult to tell if they had died by sword or creature. Bren approached him as he stood near the bodies of his fallen men.

"Sergeant Fenlow was going on leave next month to see his girl. Corporal Rowan was due a promotion. It was going to be a surprise," Bren murmured.

Colin's breath caught in his throat before erupting into a growl. "That bastard sent Karr to kill us. He is responsible for the deaths of these men!"

"Why would he have done this? We were on our way."

"I don't know, but somehow, I believe he found out about my trip to see Alec. He never wanted Elaris to find out about her powers. I interrupted some plan of his."

"Speaking of Elaris," Bren said, pointing to Briggs running toward them.

Out of breath, he panted, "She's gone."

"What do you mean, 'she's gone'?" Colin snapped, grasping his side as pain shot through his still-healing wound.

"She's not in the cave. I looked over the whole area. There is no sign of her except this," he said, handing Colin a bloody rock.

Colin took it in his hands, turning it over. The blood was sticky and dark, clinging to the jagged edge of the rock—still fresh. Horrible thoughts raced through his head—what happened to her? Where was she? Who could have done this? Was she hurt?

Looking for Thistwyn, he called for her. Hearing the panic in his voice, she rushed over to the men.

"Elaris. Where is she?" he demanded.

"She should be in the cave," she answered, frowning in confusion.

"She is not, and Sergeant Briggs found this nearby," he snapped, handing her the rock.

Thistwyn took it, staring down at it for a long moment. "We were distracted by the Shriven," she said quietly.

"That was probably the plan," he ground out.

"Claudius?" Bren asked.

"I'm willing to bet," he spat.

"I have failed her," Thistwyn said, hanging her head.

"No. I have failed her," Colin said through clenched teeth.

Colin thought about Claudius taking Elaris. He knew the wizard wanted her dead. Why take her instead? He needed to find her before Claudius enacted whatever plan he had up his sleeve. The thought of her hurt... possibly dying... was like a punch to his gut. Images of her violet eyes and her sweet smile flashed through his thoughts.

She had become so much more than a mission.

Colin knew he needed to move if he was going to save her in time.

"Bren. I am going after her. Will you stay and deal with this?" he asked, sweeping his hand toward the aftermath of the battle.

"You mean *we* are going after her," Bren corrected.

"I don't know if you've noticed, Bren, but we are now enemies of Ashcar—no longer part of the Guard. I can't order any of you to follow me," he responded quietly.

"You don't have to," Briggs stepped in. "We would follow you anywhere, Sir—especially if it means saving Lady Vaelora."

Bren smiled at this response and nodded. "Briggs is right. These men would fight and die for you. You have earned their loyalty. Your chances of saving her are better with us at your side."

Colin hesitated. He thought about the road ahead. Mordane wanted him and his men dead—that was clear. There was nowhere for them to go, no safe haven. They would be on the run. Even their families, if they still had one, were in danger from his wrath. He didn't want to ask this of them.

Taking one more look at Briggs and Bren, he realized that there was no arguing with them.

"Alright. But I want each man to make the choice on his own. There is more at stake here than their place in the Guard. Their lives—and the lives of their families—are also at risk."

Bren nodded. "I will gather the men."

Twenty minutes later, with the camp stabilized and decisions made, Colin's men stood in formation—Bren and Briggs in their usual positions up front. Colin looked closely at each of them. Some men were older and probably ready to leave the Guard and start a new life. Some were young, with their whole lives ahead of them. He wondered how many would stay—and how many would opt to take the opportunity for freedom.

Taking a deep breath, he addressed the company, perhaps for the last time. "Guard. You fought bravely today. Many of you are probably wondering why we were attacked by our own people. I'm not going to keep the truth from you. It was Lord Mordane. He ordered Captain Karr here to kill us."

There was murmuring amongst the men, but he continued, "I made the choice to help Lady Vaelora understand what was happening to her by seeking assistance from a wizard. Lord Mordane found out and sent Captain Karr and his men after us. I'm afraid our time as the Royal Guard is over."

The words felt heavy on his tongue, like closing a door that would never reopen. He could hear whispers coming from the back of the formation.

"Where is Lady Vaelora?" Sergeant Keswick yelled from the back.

"She has been taken—by the same man who arranged the attack at Lake Rehl."

"Sir—we must find her!" Sergeant Linwood yelled.

"I intend to do just that. But I can't ask you to come with me. I am no longer your captain, and you are no longer members of the Royal Guard. Your lives are your own."

"When do we leave, Sir?" Sergeant Darrow asked loudly.

Bren smiled, flashing his friend a look that said, *I told you so*.

Colin took another hard look at his men, each of them with an expression of determination and pride. He didn't know what to say, so simply said, "Thank you."

"What of Karr's men, Sir?" Briggs asked.

"We will deal with them once we have paid honor to our dead."

All the men nodded in agreement.

"Prepare the fallen," he ordered.

The men broke formation and started building ten pyres—two for their men and eight for Karr's. Captain Karr's body, however, was dragged to a nearby swamp, left to rot.

The funeral was short, Colin giving honor to his men, and recognizing the lives of the enemy soldiers.

"We lost good men today. Sergeant Fenlow and Corporal Rowan fought with honor. We will carry their memories with us from this day forward. But they aren't the only ones who died in the bloodshed.

"With them, eight others lie—soldiers who once swore the same oath we did. These men might have been allies had they been led by someone with more honor. We don't mourn the choices they made, but who they could have been."

Colin paused for a moment, then took a torch from Briggs and lit the pyres. "We give them the dignity they were denied in life."

The company watched as the pyres burned, the smoke rising to the heavens above. Their eyes remained focused on Rowan and Fenlow. After a few minutes, they slowly broke away, going off to prepare for the journey ahead.

Bren approached Colin and asked quietly, "What do you want to do with the prisoners?"

"Bring them to me," he answered, his voice hard.

As the rest of the company packed up the camp, Colin stood, waiting. He watched as Bren and Briggs led the five men who had surrendered to stand in front of him. He noticed right away that they were tired, dirty, and broken—their heads hung in defeat as they waited for their judgement.

"Who is the ranking soldier among you?" Colin asked, his tone that of a captain in command.

"I am, Sir—Sergeant Hill, Sir," the soldier saluted formally.

"You and your men made a deadly mistake today, Sergeant," Colin snapped.

"Yes, Sir—we did," Hill replied softly, lowering his head.

Colin paused for a moment, analyzing the sergeant and his men. "I understand you all surrendered immediately without harming anyone."

"We had no desire to be here, Sir—or to fight fellow members of the Guard," he replied.

"Because of the wisdom of your decision, your lives will be spared. Unfortunately, I'm not sure that we are doing you any favors."

"Sir?" the sergeant asked, confused.

"You were sent to kill me and my men, Hill. You have failed. In the eyes of Lord Mordane, your lives are forfeit."

The men's expressions changed from humility to shock.

"We... we understand, Sir," Hill stammered.

Colin looked into their eyes. Two of them looked like they were barely twenty years old. He sighed deeply as he made a decision that he hoped he wouldn't regret.

"You have a choice, Sergeant. You can flee and try to live your lives in hiding, hoping that the Guard doesn't find you—or you can join us."

Hill looked up to him with hope in his eyes. "Join you, Sir?"

"Yes," Colin explained, "But understand this—we are no longer Guard. We are being hunted by Lord Mordane. Our mission—our only mission right now—is to save Lady Vaelora. Many of us may die in this pursuit. You may be safer on your own. You must also think of any family you may have. They will be hunted as well."

Sergeant Hill looked back at his men, many of whom looked to be deep in thought. "I shall discuss it with the men, Sir."

"Make it quick, Hill. We leave within the hour," Colin ordered.

Colin walked away, Bren at his side.

"How many do you think will join us?" Bren asked.

"I hope none," he replied.

Seeing Bren's confusion, Colin explained, "They will have no friends here—at least until they prove themselves. We can't offer them anything. I meant what I said—they would be safer on their own."

Thistwyn came to them then, a look of pure determination on her face. "Human—the Alari shall join you, with Lumirien's blessing."

"We welcome the help," Colin said, bowing.

Bren ran over to assist in securing the rest of their gear while Colin discussed a plan with Thistwyn.

Looking over a map she drew in the dirt, they plotted the fastest route out of the forest.

"Some of our scouts found several dead Shriven deep in the forest. They had been killed by wizard's fire. We believe Claudius is using their roads to flee the forest. It is a much more direct route," she explained.

"Then that's the path we take as well," he declared.

Feeling the presence of someone behind him, he turned to find Sergeant Hill and another soldier standing at attention, waiting for him.

"I assume you and the men have reached a decision," Colin said.

"We have, Sir. Three of the men shall depart. They have families they wish to protect. Corporal Hewitt and I will be joining you."

Colin nodded slowly. "Understood, Sergeant. Where did you leave your horses and gear?"

"Just over the ridge to the east, Sir," he answered.

"Go collect them and get back immediately. We won't be waiting for you."

"Yes, Sir," he replied.

Turning to leave, Hill paused for a moment and said, "Sir—I just want to thank you. For honoring our dead. I wanted to serve with you once. I see now I was right."

Colin gave a hard stare and nodded once as Hill and Hewitt turned to leave.

Walking to the edge of the camp, he looked to the south—toward Elaris. Every moment they delayed was a moment she was in danger.

He would find her. And when he did—he would kill the man who dared lay a hand on her.

CHAPTER 26

In a dark room, deep in the heart of the palace, Draegor sat. In front of him stood a large table with a map of Ashcar carved into it, with flags of different colors placed at various points.

Sitting at the table with him were his scribes and advisors, all desperate to win his favor. But he was in no mood for any of them. His thoughts were only on Elaris.

Almost thirty years ago, when he knew the time was drawing near, he enlisted several spies to go out to the villages and watch. Their instructions were simple—find a baby with violet eyes. The search had taken almost ten years, but then, like fate itself had intervened, she was found.

Taking her from her mother had been difficult, or so he had heard.

She had been too young to be of use, of course, so he'd had her taken to Pyete to be hidden away until she was old enough.

Draegor ensured that she was surrounded by the right instructors and mentors—people who would teach her what he wanted her to know and nothing more. After all, he didn't want her to know *too* much. He had waited nearly two decades to finally have her in his grasp, to finally fulfill his plan.

Now, she was out there—awakening to powers she had no right to. He had to get her before it was too late.

Standing abruptly, he walked to a window overlooking the palace grounds. In the distance, the village of Houck stretched beneath a haze of morning mist—its people as insignificant as the fog that cloaked them.

"My lord, our men in the south report King Thadius has moved a thousand troops closer to the border. This makes three different divisions he has repositioned in the last month," one of his advisors reported.

"He is clearly preparing for an attack," another advisor interjected. "We should move our men to the border. We can't chance him gaining more ground."

"King Thadius will soon know the despair of defeat," Draegor mumbled.

"My lord?" the first advisor questioned. "Do you wish for our men to attack, then?"

Draegor sighed, "Not yet. The time will come… soon."

The man bowed slowly, backing away and returning to his seat, clearly perplexed.

A third advisor, this one a balding man with a thick beard, spoke up. "We need to make a move now. Our border villages are at risk. We have a mining community a day's ride from his troops' last known position. We are in serious danger of losing that resource!"

Draegor slammed his fist on the table, growling, "I said. NOT. YET. I have a wedding to focus on."

His scribes and advisors all looked to one another, exchanging expressions of concern and fear.

"My lord… your wedding is of utmost importance to the kingdom, to be sure, but…" the first advisor began.

Draegor glared at the man. "But… what?"

Just then, the doors burst open and Draegor's little son ran into the room.

"Ah! If it isn't little Prince Orran!" one of the scribes cooed.

"He has grown so quickly—and he looks so much like you, my lord!" an advisor said. "He will make an excellent ruler when the time comes!"

Draegor turned to them, disgust and annoyance riddling his features. "If his blood is strong, he won't need your hollow compliments. If it isn't, your flattery won't save him."

The men took a step back, lowering their heads.

He bent down to the child and grabbed his face, squeezing it to expose his teeth and causing the child to cry. "Still crooked," he mumbled.

Perhaps he needed to breed with a different woman—one who could give him a son worthy of his parentage, he thought.

The child continued to cry, reminding him of so many others before him—all sniveling brats who couldn't live up to his expectations. He had hopes for this one, but he was beginning to wonder…

The last one had made it to twelve before he showed signs of being unworthy.

He had demonstrated great potential, initially. He learned to speak quickly and was an excellent student. His features were very similar to his father's—same dark brown eyes, same light brown hair. His teeth were perfectly straight, unlike this child's.

That boy had unfortunately let Draegor down when he had made the critical error of falling off his horse and breaking his nose.

He had to go.

Draegor looked to this boy and wondered how long it would take him to fail as well.

If only he could find a way to make a child purely from his blood instead of contaminating the line with the blood of the mother.

The child's caregiver rushed in, clearly frazzled. "My apologies, my lord!" she pleaded. "I only turned for a moment, and he was gone!"

Draegor glared at her. "Take him away," he said coldly.

The woman scooped the child into her arms and practically ran from the room.

One of the advisors cleared his throat in an attempt to get Draegor's attention back on matters of war.

"Concerning the troops in the south, my lord..." he began.

The advisor was quickly interrupted by Kaz entering the doorway. He stood in it, blocking the light from the hall, his posture shrinking in obvious fear.

"What is it, Kaz?" Draegor snapped.

Kaz twisted his hands nervously and replied, stammering, "My lord... I have news... of great importance."

Draegor glared at him. He gave himself a moment imagining the feeling of wrapping his hands around the man's neck until he drew his last breath. He looked forward to the day that dream could be fulfilled. For now, he was still needed.

"Leave us!" Draegor bellowed, ordering his men to leave the room.

Kaz stepped aside as the advisors and scribes quickly shuffled out, many of them giving him looks of pity as they left.

"Kaz. Let me make something very clear to you. I want all relevant details. Your life depends on it," he growled through gritted teeth.

"Yes, my lord—of course, my lord!"

"Now, Kaz!" he barked.

"They are dead, my lord," Kaz blurted.

Draegor wasted no time—he had his hands around the man's neck in seconds, squeezing tightly. Kaz choked and gasped in an attempt to get air, but it was no use.

His face turned blue as he reached up to grasp the hands around his neck, clawing for survival.

"All. Relevant. Details. Kaz," Draegor growled, digging his nails into his neck.

Kaz tried to cry but failed. He pulled at Draegor's hands, but he was too strong. The world turned dark as he began to lose consciousness. Just as he was about to pass out, Draegor released him.

He fell to the floor in a heap, blood trickling down his neck from Draegor's nail marks.

"Let's try this again," his master purred.

Kaz pulled himself up to his knees, still clutching his neck and rubbing it, trying to calm the ache. "My lord," he croaked, "Captain Karr and some of his men are dead."

Draegor blinked, then turned. He walked the perimeter of the room slowly, each step deliberate.

"And Captain Aedric?" he asked quietly.

"He lives, my lord. Two of his men are dead."

"I am assuming that Lady Vaelora is with him, unharmed."

"I'm unsure, my lord. She was separated from the captain and the Guard and used her magic. But then I sensed Claudius next to her, using his magic. He now moves south—I sensed him use his magic again in the dark part of the forest."

Draegor paused where he was, his back to Kaz, fists balling up. In a moment of pure rage, he let out a primal scream and smashed the cabinet in front of him into pieces, shards of wood splintering and landing all around them.

Kaz cowered on the floor, hiding his face from his master.

Draegor stood motionless, his hands tight. "I need her, Kaz. I need her here. Now. Everything depends on it."

"My lord... will Captain Aedric not bring her to you still?" Kaz coughed, his voice hoarse.

"Captain Aedric will have figured out that I sent Captain Karr after him. He will not willingly bring the girl here."

Kaz lowered his eyes again, afraid to speak.

"However," Draegor added quickly, "Captain Aedric is a man of honor—a *disgusting* level of honor, actually. He won't leave the girl to Claudius, if he has her."

"Yes, my lord," Kaz could only agree.

Draegor began pacing again, looking down at the floor with every step. On his second turn around the room, he stopped, an idea coming to him. "Kaz. You will go to

Claudius's home. If he has her, he is sure to bring her there. Kill him and bring her to me."

"My lord," Kaz sputtered, "Claudius is very powerful."

"You are more powerful," Draegor answered simply.

"What of Captain Aedric?" Kaz argued.

Draegor shrugged. "Kill him as well."

Kaz frowned, knowing the task was not as simple as his master was making it out to be.

"My lord, the captain will not be easy to kill," he appealed.

"Stop sniveling, Kaz. You are a wizard. He is a mere man."

Knowing there was no sense in arguing further, Kaz replied softly, "Yes, my lord."

"Do not fail me, Kaz. You know what I will do if you do not return with her."

Kaz immediately thought of the jar and its swirling contents.

Yes, he knew his fate should he not succeed.

Bowing to his master, he replied, "I will not fail you, my lord."

"Now go," Draegor snapped.

Kaz bowed again and backed out of the room, closing the door behind him.

Alone in the room, Draegor walked to the window and looked out to the land before him. He had waited what seemed like an eternity for her. She was out there, but she was out of reach. He was so close—he could almost taste it.

Slamming his fist into the wall and screaming again, he turned on his heel and stormed out of the room, flinging the door open in a rage.

As he walked down the hall, he passed by portraits of the rulers that had preceded him.

Thirty-four generations of Mordanes, all strikingly similar. Draegor paused to look at the picture of his predecessor and compared him to the child that was to be his heir. He didn't see the resemblance, but, then again, he never had.

Completing his journey down the hall, he entered his room and slammed the door, rattling a number of items on the shelves nearby. He made his way urgently to a cabinet in the corner, pulled a key from his pocket, and unlocked it. Inside, he found his most prized possessions.

Ten jars, all lined up neatly on the shelf in the cabinet, all containing colorful swirls of light. He picked one up and tilted it to the side, enjoying the way the tangled threads shifted and vibrated with every motion. Holding it to his ear, he listened to its gentle hum. The sound calmed him.

Seeing the jar he had brought to Kaz, he picked it up and turned it upside down, shaking it roughly. He held it to his ear like the one before, but this one had a high-pitched tone. He held it at arm's length, tempted to drop it to the floor. No—not yet, he thought.

Putting the jar back on the shelf, he picked up another. This one, he examined closely. Its ribbons of color excited him. He delighted in their movement, the energy he could feel through the glass. The sound this one made was nothing short of alluring.

He brought the jar up to his face, holding it next to his cheek.

"Soon," he purred, stroking it softly.

CHAPTER 27

It was almost noon by the time Colin and the thirteen men lined up to leave the camp, Thistwyn and several of the Alari standing by. The funeral pyres still burned, smoke rising above them, but there was no time to wait—they needed to find Elaris.

Colin looked closely into each soldier's eyes, seeing grit and determination looking back at him. Reaching up to his neck, he unfastened his black cape with the gold falcon embroidered on it and let it drop to the ground—the final death knell for his time in the Royal Guard. Each of his men followed suit, letting their capes drop into the muddied earth.

Colin took a deep breath and called for them to move out, taking the lead—the horses trampling the once-prized symbol of their allegiance. Thistwyn and her people took flight, scanning the route for possible foes. They would be heading into the darkest part of the forest today, to the road that Claudius had taken.

After the camp was far behind them, Bren rode up next to him.

"Will we make it out of here today?" he asked.

"We won't rest until we do," he answered soberly.

Bren glanced back over his shoulder. Speaking low, he murmured, "The two additions have already made some enemies."

Colin wasn't surprised. "Who have they managed to offend?"

"Sergeants Bower and Renshaw. Apparently, the corporal was caught taking additional rations. His sergeant had to step in to defend him."

"They look like they haven't eaten in days," Colin noted. "Make sure they get an additional portion—out of sight from the others at next meal."

"Is that a good idea?" Bren questioned.

"I'm not going to have two of our men drop from hunger during battle."

Bren nodded. Shifting in his saddle, he opened his mouth to speak but then quickly shut it.

"What is it, Bren?" Colin sighed.

"Captain... what if... what if she's dead?" Bren asked softly.

Colin's chest tightened, and his vision grew momentarily blurry. "She isn't dead," he snapped.

Bren took a deep breath and pressed again, saying quietly, "Colin... Claudius wanted her dead. Everything Briggs found out in Glendale supports that. And... the blood on the rock..."

Colin couldn't deny he had the same thoughts, but he knew she was still alive. She had to be.

The memory of her face, her laugh, her smile—all came flooding back to him. He swore he could feel her presence—

like her soul was calling to him. He felt like he could almost reach out and touch her. He couldn't explain it.

"Bren," Colin sighed. "I understand your concerns. All I can say is, I just know she is alive."

Bren gave his friend a half-smile, wondering if hope alone could hold a man together. "I'm sure she is, my friend," he said softly.

The two men rode side by side quietly until Thistwyn flew down, intercepting them.

"There is trouble ahead in about a mile—several dark creatures. They hide in the trees," she reported.

Turning to his men, Colin signaled for them to draw their weapons. "We move quickly," he ordered. "We grant no quarter today."

The men all growled in agreement.

Thistwyn took flight again as the men picked up their pace, matching Colin's lead.

Colin and his company were ready when the attack came—at least two dozen creatures of several species emerging from the trees. The memory of their loss earlier in the day still fresh in their minds, the men charged into the enemy, running down some while slicing through others.

Arriving from above to support, the Alari quickly discovered that their help wasn't needed for this fight. The creatures that remained screamed out in fear as the men dismounted their horses and chased them down, finishing off the last of the enemy.

Thistwyn seemed surprised, turning to Colin to say, "I won't say that your methods aren't... effective."

Bren grinned at her. "You should see us on a good day," he said with a wink.

Thistwyn rolled her eyes and took flight again, going off to scan the road ahead.

"I think you're growing on her," Colin said.

"You think so?" Bren replied hopefully.

"No."

The men cleaned their swords on the underbrush, mounted their horses, and fell back into formation.

Colin signaled for them to proceed, and they continued their journey down the road.

After several hours of traveling with no indication of enemies, Thistwyn returned.

"Human, there are signs up ahead. The wizard has passed through here," she said urgently.

"What signs?" Colin demanded.

"Runes burned into the trees—and the smell of fresh blood... human blood," she murmured, her face hanging low.

Seeing Colin's expression of rage, Bren tried to steer his focus to the problem at hand. "Why runes? What is he doing?"

"Using magic to block creatures from following him," she replied. "We felt a resistance when approaching them. We cannot travel there."

"He's got to be close," Colin said through gritted teeth. "We need to keep moving."

"Captain, the men need to rest," Bren interjected.

Colin looked back at them, knowing that each one would press on with no complaints, but he needed them ready for the fight that was coming.

"We rest here," he ordered.

The men dismounted, moving off to tend to nature's call and grab a ration of food.

Thistwyn was about to leave when Colin called her over.

"I need a favor," he whispered.

Thistwyn looked suspicious but inclined her head to him, indicating she was listening.

"I need to know more about what happened with Claudius. He was clearly in league with the Shriven, organizing that distraction during the battle so he could take Elaris. They may know where he went and what he's planning."

Thistwyn's expression turned thoughtful. "I have an idea," she murmured.

Before Colin could reply, she turned her back and flew away into the trees, leaving him wondering what she had planned.

The company's rest didn't last long, each of them eager to get out of the forest and find Elaris. They started their journey again, moving into the section of the forest that Thistwyn had spoken about. Runes were burned into trees at intervals of every hundred feet. The Alari kept their distance, flying above but not coming to ground level.

The air felt thick as they traveled through the magically marked trees, a strange blue fog lying heavy on the forest floor. Eerie sounds emanated from the runes, almost as if they were humming or singing.

Sergeant Briggs, not liking the looks of them, went over and touched one with his sword, receiving a shock in return and earning a chuckle from his fellow soldiers. They quickly quieted when they saw the unamused expression on his face.

The runes may have been made to keep Claudius safe, but they had the added benefit of keeping the dark creatures out of the company's path.

After an hour, they emerged into a clearing, able to see far ahead without obstructions and free from the rune-marked trees. Thistwyn circled and landed in front of them, pulling her wings in behind her. Pointing to another Alari flying above, she said, "Human, we have a gift."

The other Alari, a tall male with chiseled features and striking green eyes, flew down to them, a Shriven resembling the ones that had attacked them at the camp in his grasp.

Bren sized the Alari up, noting the muscles bulging from his tunic, and frowned.

The Shriven screeched loudly, flapping his wings and attempting to grab the Alari with his talons. His attempt was futile, however, as the Alari was easily ten times his size.

"Enough!" the Alari snapped, squeezing the creature's neck tightly.

The beast screeched again, fighting for its freedom.

"What have we here?" Colin asked, glaring at it.

"Adam has brought you one of Claudius's Shriven," Thistwyn said, smiling at Adam.

"*Adam?*" Bren scowled, glaring at the man.

Colin wasted no time, closing in on the beast. "Where is Claudius?" he roared.

The Shriven cried out in anger. "Gone! Burned us!"

"Did he have a girl with him? Beautiful, with violet eyes?" he asked desperately.

The creature made a sound resembling a laugh, causing Adam to tighten his grip.

"Girl! Yes!" it gasped as its throat was pinched tighter.

236

"Where did they go?" Colin growled, tempted to drive his sword through it.

"South! Raven!" he replied, beating its wings in a desperate attempt to free itself.

"Raven?" Colin questioned.

"He probably means Ravenwood," Thistwyn answered.

Colin placed a hand on Adam's shoulder, saying, "Thank you, Adam," before turning to get back on his horse.

"We ride to Ravenwood!" he called.

Bren watched with reluctant awe as Adam snapped the Shriven's neck in one easy move.

The men got back into formation and rode forward, fresh determination coursing through their blood. Colin could feel they were getting close. Elaris was alive. The Shriven had confirmed it.

His desperation to reach her grew with every mile they traveled. He thought about the day he had met her, just a couple weeks ago, and the mission he had been given—to bring her to Lord Mordane. The thought of that bastard having her sickened him now. He promised himself that, when he found her—and he would find her—he would do everything in his power to convince her to stay with him.

To hell with her duty.

The idea drove him forward even harder.

The men rode quickly and quietly, each of them lost in their thoughts. Colin looked to Bren riding next to him, seeing that his expression was one of disgust.

"What's on your mind, Bren?" Colin asked, afraid he already knew the answer.

Bren scowled. "Do you think they are *together*?" he asked.

"Who?" Colin sighed, choosing to make his friend tell him what was obvious.

"Thistwyn and that... *Adam*," he replied, nose scrunched as if he smelled something awful.

Colin adopted a very serious expression. "Oh, I wouldn't doubt it! Did you see him? He looked like he could lift twenty men with those arms! And those eyes! I'm sure many a maid has fallen prey to them."

Bren threw daggers at him with his eyes, seeing that his friend was poking fun at him.

"Just wait until you are in love," Bren bit out.

"Too late," Colin whispered to himself.

CHAPTER 28

A cold wind blew, and Elaris could feel a chill deep in her bones. The damp earth beneath her did nothing to provide warmth, nor did the thin dress she wore. She rolled to her side, trying to adjust, but was limited in movement by the bindings on her wrists and feet, her waist tethered to a nearby tree. Her head ached where she had been struck, with dried blood still on her face. Her arms bore fresh gashes from the Shriven's talons.

She looked at her surroundings, noticing faint light peeking through the trees.

Morning.

Nearby, Claudius slept.

They had traveled continually the day before with no rest. He had pulled her mercilessly along the path, only stopping to perform spells on the trees and surrounding areas. She had done everything in her power to slow their progress— tripping over branches, dragging her feet, begging. Nothing had worked. Claudius had only persisted, hitting her in the face and threatening to take her life if she didn't comply. She was now bruised and bloodied, and still his captive.

Elaris adjusted again, thinking of the events of the day before. Her eyes began welling up with tears.

Colin.

The image of him lying on the ground with a sword penetrating his back caused bile to rise in her throat. He had died protecting her. He had been nothing but kind and honorable, and a friend to her. After Hatti's death, he had been the one she could count on and trust.

Elaris sobbed silently, burying her face in her bound hands. Every day, she had looked forward to seeing him. She loved their private moments and the conversations they shared. She felt safe with him—and loved. Her breath caught in her throat.

She had grown to love him.

She was responsible for his death.

Her—and Lord Mordane.

Her chest tightened.

She knew that her betrothed had played a part in it all. She didn't fully understand why—Colin hadn't had time to explain what Thistwyn had found out during the chaos before the attack. But she had overheard enough of his conversations with his men: Karr was coming, sent by Lord Mordane, tasked with killing Colin and his company and taking her to the palace.

If Mordane were standing in front of her now, she would kill him.

Claudius snored loudly, mumbling in his sleep. Elaris breathed deeply and tried to focus on the problem in front of her. Her powers had been taken away—she assumed temporarily, as he had performed a similar ritual to Hatti's nightly blessing on her last night. With time, they should return.

She was much younger than him and knew that, if given the chance, she could outrun him—if only she could escape her bindings and distract him in some way. Fighting him was out of the question. He had proven to be very strong, she thought, as she touched her bruised cheek where he had last struck her.

She had asked him multiple times the day before what he wanted from her, but he gave no answer.

Claudius stirred again, this time waking with a start, sitting up and yelling, "Sophie!"

He looked around at his surroundings, disoriented, finally fixing his gaze on her. "Sophie?" he asked, his voice full of a mix of hope and sorrow.

Elaris remained silent.

After a few moments, he rubbed his eyes and looked at her again. This time, he seemed to recognize her, and his expression changed to loathing.

"Get up!" he ordered, pulling her to her feet.

"Where are you taking me?" Elaris demanded.

Claudius ignored her, untying her from the tree. He pulled her roughly, finding the path they had been traveling earlier, and continued down it.

After an hour, the forest thinned and eventually opened to an endless horizon—wheat fields as far as the eye could see. They were out.

Elaris turned and looked at Vale Forest behind her. She knew Colin would not be coming for her. Would anyone be coming for her? She had wanted nothing more than to leave the darkness while she was there—and now, she wanted nothing more than to return, to find safety away from this man.

Claudius pulled her again, jerking her onto a country path to the west. She dug in her heels and snapped, "Where are you taking me? And who is Sophie?"

Claudius came to a dead stop upon hearing his daughter's name. He turned to Elaris and, in a rage, slapped her.

"Don't you ever say that name again!" he screamed, jerking her forward.

Cradling her cheek, Elaris smiled inwardly. She had found his weakness.

The sun made its way higher into the sky as the morning progressed. Elaris could see farms on the distant horizon as they walked, catching sight of farmers working in the fields. She hoped that they would pass someone on the road, but no one came.

Claudius gave them a brief stop by a tree along the road, unwrapping a crust of bread from his pocket and throwing it to her. She looked at it in disgust and tossed it in the dirt in defiance, preferring to starve. He didn't seem to care—only shrugging and pulling her back to her feet to continue their march.

It was around noon by the time they reached their destination. Elaris saw a small village coming up on the road and was hopeful they would pass through—planning to yell to the first person they saw. But they went down a path that branched off just before it instead. A short walk down a winding lane later, and they had arrived at a small cottage.

Elaris noticed immediately that it looked like it hadn't been lived in for many years. Weeds were overgrown in the gardens, paint was peeling, windows were broken, and cobwebs had overtaken every inch of the doorway.

She panicked as Claudius opened the door and tried to pull her in. She grabbed the doorframe, dug her feet into the dirt, and held tight, refusing to enter. He seized her wrists and yanked her off her feet, slamming her onto the dirty floor.

The smell of mold immediately assaulted her nose. Dust covered every surface, and leaves littered the floor from a hole in the roof.

Claudius slammed the door and went about lighting a fire, completely ignoring her. Elaris stood slowly, careful not to bring attention to herself. She quickly scanned her surroundings. The cottage was small—just two stuffed and torn chairs in front of the fireplace, a kitchen table with four chairs around it, a bookcase full of dusty tomes, and a small kitchen with what smelled like rotted food on the counter. There was a door down a hallway to the left, which she assumed led to a bedroom.

Above the fireplace was a painting of Claudius, an older woman, and a young girl.

Walking slowly toward him, Elaris looked up at the painting, examining it closely. Claudius continued ignoring her, stoking the fire he had made.

Looking at the painting of this man with what she assumed was his family, Elaris made a decision. She needed to change her strategy.

Speaking calmly and peacefully, she asked sweetly, "Is this your family?"

Claudius didn't look at the painting but answered her quietly with a simple, "Yes."

Progress.

Elaris steadied her breath, knowing she had to be careful. "A lovely family," she said with a soft smile.

He breathed deeply, responding with a raspy voice, "They were."

Elaris paused, recognizing she was entering dangerous territory. "Claudius—why have you brought me here?"

Claudius jammed the fire poker in the fire roughly, causing embers to fly out. He looked like he was deciding whether to answer her when he finally replied, "To bring them back."

Elaris stood speechless. She assumed his family was dead—everything pointed to that. How did he think she was supposed to bring them back?

"I don't understand," she said.

"You will bring them back. We will be a family again," he responded flatly.

"Claudius… I can't bring people back from the dead," she said softly.

In one swift movement, he was on his feet, gripping her by the arms, fury in his eyes. The pain from her wounds was overwhelming.

"I saw you save that soldier. If you can save him, you can save them!" he spat.

Elaris winced as he held her arms tighter. "Yes—I did save him, but I can't save someone who is already dead!" she pleaded. "I can only change the fates of the living!"

Claudius slapped her again, making her cry out. Elaris cradled her cheek and looked at him in horror.

Suddenly, his face changed and softened, agony in his eyes.

"Sophie! I'm so sorry, Sophie! I didn't mean to hurt you!" he said as he pulled Elaris into his arms, holding her tightly.

She fought against him, pushing against his chest, struggling for freedom from the embrace.

"My sweet Sophie. I would never let anything happen to you!" Claudius murmured as he pulled back and stroked her bruised face, tears streaming from his eyes.

Elaris froze in fear. The man was insane.

He continued to stroke her face, smoothing strands of her hair back. She forced a smile to appease him. It seemed to work, as he turned and sat back down next to the fire, picking up the poker and continuing to stab at the logs.

Elaris carefully took a seat opposite him at the fireplace. Being cautious not to anger him, she held her hands up to him and said softly, "Can you please remove my bindings?"

Claudius seemed to still be caught up in his fantasy. He turned to her, leaned forward, and quietly started untying her. Elaris held very still, careful not to move.

The bindings fell freely from her hands to the floor, and Claudius returned to his position, looking into the fire. Elaris's heart raced. She was afraid he would hear her heart beating through her chest. This could be her only chance, she thought.

Moving quickly, she stood and ran for the door. Finding the handle, she turned it and pulled the door open to freedom. She screamed in pain as Claudius rushed up behind her and grabbed her hair, pulling her back into the dark cottage and to the floor.

His face was back to pure rage. Whatever place he had visited in his mind before, he was back now. Elaris feared he was here to stay.

Grabbing her hair in his fist again, he dragged her body swiftly down the hall.

Elaris fought to gain her footing and pull herself up, clawing at the floor, but it was no use. He pulled her into a bedroom in the back of the cottage, picked her up, and threw her on a damp, dirty bed, making her hit her head against the headboard.

With not another word, he turned and left the dark room, slamming and locking the door behind him.

Elaris jumped up and ran to the door, pounding on it until her fists bled. She stumbled back, gasping for air as the panic set in. It was dark. There was not a window to be found. She was alone. Colin was dead. She screamed out for help.

But no rescuer came.

CHAPTER 29

They were no more than a few hours behind Claudius and Elaris—perhaps half a day at most, judging by the fresh tracks pressed into the earth. Colin was convinced that Claudius had laid some kind of spell over the final stretch of the forest to slow their progress, as every step they took had been fraught with unseen resistance.

A strange fog had formed, making it difficult to see even their hands held out in front of them. Although there had been no rain in the area, the horses' hooves sank deeply into the earth, making riding them impossible. Even the plants worked against them, vines reaching out to grab limbs, spores shooting from flowers to cloud their vision.

As the sun reached its peak, the fog parted, revealing the exit to Vale Forest—as well as Lumirien, Thistwyn, and several of the Alari waiting for them.

Colin approached the queen respectfully, bowing in greeting. "My lady, you honor us."

"I come to bid you farewell, Captain. The Alari cannot pass this point," she said somberly.

"Thank you for your assistance." He bowed again.

Lumirien's expression turned sorrowful, and she murmured, "I'm only sorry we failed to protect the Fatewaker."

Colin understood her grief. He felt it too.

"We will find her, my lady. We will find her and bring justice to the man who took her," Colin vowed.

Lumirien nodded. Pulling a silver ring from her pocket, bearing a white stone, she handed it to Colin, saying, "When you find her, give her this—a sign of friendship from the Alari. It holds no magic, only a promise to aid her when her time comes."

Colin looked down at the ring, turning it over in his hand. He knew the Alari believed that Elaris was meant to bring peace to the creatures. What exactly did Lumirien mean by "when her time comes?"

"I will ensure she gets it," he said, while securing it in his pocket.

"One more thing—the man you serve is dangerous. He will use the Fatewaker to his own ends," she warned.

"We serve no one but the Fatewaker. And he isn't going anywhere near her if I have anything to say about it," Colin declared, a rumble of agreement passing through the company.

Lumirien smiled in response. "I'm glad to hear it. Safe journey to you and your people."

Bowing again, Colin mounted his horse and turned to leave, nodding at Thistwyn as they rode away.

The company turned down the road to Ravenwood, happy to be out in the sun and seeing farms and wheat fields instead of endless trees. Bren made his way forward to ride at Colin's side. He sighed dramatically.

Colin ignored him.

He sighed again, this time earning a smirk from his friend.

"What, Bren?" Colin asked, as if he didn't already know.

"There goes my heart, my soul, my one true love!" he moaned.

"You knew her for five minutes," Briggs muttered.

"You'll find another lady by sundown," Sergeant Linwood yelled from the back, causing the rest of the company to laugh.

Bren adopted a hurt expression and looked to his friend for help.

"Don't look at me. I doubt she even knew your name," Colin said with a shrug.

"Someday, they'll sing songs about this heartbreak," he muttered, producing new bouts of laughter from the men.

Colin smiled to himself as he set a quicker pace, leaving Bren sulking behind him.

Before long, they reached a tree on the side of the road, the broken brush around it showing signs someone was recently there. Colin and Briggs got down to look.

"There are fresh foot impressions here, Captain. Small—a woman's foot. And over here—a crust of bread," Briggs said.

"We're close," Colin declared.

The men pressed forward with new determination, arriving at the village of Ravenwood in the early afternoon. Colin gave the signal for the company to circle around him.

"I want you to spread out," he ordered, "Find out where Claudius lives—someone in this village must know something. Report back here as soon as you have something."

The men dispersed, some choosing to go door to door, others questioning people at the marketplace or the tavern. It didn't take long before they found the information they were looking for.

Sergeant Colburn was the first to return, having gone to a local shop to ask the shopkeeper.

"His cottage is just up the road there, Captain," he said, pointing to a lane that branched off before the village entrance.

"Call the men back," Colin ordered.

Sergeant Colburn pulled a small horn from his side and sounded a single, long blast. Within moments, the men were running back to fall into formation.

"He's close, men," Colin announced, pointing to the road. "We go in quietly, on foot. We'll leave the horses here at the stable."

The men did as they had been ordered, securing their horses and falling back into a tight formation. Colin led them back out of the village and down the side path. When the cottage came into view, he signaled them to stop.

Smoke curled from the cottage chimney—a sure sign someone was inside.

Gathering the men around him, Colin gave his orders, "Keswick, Linwood, Knoll, and Darrow—circle to the back. Make sure he doesn't escape. Lieutenant Holt, Colburn, Hill, Finwick, and Bower—hold the front and the road. Be ready to move if we need you. Briggs, Bryant, Renshaw, Hewitt— you're with me. We go in fast. We are dealing with a wizard— don't give him time to fight back. Take him down quick."

The men nodded, their faces grim with determination and rage.

"Lady Vaelora is in there. Let's go get her," he growled.

The men quickly dispersed to take up their ordered positions. Colin quietly led his four to the cottage, sneaking slowly up the path to the door.

In one swift kick, Colin had the door down. Dust flew up from the floor as it made contact, causing a thick haze to block their view. In a flash, bright ribbons of fire were coming at them.

Colin rolled on the floor, standing swiftly once he had cleared the blast. Briggs, Bryant, and Hewitt followed suit, rolling and finding themselves positioned next to a kitchen table.

The blasts of fire continued, but they were randomly directed.

As the dust settled, Colin caught sight of Claudius. "He's by the fireplace!" he yelled.

Corporal Hewitt wasted no time—rushing forward to tackle him. Before he could reach the wizard, he was hit with a thick band of fire, knocking him to the ground.

The maneuver was enough, however, to pull Claudius's attention away. Colin was on his feet in a heartbeat, jumping over a chair and driving his sword deep into the man's chest.

An eerie silence fell on the room. Corporal Hewitt stood, grasping his arm where he had been hit, the injury significant but not life-threatening. Claudius lay on the floor, bleeding.

"Where. Is. She?" Colin growled, twisting his blade.

"I tried... I tried to stop it..." he sputtered as blood came from his mouth.

"Tell me where she is!" Colin roared.

"You... don't know... what you've unleashed..." he coughed, taking his last breath.

Colin looked down at the man with fury in his heart.

"Captain!" Briggs yelled. "There's a door down the hall!"

Colin dropped his sword and ran down the hall, finding the door at the end of it locked.

"Elaris!" he called. "Stand away from the door!"

Slamming into the door, it fell easily to the floor. Inside the room, Colin found Elaris, huddled in a corner on the floor, her face hidden.

"Elaris!" he called as he rushed to her.

Looking up at the sound of his voice, Elaris sobbed, "Colin!"

In one smooth movement, Colin had her in his arms, holding her tightly.

"You're safe now. I have you," he soothed.

"I... I thought you were dead! I saw you die!" she cried.

Colin pulled back, looking at her face and seeing the damage he had done to it.

"What did that bastard do to you?" he growled.

"Claudius! Colin—he's insane!" she cried in fear.

"He's dead, Elaris. We saw to that."

She seemed to relax in his arms, making no attempt to pull away.

"I thought you were dead," she repeated quietly into his chest.

"I'm alright. I was injured, but Thistwyn healed me."

Elaris clung to him, her breath slowing. "I thought I had lost you," she whispered.

Colin smiled into her hair. "I thought I had lost you too."

CHAPTER 30

Colin stood over Claudius's body, staring down at him. Elaris sat in a chair at the table, a warm blanket wrapped around her—a kindness from Briggs. Looking at her bruised face, Colin wished he could bring Claudius back to life so he could kill him again.

"Take this filth out back and bury him," Colin ordered Sergeant Colburn and Corporal Knoll. The only reason he was getting a burial rather than being left in the woods to rot was because Elaris had requested it. She had looked at the painting above the fireplace and, seeing him with his family, had whispered that even monsters had once belonged to someone.

The two men carried the body out, being careful not to alarm the lady in the room. Briggs busied himself looking through the small cottage, while the rest of the men searched the property for clues about Claudius and his purpose.

Corporal Hewitt sat in a chair behind Colin. Seated next to him, bandaging his wounded arm, was Sergeant Renshaw. Colin smiled to himself at the pair. Just yesterday, Renshaw had wanted to throttle Hewitt for taking an additional ration, and now, just a day later, he was tending to his wounds. Apparently, the young corporal had proven his worth during the fight with Claudius.

Bren walked in, wiping his boots out of sheer habit at the door, and smiled warmly at Elaris as he passed her.

"I have guards posted on every side. The rest of the men are combing the woods and the area around the house. There is something strange about this place," he said, scratching his head.

"Such as?" Colin asked, concerned.

"The cottage seems larger on the outside," he replied, stepping back to the door, turning, and walking across the room one long step at a time.

"What is it, Bren?" Colin asked.

"It takes ten paces for me to get across this room—but it takes at least fifteen for me to walk from the front of the cottage to the back on the outside."

Colin looked to the back wall, noticing there were no windows, much like the room Elaris had been held captive in. Walking outside with Bren, they went around the perimeter of the cottage, examining the walls. They made their way back to the front door, and reentered the cottage.

"It has to be a hidden room," Colin announced, going to the back wall and feeling along the cracks. Bren and Briggs joined in, running their hands over every surface, looking for anything odd in the floor or ceiling.

Bren walked over to a bookcase positioned at the end of the wall. The bookcase, heavily laden with books, was impossible to move easily.

"Briggs, a little help here," he called.

Briggs made his way over and, grasping the bookcase by the side, pulled hard, wrenching it free from the thick carpet of dust that had settled around its base.

As the heavy shelf scraped aside, a cold draft rolled out from the wall behind it, carrying the stench of mildew and rot. Bren stepped forward, peering into the space they had uncovered—a narrow, dark corridor hidden behind the heavy bookcase all along.

"Found it," Bren reported.

Colin walked over to take a look.

Seeing the darkness within, he turned to Briggs and said, "You stay with Lady Vaelora. The lieutenant and I will be going inside."

Bren lit a lantern from the fireplace, preparing to enter. Colin took one look back at Elaris and said, "We'll be right back," with a warm smile.

Elaris smiled shyly and nodded in response.

Stepping into the darkness, Colin and Bren made their way through a small passage so narrow they had to turn sideways to get through.

"I think I need to cut back on my portions," Bren joked as he sucked in.

At the end of the passage was a door that opened to a room filled with books, vials, desiccated animals, scrolls, cauldrons, and the like.

"Wizards," Colin grumbled.

Hanging the lantern on a hook, they examined their surroundings—Bren heading over to the nearest bookshelf and Colin moving to a large chest positioned against the wall.

Flipping randomly through the books on the shelf, Bren paused on one and said, "Claudius has a lot of information here on the Fatewaker."

Colin looked up from the chest he had just managed to pry open. "That will come in useful," he mumbled as he pulled a handful of drawings out.

"He has multiple drawings of the women from the painting. Elaris said he kept saying, 'Sophie.' She thinks it was his daughter."

He held up a sketch of a young woman with her name— Sophie—written on the bottom corner.

"Colin—these books discuss specific powers of the Fatewaker," he said, flipping through a brittle page. "They go into considerable detail. Why would he have these?"

Colin frowned. "He apparently believed Elaris was going to bring destruction to us all. Maybe he thought he could control her somehow."

Looking back at the sketch and studying it, Colin murmured, "Elaris said he was... confused. He called her 'Sophie' and spoke of her bringing his family back."

Colin dropped the sketch back in the chest with a sigh. "Either way, he failed."

Wanting to get back to Elaris, Colin grabbed an armful of books and squeezed his way back down the corridor, Bren following closely behind.

"Find anything?" Briggs asked when they emerged.

"Creepy wizard lair," Bren shivered, smacking cobwebs off his arms.

Colin dropped the books on the table, sending dust flying. "We also found these—with plenty more where those came from."

Elaris reached forward and took one, opening it to the middle and reading:

The hand of the Fatewaker may sever the living from the stream of time, and none shall call them back…

The men exchanged uneasy glances.

"Remind me to stay on your good side," Bren laughed nervously.

Elaris threw him a half-smile. "You have nothing to worry about yet, Lieutenant. My powers are just starting to return," she paused, her eyes glinting, "Tomorrow, however…"

Bren stood with his mouth open, not knowing what to say.

Colin burst out laughing at the look on his face, the sound breaking the quiet that still hung in the room.

Elaris smiled at the sound of his laughter, but when she turned back to the book, her smile faded away, the weight of what she had just read still lingering.

Colin could see the concern on her face. She had just found out about her powers recently—the idea she was able to kill with them was probably making her uneasy.

Wanting to distract her, Colin touched her shoulder gently and asked, "Would you like to go outside and get some fresh air before it gets too dark?"

"Yes, please." She smiled gratefully, standing up.

Before going outside, Colin gave orders to Bren to get the camp set up, as they would be staying a few days. Speaking softly, he said, "I want to give Elaris time to heal, get her strength back, and maybe have time to study those books. Besides, this place is as good as any to plan our next move."

"Good idea," he agreed, "I'll have someone clean up that room for her so she can have a real bed to sleep on."

Colin gave him a look of appreciation and then went to place a wrap around Elaris's shoulders and walk her out of the cottage.

She immediately stopped and took a deep breath, savoring the fresh air.

"I didn't realize just how dusty it was in there," she said.

"It looks like Claudius hasn't been here for quite a while—probably since before he began his search for you."

They walked down the road a bit, stopping under a tree. Elaris sat down on a rock, enjoying the last colors of the sunset on the horizon. Colin took a knee next to her, pulling out the ring from Lumirien and placing it in her hand.

"What is this?" she whispered, holding it carefully.

"A promise from the Alari—that they will be there for you when your time comes."

Elaris was silent, turning the ring over in her hand. After a long moment, she took it and slid it onto her right hand.

"They seem to think I will bring peace to them," she murmured.

Colin chose his words carefully. "Maybe you will—someday. For now, we focus on your healing and keeping you safe."

"Will he come after me?" she asked, looking intently into his eyes.

Colin nodded slowly. He didn't need to ask who she was speaking of. "He will. He is not a man who takes kindly to disobedience. We will be prepared when the time comes."

Elaris looked back to the horizon, now darkening. "I still don't know what he wanted from me—why, if he wanted me to use my powers, he didn't train me sooner."

"Lord Mordane always has a plan," Colin sighed.

258

The two sat quietly for a bit longer before heading back to the cottage. When they returned, supper had been prepared, and everyone not on guard duty was inside, gathered around the fire enjoying their meal. When Elaris entered, they all stood and smiled at her.

Briggs handed her a bowl of stew and offered her a chair close to the fire. She took it gladly and sat. The men resumed their conversations, entertaining her with stories of their harrowing battles with the dark creatures on their way to find her. They were clearly happy to have her back.

When Colin noticed that her eyes were getting heavy and she had yawned several times, he welcomed the company to depart from the cottage and go to the camp set up outside so she could get some rest.

Walking down the hallway to the room, Elaris turned and smiled at him. "Thank you, Colin—for coming for me," she said shyly.

Colin smiled warmly at her. "There was never a question, Elaris," he said quietly. "I'd find you—no matter what it took."

Elaris took a moment longer to gaze at him before going to the room and finding it swept and dusted with a clean blanket laid out for her.

Colin went to the fireplace and sat in one of the chairs, looking into the fire. Elaris's question about Lord Mordane was his next problem. He would come for them—for her—and they needed to be prepared. For now, he hoped the cottage would provide some sanctuary.

Drawing his sword and laying it across his legs, he settled into the chair for the night. No one would be taking her or harming her again—he would make sure of that.

As he sat keeping guard, his thoughts drifted to Elaris. Her eyes, her smile—the way she had clung to him earlier.

She had called him Colin.

CHAPTER 31

Elaris woke to the sound of birds chirping outside and the smell of eggs cooking. Her stomach growled in response, motivating her to get up quickly and join the company for breakfast. Stepping out of her room, she found Colin standing at the kitchen table, looking down at an open book.

"Good morning," she said, singing the words.

Colin turned and smiled at her. "Sleep well?"

"Oh yes. I forgot how nice it was to sleep under a roof," she laughed.

Colin grinned. "Well, I believe breakfast is ready, if you're hungry."

"Starved!" she said, pressing a hand to her stomach.

The two walked outside, greeting the men who were just waking up and making their way to a fire that had been built near the edge of a clearing.

"My lady!" Sergeant Hill stood, greeting her with a dip of his head.

Elaris, not recognizing him, looked at Colin, confused.

"Sergeant Hill and Corporal Hewitt joined us recently. They were previously part of Captain Karr's company," Colin informed her, pointing out the injured corporal sitting nearby.

"Oh!" she exclaimed awkwardly. "Well... welcome!"

The sergeant smiled at her, seeing her discomfort.

"Don't worry, my lady. We follow you and Captain Aedric," he said with conviction.

Elaris smiled warmly at him.

"Thank you, Sergeant," she said, continuing on to get some breakfast. Colin veered off to speak with his guards.

Arriving at the fire, Elaris took a seat next to Sergeant Keswick. He grinned at her and handed her a plate of food.

"Good morning, my lady."

"Sergeant Keswick—I am so happy to see you are well," she said with a smile.

"I am told that I owe you my life," he murmured.

Elaris paused. Did he remember what she had done for him on the battlefield?

"I..." she began, stopping when she couldn't find the words.

"Some of the men told me that I was about to die, and that you used your powers to save me. They saw those... currents? All around. I don't remember, though."

"I may have... helped," she said softly.

"Well, whatever you did—thank you."

Keswick smiled at her again, his eyes deep with emotion, as he got up to clean his plate.

Elaris sat quietly, thinking about the battlefield and almost losing Colin because of her magic. She had saved the sergeant, but Colin would be dead now if it wasn't for

Thistwyn. If she ever used her magic again, she would have to be much more careful.

Once she was done eating, she returned to the cottage, finding her blanket and pulling it tight around her as she settled by the fire. Determined to begin searching the books from Claudius's collection, she picked up her first volume.

Many of the books were filled with information she already knew: how a Fatewaker could find and manifest Embercurrents, how they could influence and alter the chosen paths of others.

One book in particular caught her attention—a history of Fatewakers, dating back several thousand years. Unlike the last Fatewaker, the ones before had been instrumental in ensuring the peace of the land and fostering the growth of nations.

One, a Fatewaker named Aladriel who lived three thousand years ago, had saved an entire village from a plague and became an honored friend of the emperor of that time. She lived to the age of eighty, spending her life helping others and assisting the emperor in bringing peace to his lands.

As Elaris read, a realization sank in: she was part of a long, proud legacy—a lineage that once used their powers to help the world.

But not all had used their powers for the betterment of others.

The last Fatewaker—unnamed in the texts—had wielded his powers to gain control. The books spoke of him using his abilities to sever souls from the mortal plane.

Elaris shivered, remembering the book passage she had read the night before:

The hand of the Fatewaker may sever the living from the stream of time...

In that moment, Elaris made a promise quietly to herself. "I will not be like him. I will not let this gift become a curse."

For the next several hours, she read, learning more about Fatewakers from times past, as well as writings on the Embercurrents themselves—much of which was written in an ancient language that she couldn't decipher.

One book that caught her eye discussed the possibility of changing a person's past as well as their future—something she remembered Alec mentioning.

Later that evening, Bren braved the dark corridor again to bring her more books when she had finished searching through the pile. Upon opening the top one, a small book that was tucked inside fell out.

Picking it up, Elaris discovered that it wasn't a book at all, but a journal—Claudius's journal.

She paused before reading it, almost afraid of what she may find within. Opening to the middle of the journal, she found a short, broken passage written in hurried handwriting:

He came for her last night—the sorcerer.

The right hand of the devil himself.

I couldn't get there in time.

He killed her.

He killed my Sophie.

Elaris looked up to the painting above the fireplace and to the young girl next to Claudius. She was so young.

Turning the page, she was surprised that the next entry did not mention Sophie. Instead, he spoke of her:

He has chosen a bride.

They say she resides in the north.
Why does he choose her?
What does she have that he wants?

Elaris turned the page, frustrated to find entries about spells and research Claudius was conducting on the creatures of Vale Forest, as well as the training of two apprentices.

"Find anything interesting?" Colin asked, taking the seat next to her.

Elaris looked up from the book with a frown on her face. "I found his journal. He has an entry here about me, but then goes to talk about something else."

Elaris passed Colin the book, showing him the entry she had found. He thumbed through several more pages, skimming each one quickly.

"Here we go—another mention of you," Colin said grimly.

I have discovered his plan! She is the Fatewaker.

He means to bind her to him—not with chains, but with the current itself.

She must give herself freely. It will not work otherwise.

Once the vows are spoken and the bond sealed, he will share her power.

Elaris sat back in her chair, stunned, the weight of the words pressing down on her.

Colin continued to skim the journal, desperate to find something more.

"The journal ends shortly after that entry," he said quietly.

They both sat in silence, looking into the fire. Elaris thought back to her years at the monastery, all in training for her life with Lord Mordane. He had never wanted her to know about her powers. He wanted them for himself.

"My whole life has been preparation for a lie," she whispered.

Colin leaned forward, looking at her intently. "But you found out before it was too late. He can't use you now. He needs you to give yourself freely."

Elaris nodded slowly. "In a strange way, I have Claudius to thank, in part. If not for his attack, I would be arriving at the palace, preparing to be bound to that monster."

Colin reached over and took her hand. "You're free now. He will never touch you," he said firmly.

Just then, Sergeant Bryant, who had been standing watch, ran into the cottage.

"Sir—someone is coming down the road."

Colin stood, pulling Elaris with him. "Go to the room and hide," he said firmly.

Elaris started down the hall just as a ball of fire came blazing through the front door, crashing into the back wall, leaving embers scattered across the floor.

Colin ducked down, pulled his sword from its sheath, and moved quickly to the door. Taking one final glance back at her, he pointed sharply to the room, indicating she should go.

She did so reluctantly, taking refuge under the bed, pulling the blanket down over her to hide.

She pressed her hand over her mouth to muffle her breathing, but nothing could block out the sounds of battle coming from outside.

CHAPTER 32

The cottage was on fire. The doorframe burned steadily, causing Colin to cover his face as he exited the building. Outside, his men were already in position, taking cover behind trees and rocks as they dodged the incoming fireballs while advancing.

In the middle of the road was the last man Colin wanted to see other than Lord Mordane himself—Kaz.

This fight would not be an easy one.

The sorcerer wore his standard cloak of dark crimson. His face was calm, his expression one of unwavering purpose.

"Kaz!" Colin bellowed as he walked boldly through the burning brush toward the road.

Kaz stopped his advance, focusing on Colin in pursuit.

Some of the company attempted to move forward but were halted with a wave of Colin's hand.

"Ah, Captain Aedric," Kaz purred, holding a ball of fire in the palm of his hand.

"How did you find us?" Colin questioned, looking for places to take cover should the need arise.

Kaz let out a low, mocking laugh. "You didn't actually think that was a blessing I gave you before you left, did you?"

"You've been tracking us," Colin said coldly.

"Of course. Lord Mordane doesn't let his dogs roam freely without a leash," he bit out.

"My understanding of magic tells me that a spell dies when the caster does," Colin replied with a grin.

Kaz responded by throwing a ball of fire directly in Colin's path, missing him by a few feet.

"Now, now, Kaz—don't lose your temper," Colin mocked.

Another ball of fire shot toward him, this one flying over his head and landing dangerously close to the cottage.

Colin could see Bren off to the side, creeping slowly to get behind Kaz.

The sorcerer moved forward a step. Colin readied his sword in response.

"Not one more step," he ordered.

"I am here for the girl. If you get in my way, you and your men will die."

"You aren't touching her—and you will be the one to die tonight," Colin growled as he charged.

Colin moved swiftly, swinging his sword at Kaz's neck. Bren charged in from behind, aiming to take out Kaz's legs.

But the sorcerer moved too quickly. With a sweep of his hand, he threw Bren twenty feet into a tree, the sickening thud echoing across the clearing, even as he dodged Colin's blade.

Too fast for a mere man, Colin thought grimly—he was using his magic to speed his movements.

Before he could swing again, Kaz had jumped into the air, taking flight as if he had wings, and landed several feet back from Colin.

"Turn her over, Aedric," Kaz growled.

"That's not going to happen," Colin warned.

Kaz sighed, lowering his hands and folding them in front of him.

"You always struck me as a man of reason, Aedric."

"The problem is, Kaz—you are trying to take something that was never yours to claim."

Kaz nodded once, dropping his head slightly, as if weighing his next move.

"You see, Aedric—Lord Mordane has something very dear to me. If I don't bring the girl back, he will destroy it," Kaz said, his voice steady but taut.

"You'll have to find another way, Kaz. It won't be by taking Elaris," Colin answered, tightening his grip on his sword.

The change in Kaz was instant—his calm shattering into rage and grief.

"I need to save her!" he roared. "I swore loyalty to him for her life! That girl—your Fatewaker—she's the only thing that stands in my way!"

Colin held his ground, sword ready. "Save who?"

Kaz laughed darkly.

"His own flesh and blood," he snarled. "Amara—his daughter. He holds her Embercurrent—and the currents of his other children. He promised he would release her if I served him!"

Kaz's voice cracked on the last words. Without hesitation, he raised his hands, summoning a torrent of magic aimed squarely at Colin.

Elaris huddled under the bed, listening to the chaos outside.

Right after Colin left, she heard him scream a name she didn't recognize—Kaz.

Desperate to see what was happening outside, she closed her eyes and focused on the people around the cottage. Finding the enemy was easy. While the men of Colin's company all had bright, vibrant Embercurrents, this stranger's current burned a dark red—almost black.

She breathed deeply and reached for his chosen current, moving upstream to his past.

The world shifted and she emerged in a bright room. A young man—Kaz, she assumed—stood at a window, staring down at a garden below. His eyes were transfixed on a young woman walking among the flowers, her long blonde hair shining in the sunlight.

He smiled to himself as he watched her move.

The woman paused, sensing his gaze, and looked up.

While Kaz's face lit up with unguarded joy, she returned only a look of warm friendship.

The change in his expression told Elaris everything.

His love was not returned.

Pulling away from his current, she moved forward to another point, further in the future.

270

She surfaced in a dark room with rock walls, manacles hanging ominously.

Kaz, looking slightly older, stood in a corner, examining a book of some sort. A man approached. She recognized him from a painting she had studied since she was a child. He looked so much like he did in her dreams that she almost cried out.

Lord Mordane.

"Kaz. I hear you plan to leave the palace."

Kaz turned slowly, bowing to Mordane.

"Yes, my lord. I wish to join Alec."

Pulling a jar out from behind him, Mordane shook it, sending its contents swirling madly.

Kaz stood frozen, confused.

"It's a pity. Amara will miss you."

The expression on Kaz's face changed to pure horror.

"What have... what have you done to her?" he cried.

"The same thing I do to all my children who are no longer needed," Mordane shrugged.

"Please... I beg you... please let her go. I will do anything you ask," Kaz pleaded, dropping to his knees.

Elaris was pulled back by the sound of explosions outside.

Scrambling out from under the bed, she ran down the hallway and looked out the broken window to see Kaz throwing balls of fire at Colin, who had taken refuge behind a rock.

She knew she had to do something. The thought of moving Kaz to a new current frightened her. The last time she had manipulated an Embercurrent in that way, Colin had almost died.

Seeing Kaz preparing to advance closer to Colin, she focused on him and looked to his chosen current again—this time to his future.

She was suddenly outside, the cottage on fire. She could see herself being dragged away, Colin and other members of the company lying dead on the ground as she passed.

Bile rose in her throat at the image, but she pressed on.

Finding an alternate current nearby, she looked at its fate but found only the death of Colin and the company again.

Opening her eyes, she looked through the window to see Kaz standing mere feet from Colin and several of the men.

She was out of time.

Thinking back on her studies that day, she knew what she had to do.

Running down the hall to the door, she stepped through the burning frame and stood boldly in the open.

Kaz's attention was immediately drawn from Colin, who screamed her name in panic.

She steadied herself, controlling her breathing. Closing her eyes, she found Kaz's chosen current and, opening them back up, manifested it. Dark crimson streams flooded out from her fingers, flowing to him.

Kaz stopped in his tracks, horrified at what he was seeing.

"What are you doing, girl?" he called.

"I'm sorry," she whispered, as she pulled the Embercurrent from Kaz and released it into oblivion.

The light in Kaz's eyes flickered—and went out.

CHAPTER 33

Kaz collapsed, and the camp went silent. The only sound was the crackling fire consuming the trees, bushes, and cottage. The smell of smoke filled the air.

Colin stood slowly from where he had taken cover, carefully watching the body lying motionless on the ground, waiting for it to move.

Just outside the cottage, framed in fire from the doorway behind her, was Elaris. She stood with her hands still extended, her arms shaking.

"Elaris!" Colin yelled, running to her.

She didn't seem to see him. She stood frozen.

"Elaris! Are you alright?" Colin asked frantically, coming to a sudden stop in front of her.

She didn't answer. Her eyes were glazed, and she was unblinking.

"Elaris... Elaris—it's me, Colin," he pleaded softly, reaching out to touch her extended hand.

As soon as he touched her, she jumped, pulling it back as if burned. She turned her face to him, her eyes focusing slowly.

"Elaris—are you alright?" he asked again.

"I... I killed him," she gasped.

Colin took her hand and led her to a chair by a tent.

The men began to come out from their shelters, slowly analyzing the destruction. Briggs ran to Bren, who was still reeling from being thrown into the tree.

"Get the fires out!" Colin ordered.

The men ran to grab buckets from the well nearby, throwing water on the doorway of the cottage to snuff the flames.

Turning back to Elaris, he squeezed her hand and whispered, "Rest here. I'll return soon."

Running to Bren, he confirmed that the impact had left him slightly shaken, but he was otherwise unharmed.

"I'm sure this bump on my head will make me even more irresistible to the ladies," Bren joked, trying to ease his friend's obvious concern.

"Any time you want to improve your looks, just let me know," Colin said with a smirk. "I'll grab a hammer."

After confirming that no one had sustained serious injuries, Colin helped the men douse the last of the flames. Unfortunately, much of the cottage had been burned, making it unlivable.

"We were able to save many of the books, Sir—and I believe the hidden room still stands," Briggs reported, knowing how important this would be to Elaris. "We also removed the body," he added quietly.

"Good work, Sergeant," Colin said gratefully. "Do one final sweep and then post additional guards. We don't know if Kaz was alone. There may be others coming."

Briggs gave a quick salute and left to implement his captain's orders.

With the chaos over, Colin turned to Elaris, who sat quietly in the same chair he had left her in, staring straight ahead as if in another world.

He recognized that look. He had seen it many times on the battlefield.

Walking slowly to her, he lowered himself to a knee in front of her and spoke softly. "Elaris. I want you to know that you saved us. If you hadn't been there, Kaz would have surely killed us."

She blinked and nodded once, a tear escaping her eye and rolling down her cheek.

"He wasn't going to stop until we were dead, and he had found you," Colin continued, taking her hand and squeezing it.

Another tear came, and Elaris swallowed a sob. "I killed him," she whimpered.

Colin had no words that would comfort her. Killing someone, no matter who they were, left a lasting impact on one's soul.

Colin sighed, regretting what she had been forced to do.

"I know you didn't want to kill Kaz," he said gently. "I know you did what had to be done to save us. You will carry this pain with you, Elaris—but I promise you this—it will change with time. You will grow and become stronger from it."

"He loved her…" she cried softly. "Amara."

Colin frowned for a moment, thinking back. "We were told she died of a sickness."

"No—Lord Mordane captured her Embercurrent somehow. He used it to control Kaz," she explained, wiping her eyes.

"His own daughter..." Colin breathed, shaking his head. "He mentioned other children as well. Who knows how many he's done this to."

Elaris hesitated, then asked quietly, "Does he have many?"

Colin's expression darkened. "He may have hundreds. Right now, the only legitimate one is little Prince Orran."

Seeing the shock on her face, Colin hurried to explain. "He has taken many... mistresses."

He didn't have the heart to explain that many hadn't volunteered for the job.

"Oh..." Elaris said simply, dropping her gaze to the ground.

They remained quiet for a long moment, watching the men work around them.

Colin cleared his throat and broke the silence.

"We will unfortunately need to move tonight. Mordane knows where we are—and will soon discover that Kaz failed. He won't make the mistake of sending just one wizard next time."

She nodded her understanding. "I will gather a few books, if I may?"

"Of course. Just give what you need to one of the men."

Standing up, Colin gave her a gentle smile.

"All will be well, I promise," he said as he left to arrange for their departure.

Elaris gave a faint half-smile in return, standing to go into the burnt-out cottage.

Colin found Bren and Briggs standing by the campfire, discussing the night's events.

Seeing him approach, Bren grabbed a map of Ashcar from a sack and rolled it out onto a small table nearby.

He knew what was coming.

"I think we can make it to Timbrow if we cut through the pass," he started.

Colin looked at the map, his expression one of annoyance. There was no place in Ashcar where they could hide.

"No," he said firmly.

"No?" Bren asked, confused. "We may be able to make it further east, but the travel will be hard on Lady Vaelora…"

"We aren't going to Timbrow or any other safe haven," he answered firmly. "Gather the men."

Several minutes later, the company stood in a loose formation in the center of the camp.

Colin stood in front of them, as he had hundreds of times before.

But this time was different.

They were outlaws now.

And he was their leader.

Thinking of the path that lay ahead—the sacrifices it might demand—he found it difficult to ask it of them.

"Men," he began, speaking with conviction. "The days of being hunted are over. Lord Mordane will soon discover his Royal Sorcerer is dead. He will send even more wizards next time. We could stay and fight, but he will not stop until he gets what he desires. I don't intend to waste my time fighting his pawns while he sits waiting in the comfort of the palace."

The men cheered in agreement, raising their swords high.

"We leave tonight," Colin called. "Our destination is the palace of Ashcar. Our target—its ruler."

A resounding roar answered him.

"Hear me well," he said, his voice steady. "What I ask demands great sacrifice. We may perish before we even reach the gates. If any of you chooses not to follow, there will be no judgement. All I ask is that you take up another task just as vital—protect Lady Vaelora with your lives."

The men slammed the hilts of their swords against their chests in salute, their eyes full of sheer grit and determination. They would follow him into hell, if need be.

"Sir," Briggs said firmly, nodding to indicate that they had a visitor.

Stepping from the back of the assembled company was Elaris.

"I am coming with you," she said firmly.

The men grumbled in response, clearly not in agreement.

"I'm sorry," Colin responded. "It's too dangerous. A few of the men will stay back with you."

"You need me. I can be of help," she answered.

Colin hesitated, not knowing what to say.

"You *need* me," she repeated.

Colin saw the look of determination in her eyes and sensed he was about to lose. "I'm sorry, but no."

Elaris stood firmly, bringing her hands to her hips and raising her eyebrow in defiance.

"Captain—I am going to the palace. With or without you."

Colin looked to Bren and Briggs, both of whom only shrugged helplessly in response.

The other men looked away, afraid to meet his eyes.

Colin sighed, knowing he had been defeated. "You may go," he said.

Elaris started to smile but was quickly interrupted.

"But! You will stay with Sergeant Briggs and will not be entering the palace itself," he said firmly.

Colin gave Elaris a hard gaze, indicating he would not budge on this.

"Agreed," she answered.

Colin dismissed the company, and the men went to pack up the camp. Elaris stood off to the side, watching him.

Approaching her, he shook his head. "This is a bad idea, Elaris."

"You are probably right," she agreed. "But I want to be of help to you. Besides, I have a plan."

"Oh?" he asked, curious what idea she had come up with.

"Yes. But I'm going to need you to bend that rule about me going into the palace a bit," she said with a mischievous glint in her eye.

CHAPTER 34

Colin hated traveling at night—especially this close to the border of Vale Forest. But there had been no other choice. The company had packed quickly and set off east, aiming to reach the main road heading south that would carry them to the palace.

It wasn't the most concealed route, but it was the fastest. Speed mattered more than stealth. The challenge now would be avoiding any unfriendly eyes—or creatures—along the way.

Colin estimated that they had two, maybe three days before Lord Mordane realized Kaz had failed. That was assuming it took Kaz that long to find Elaris and bring her back.

With the Royal Sorcerer now dead, Colin hoped the tracking spell had died with him. But if it hadn't... they might already be hunted.

He glanced over his shoulder. Elaris rode beside Briggs, deep in conversation. Before they'd left, Briggs had retrieved a handful of books and notes from the hidden room—documents Elaris had specifically asked to keep.

Colin could only hope she found something useful within them—something they could use, because the battle ahead wouldn't be won with strength alone.

Bren rode up beside him, looking troubled. "I'll be happy when we are away from this cursed forest," he grumbled.

"Really? I thought you'd appreciate another chance to see a certain redhead," Colin joked.

Bren's expression quickly changed to a grin. "Thistwyn hasn't seen the last of me."

"That sounds mildly threatening," Colin laughed.

Bren only smiled wickedly in response.

Colin turned to check on Elaris again, seeing that her conversation had ended, and she was now riding with her eyes closed. He guessed she must be practicing her magic.

"So, do we have a plan yet?" Bren asked.

"Somewhat. Elaris says she has something in mind."

"If it's anything like what she did to Kaz, then we're in good hands," he said, his tone serious.

"She took it hard," Colin said quietly, glancing back at her.

"I imagine she did," Bren murmured. "I hope she knows how much the men appreciate what she did. We would all be dead if not for her actions."

Colin nodded. "I think it will just take some time. You remember how it was—the first time."

Bren's eyes glazed for a moment, and he seemed to be lost in thought. "Yes. It's good she has you, Colin. Just like I did."

Colin smiled at him, appreciating his words.

Anxious to lighten the mood, Bren sat up straight in his saddle. "What I wouldn't give for a pint," he sighed.

"When we complete this mission, drinks are on me," Colin grinned.

"You and I should open a tavern when this whole rebellion-against-Mordane thing clears up," Bren said lightly.

"A tavern?" Colin laughed.

"Sure! I could charm the customers while you pour the drinks," he said with a wink.

Colin snorted. "So, I run the tavern while you flirt in the corner."

"Division of labor," Bren replied proudly.

Colin just shook his head, laughing.

The company stopped early in the morning at a small farm that looked to be abandoned. Far from the road, it was perfect for getting some much-needed rest while staying away from prying eyes.

Sergeants Bryant and Colburn worked to get a room in the small home ready for Elaris, while the other men prepared food or stood guard.

After ensuring that all tasks had been completed, Colin went to find Elaris, spotting her sitting under a tree by the barn with a book in her lap.

The sun had crested the horizon, letting rays of light shine down on the farm. Colin noticed that Elaris had changed into her blue dress. With her current surroundings, she looked every bit like a country lass.

She was barely recognizable as the girl veiled in black from weeks ago.

"Have you found anything helpful?" he asked, sitting down next to her.

"I think so," she murmured, turning a page in her book. "I think I know what Mordane is doing with his children's Embercurrents."

"Oh?"

"Yes... this text describes the act of stealing someone's Embercurrent. It keeps the person frozen between life and death—their fate sealed away. It's quite different from the act of removing the Embercurrent completely, essentially destroying it and killing the person in the process," she said quietly, remembering Kaz.

"But for what purpose?" Colin asked.

"To feed off of it—to gain power," she replied solemnly.

Colin frowned. "But why his children? He has any number of other subjects to choose from."

"I suspect I found the answer to that question," she said, opening and reading from another book nearby:

Of all the sources, none grant greater power than the Embercurrent of one's own blood. Bound by shared essence, it endures longer, burns brighter—but always at a price, for such ties are not easily severed.

Colin leaned back against the tree. "Is he a wizard then, to be able to accomplish this? Or did Kaz help him?"

"Kaz didn't help him take Amara's Embercurrent. He was devastated over it," she said sadly.

Colin looked toward the sunrise—his expression thoughtful. "We know he is somehow related to the last Fatewaker. Could he have inherited some of that power?"

Elaris shook her head. "I don't know. I have found no mention of such a thing yet. Perhaps I will find more in some of the other books that Sergeant Briggs recovered for me."

Seeing her stifle a yawn, Colin stood, holding out his hand to help her up.

"You should try to get some rest. We won't be staying long. We need to keep moving."

Picking up her books and taking his hand, she stood and brushed off her skirts.

"Will it take long to reach the palace?" she asked as they walked back to the house.

"If we make good time, we should be within sight of it by tomorrow night. Getting there as soon as possible is key to taking him by surprise."

Elaris nodded quietly as she stepped into the home. She paused, smiled faintly at him, and shut the door.

Elaris barely slept a wink. Her mind was focused on the task ahead. She had spent most of the time on the journey practicing—finding the Embercurrents around her while keeping her eyes open and alert.

She was becoming increasingly successful, having managed to view the currents of the company, eyes open wide, while quietly riding. It took an immense amount of concentration and breathing, but she believed that with more time, she could perfect it.

The problem was: time was running out.

Her plan for confronting Mordane depended on gaining more control of her powers. But the discovery in Claudius's books had shaken her. She had expected to face a man— dangerous, yes, but mortal. Now she knew better. Mordane possessed a power of his own, and that changed everything.

She peeked out the house's window and saw the sun dipping lower in the sky. They would be leaving soon.

She gathered her books and stepped out into the dwindling sun, greeted by several members of the company.

"Would you like something to eat, my lady?" Sergeant Linwood asked her.

"That would be lovely, thank you." She smiled, causing his ears to turn red.

She took a seat next to the fire, the smell of smoke and stew drifting around her as she watched the company prepare to leave. She thought about what they were about to do, and the impact that would have on their lives.

None of them would ever be able to go home—not while Mordane lived. They had lost everything—their country included. What they were left with was the brotherhood they had created.

Elaris suddenly felt a wave of emotion, looking at her new family. They had done so much to protect her and were now marching into hell to ensure her freedom.

She made a silent vow that they would all get out alive.

Standing and walking to Colin, who was packing up his horse, she announced, "Please assemble the men. It's time we discussed my plan."

CHAPTER 35

Colin couldn't believe what he was hearing.
"Absolutely not," he said firmly.
Bren shifted from one foot to the other nervously.
"It may work, but I don't like it." He hesitated.

"I'm with the captain. Bad idea," Briggs grumbled.

Elaris sighed. She had asked to speak to all the men at once about her plan to avoid this conversation, but Colin had insisted that he, Bren, and Briggs hear it first.

"It will work. If there is one thing I have learned about Lord Mordane over the course of this trip, it's that he hungers for more power. This is the perfect way to use that against him."

"Elaris. There are too many things that can go wrong—several of them ending in your death. We will come up with another plan," Colin insisted.

Elaris decided to change tactics. She turned to Briggs and smiled sweetly. "Sergeant, you know that Lord Mordane will never stop coming after me."

Briggs stood up straighter, the idea clearly upsetting him. "Yes."

"This is the only way to ensure he can't do that anymore. The only way we will know for sure that he will leave me—and us—alone," she said softly, touching his arm.

Briggs smiled at the contact, an expression of fondness on his face. "If you think this will work, my lady, then I will follow you."

Colin and Bren both shook their heads, clearly disgusted.

Elaris looked to Bren next, who held up his hands in surrender. "I go where I am told to go. No need to use your magic on me," he said with a laugh.

Elaris smiled at him in response. But her last target would be the hardest.

Stepping closer to Colin, she reached out to touch his arm but was surprised when he quickly moved away, positioning himself on the opposite side of the table.

"The answer is still no, Elaris," he said firmly, folding his arms in front of him, his expression a mix of determination and fear.

"Colin—I can do this. And I have full confidence that you and the men will be there when the time comes. Please… let me try," she pleaded softly, her eyes hopeful.

Colin scowled. He looked to Bren and Briggs for support but found none.

"Briggs will be at your side the whole time," he demanded, glaring at the sergeant.

"Of course!" She smiled.

"And we will run through this *multiple* times until it is perfect. Then we will run through it a hundred times more!" he barked, clearly getting more upset at the idea by the minute.

"That is an excellent idea," she said with a nod.

"You will explain this to the men. I doubt they will be as... receptive... to your charms as Briggs," Colin grumbled, glaring at his sergeant.

Briggs hung his head, looking at the floor and avoiding his captain's eyes.

Elaris stood up straighter. "I'm sure the men will be just as wise and understanding as my friend here," she responded, patting Briggs on the shoulder.

"Thank you for trusting me, Sergeant. I will not waste that trust."

Briggs smiled at her, earning a grumble from Colin.

Considering the issue resolved, Elaris made her way to the center of the camp, where the men waited.

She took a moment to look at them each individually, wanting to capture each of their faces in her mind.

Pulling herself to her full height and clearing her throat, she began speaking. "We will arrive at the palace the day after next. There is no way we can overtake the palace guards by brute force. We must use deception."

The men shifted and nodded, seeming to like where she was going.

"I will be turning myself over to Mordane," she announced confidently.

The men responded with agitated shouts and words she had never heard before, most of which she suspected were highly improper.

Colin stood off to the side, arms folded, smiling at their response.

Elaris turned to him and frowned.

"Please," she pleaded, causing them to quickly return to order.

"Please. This will work. Because you will be there."

Ears perked in curiosity.

"My friends," she began again.

"Nice touch," Colin grumbled next to her.

She rolled her eyes at him and continued. "My friends, you have recognized the error of your captain. Your loyalty is with Lord Mordane. Mine is with him as well. You clearly need to kill your captain and bring me to Lord Mordane to carry out your mission." She smiled.

Several of the men started grumbling again, not liking this at all.

"Once I am inside, I can use my powers to shift his current. It will be fast and easy. He won't even get a word out," she said proudly.

The company looked at her with expressions of apprehension.

"Once that is complete, we can find the captured Embercurrents of his children and save them," she rushed to say.

"What?" Colin snapped, stepping forward to look her in the eye. "You never mentioned this part."

"Well, once I shift his current to something less... evil... saving his children will be easily accomplished. We can't just leave them trapped," she said simply.

Colin shook his head at her, indicating he did not believe this was going to work as simply as presented.

Colin stepped forward to address his men. "You, led by Sergeant Briggs, will be taking Lady Vaelora to our illustrious leader and will wait for her to signal should she need your help. I, Lieutenant Holt, Keswick, Bower, and Hewitt will go in through the guard's entrance at the back. We may need to deal with some of the Guard, but I am hopeful we can pass unnoticed."

The men nodded, growing in confidence.

"We will go over the details tomorrow when we stop. We need this to be perfect. No mistakes," he said firmly.

Taking one final look at them, he ordered, "We leave within the hour. Dismissed."

The company scattered to take care of final preparations for the night of travel ahead.

Briggs approached Colin, looking confused. "Sir, would Lieutenant Holt not be the better option to lead the men?"

"The Guard and Mordane know the lieutenant and I are friends. They would never believe he would turn on me."

Briggs frowned at the idea, clearly uncomfortable with even pretending to be a traitor. "I see, Sir."

"Briggs—I have full confidence in your ability to lead them. And to protect Lady Vaelora," he reassured.

"Thank you, Sir," he replied with a nod, turning to pack his gear.

Elaris approached him slowly. "This will work, Colin."

"I hope so, Elaris—because if you die—it will break them… and me," he murmured as he turned to walk away.

The sun was setting by the time they left the camp. Colin rode quietly in the lead position, going over the plan in his mind. He let out a grumble when he thought about all the risks involved.

"Thinking of the plan?" Bren asked.

"It's a horrible idea," he grumbled again.

"It is," he agreed. "But it's the only one we have that has a chance of success."

Colin remained silent. He didn't want to agree, but he knew his friend was right.

"I think Lady Vaelora is missing your company," Bren noted, turning his head to look at her riding several positions behind them.

"She has Briggs," Colin replied flatly.

"Something tells me that Briggs's company isn't quite the same as yours," he winked, laughing quietly.

Colin scowled.

"When are you going to tell her you are in love with her?" Bren asked casually.

"What... I... I have no idea what you are talking about," he sputtered.

Bren just laughed and shook his head, his expression one of pity.

A few hours later, when Colin felt it was again safe to do so, he turned his head to check on Elaris.

She was riding quietly next to Briggs, her expression focused and still. He assumed she was practicing her powers.

He thought about the things she may see when looking at Mordane's Embercurrents and became worried.

While he didn't know all the details, there were always rumors of his cruelty. He wore a façade of a generous and magnanimous ruler well, complete with his young son whom he adored.

But Colin knew from whispers within the Guard, as well as things he had witnessed himself, that it was all a lie.

What would Elaris see in his Embercurrent? Colin hated that he couldn't protect her from it.

Sitting forward and looking at the road ahead, he ran over the plan in his mind. There were several problems with it—hundreds, actually.

While he had full confidence in his men and their ability to protect Elaris should there be any trouble, only nine of them would be with her—up against the full force of Mordane's palace guards.

Elaris was still learning and adapting to her abilities. She practiced for hours every day, but being surrounded by hostile forces was very different from the situations she had faced thus far.

And then there was Mordane himself. Colin was not foolish enough to view him as weak. They had already discovered that he possessed some sort of magical powers—enough to capture the Embercurrents of his children. They couldn't make the mistake of underestimating him.

Colin exhaled and looked ahead. The plan was flawed, the risks impossible to ignore, and the person they were relying on most was still just learning who she was.

But she believed in them—trusted them to pull her back if it all went wrong.

He just hoped they were ready—because if they failed... they wouldn't just lose her.

They'd lose everything.

CHAPTER 36

T he day's first light had broken when they arrived at the lake where they would be camping. It was their final stop before reaching Houck. The small village just outside the palace was a perfect place for them to initiate their plan—it was only a few hours away.

The company moved quickly to get tents set up, seeing the first signs of rain clouds on the horizon. Elaris grabbed a quick meal and headed to her tent for some rest.

Colin went about ensuring they had proper guards posted, and then tracked down Corporal Finwick.

The corporal had just finished setting up his tent and was getting ready to take a much-needed nap.

"Corporal," Colin said quietly.

Finwick turned quickly to face his captain, standing at attention.

"Sir!" he answered stiffly.

"I have a job for you."

"Certainly, Sir," he replied.

"I need you to ride into Houck and find the Guard's supply cache. We need capes for this mission, and we all left ours behind. Ride back when you have them."

"Yes, Sir," he said, clearly happy to be chosen.

"Get some rest first, Finwick—at least a few hours. I need you sharp for tomorrow's activities."

The corporal nodded and went inside his tent, leaving Colin to find his. He doubted he would be able to sleep, his mind plagued by the details of the day ahead.

He was surprised when, six hours later, he woke up from a sound sleep. He could hear activity in the camp outside, the sound of Elaris's laughter carrying through the fabric of his tent.

Emerging into the sunshine, he could tell it had rained earlier. The grass beneath his boots was wet as he walked to the center of camp. There, sitting on a chair surrounded by his men, was Elaris. She had her blue dress on again and had pulled her hair back from her face with the scarf he had bought for her in Millcross. Her eyes shone brightly in the sun.

The image of her made him catch his breath.

"Sir?" Sergeant Hill interrupted.

"Yes, Sergeant?" he asked, clearing his throat.

"I wanted to speak to you about the mission, Sir."

"Certainly. What's on your mind?"

"It's Corporal Hewitt, Sir."

"Are his injuries still bothering him?" Colin asked, concerned.

"Oh—no, Sir. He is healing up nicely. I just wanted to say… he is very excited to be on your team for the mission."

Colin nodded once, sensing the sergeant wasn't here to talk about his excited corporal.

Sergeant Hill hesitated before continuing. "He is young, Sir. He is anxious to please and... sometimes anticipates orders before they are given."

Colin smiled slightly. "An issue we all had at one time."

The sergeant relaxed slightly. "Yes, Sir," he laughed.

"I'll watch out for him, Hill. Thank you for letting me know."

Hill gave a salute, turned, and left.

Colin returned his attention to Elaris, who was now smiling at him.

He cursed under his breath softly as his heartbeat increased. He was in trouble.

Elaris rose from her chair as he approached.

"Good afternoon, Colin," she murmured.

"Good afternoon. Did you sleep well?"

"Yes. I always love the sound of rain. It always brings the best dreams," she said with a smile.

Colin was very curious what she had dreamed about, but was once again interrupted—this time by Bren.

"Ready to go over this plan?" he asked.

"Yes. Gather the men. Has Finwick left yet?"

"He rode out about an hour ago," Bren confirmed.

"We'll fill him in on the details once he gets back," Colin replied as he walked to a planning table that had been set up.

As the men gathered around them, Colin spread out a map of Houck, with the palace featured to the right.

They went through the plan carefully, step by step. The two groups would travel toward Houck, separating about an hour from the village. From there, they would travel to their designated locations—Colin and his men to the south entrance of the palace, Briggs and his men to the front entrance with Elaris, playing the part of the blushing bride.

If all went according to plan, Elaris would be escorted to the main hall to meet her groom. The Guard in this area would be light, the majority of them posted at the gates. Briggs would insist upon escorting her himself, with the rest of the men accompanying to see Mordane, expressing the need to report on the death of the captain.

Elaris was confident that she would be able to read and manipulate Mordane's current quickly. She had apparently been able to speed up the process with concentration.

Colin and his men, on the other hand, would be accessing the main hall via the back entrance and would ensure that the Guard didn't interfere with what Elaris had to do.

"And what of these children you spoke of?" Sergeant Linwood asked.

"I should be able to see more about them and their location once I can see his current," Elaris said hopefully.

Once they had run through the plan multiple times and all questions and concerns had been addressed, the company went about preparing for the next day's events.

Elaris went to walk by the lake while Colin pulled Briggs aside.

"There are many things that can go wrong tomorrow, Briggs," he grumbled.

"You're not wrong, Sir," he replied solemnly.

"Lady Vaelora has her plan—but we need to be prepared for it to fail."

"What do you have in mind, Sir?"

"If something happens, I want you to grab her and get her out of there. She is your priority."

"Yes, Sir," Briggs said firmly.

"And Briggs... don't let her use her charms on you."

Briggs turned red and mumbled, "Of course, Sir."

Colin made his way down to the lake to find Elaris, who had taken a seat on a rock under a tree.

She looked up at him and smiled, but it didn't reach her eyes.

"What's on your mind?" Colin asked softly, suspecting he knew the answer.

"I'm worried about tomorrow. I wish there was more time to practice."

"You have already learned so much at an incredible pace, Elaris."

"I know," she half-smiled. "I just don't want to fail. You are all depending on me."

Colin crouched in front of her and gently took her hand—something he had discovered he enjoyed doing.

"You won't fail us, Elaris."

He paused, searching her face. "Even if things don't go to plan... you're not alone in this. You never have been. And you're not the only one carrying the weight."

Her lips curved slightly, but her eyes still shimmered with doubt.

He squeezed her hand. "Just be who you are. That's what's gotten us this far. That's what we believe in."

She looked out toward the lake, her expression one of concern.

"What will happen... once it's over?" she asked shyly.

"Well… depending on the current you put Mordane in, I am hopeful that things will improve, and he will leave us in peace."

"But what about… me?"

Colin let his breath out slowly. There was what he wanted, and what was best for her—and he wasn't sure the two aligned.

"Let's just get through tomorrow before we worry about that," he said as he squeezed her hand again.

Colin saw Bren signaling him from the ridge and stood up to leave, giving her a reassuring smile as he walked away.

Bren met him halfway.

"I've run through different scenarios with the two groups. I think we are in good shape for tomorrow. The flaw in all this planning is that it's all based on assumptions—that nothing has changed in their standard operations since we left."

"I was thinking the same thing," Colin said quietly, his expression worried.

"Have you thought about where we are going should this all go wrong—assuming we are still alive, of course?" Bren asked.

"I have, actually. If this falls through, we will make our way to the south. The king there may welcome some traitors with our knowledge and experience."

"Perhaps he has a tavern we can take over and live out our dream," Bren grinned.

"Your dream, friend. My dreams are far more enjoyable," he said, looking at Elaris.

CHAPTER 37

Morning broke the next day, and the company was in formation, ready to ride into Houck. Elaris stood in her black dress, Briggs helping her mount her horse. Once she was up, she pulled her black veil from a pocket and draped it over her head and face.

The men all stared at her, surprised to see her like that again. They had all forgotten the girl in black they had begun this journey with.

How much she had changed.

Corporal Finwick, who had returned the night before, passed out the capes to all the soldiers.

"I didn't think I'd be wearing this thing again," Sergeant Renshaw grumbled as he secured it over his shoulders.

"Finwick, did you pull these out of a sewer?" Sergeant Bryant complained as he sniffed his cape.

Finwick merely grinned at him, a secret behind his eyes.

Colin rode to the front of the formation, taking one last look at everyone, his eyes lingering on Elaris.

"Today is the day. You all know what you need to do. We follow the plan. We all stay alive."

The soldiers pounded their chests once, indicating they were ready.

Briggs came up and took position in front of his group while Colin and his four rode at the back. Elaris rode in the middle of the company, as was proper for an escort.

As they departed, Colin wondered how many would return. He thought about each of his men—how they had all grouped together to rescue Elaris and protect her. They could have easily killed him and turned her over to Mordane, just like their scenario. Each one had chosen his brothers—and Elaris—over Mordane's Guard.

He only prayed they would survive the day.

Two hours later, the company came to a stop at a crossroads. Colin rode up to the front of the formation to give final orders to Briggs.

"We will meet you inside. Remember your backup plan," he said knowingly.

Briggs nodded, the hard look of a warrior on his face.

As Colin returned to his group, he stopped next to Elaris. She pulled the veil up, and they exchanged a long gaze.

"I'll see you inside the palace," Colin said, his voice low and steady, before continuing to the back of the formation.

Elaris pulled her veil back over her face and moved forward as Colin and his men departed through the woods toward the palace.

Elaris couldn't believe what she was seeing. They had ridden through the village of Houck earlier—a quaint village that seemed very busy with people going about their business at the various markets. The people had seemed somewhat strange to her, dashing into their homes upon seeing the men in their uniforms.

Now, they were approaching the palace—a huge, oppressive structure on a hill, dominating most of the landscape. It looked exactly like it had in her nightmares.

At the gate, they were stopped by the guard on duty.

Briggs exchanged brief words with him, the guard glancing at Elaris multiple times. Finally, the gates were opened, and they proceeded inward.

Elaris could feel her heart racing. The company moved slowly across a bridge that led into the main courtyard. She tried to focus on the guards there, finding their Embercurrents. Breathing deeply and slowly shifting her focus to the palace, she searched for Mordane, but found only guards.

They came to a stop, and Briggs got down and made his way over to her to help her off her horse.

As he was taking her hand, he whispered, "Anything?"

"Not yet," she replied softly, adjusting her veil.

They were greeted at the door by two large guards, each with pristine golden armor. They bowed to her but seemed reluctant to let Briggs and the rest of the men inside.

"I have a report to give to Lord Mordane concerning the death of Captain Aedric and Lieutenant Holt," Briggs announced firmly.

Although the men were large, Briggs still stood a head taller, making an intimidating figure. Both guards looked at each other as if trying to decide, but Briggs made the decision for them, ordering his men to continue through.

As they walked down the hall, Elaris tried to concentrate on the area around her, searching for Mordane's Embercurrent. Her boots echoed loudly on the marble floors, making the hall seem cavernous. She looked up to see that the ceilings towered at least three stories high, making even Briggs seem small.

Briggs moved into place beside her in a protective posture. He walked cautiously, scanning every hallway they passed.

Elaris took a deep breath and tried to sense her surroundings again—first seeing the currents of the men around her, then the staff and guards in the other rooms. Finally, she found what she was looking for.

At the end of the hall, she saw an Embercurrent like none she had seen before—red and blazing, like fire. She could hear it crackle loudly—its energy bursting in rivers in all directions. It made her skin crawl.

This had to be Lord Mordane's current, she thought.

"I found him," she whispered to Briggs.

Briggs stiffened, slowing his pace significantly. The rest of the men adjusted their speed to match. They wanted to give her as much time as possible.

Elaris found Mordane's chosen current. She had no intention of looking into it, trying instead to find an appropriate alternate current, but was pulled forcibly in, unable to escape. It moved her backward, upstream.

She emerged in a dark room. The smell of sulfur and blood hit her nose.

Mordane stood next to a table, several jars lined up on it. Kaz approached him slowly.

"It is time, my lord," he said.

Mordane smiled wickedly, took one of the jars and, opening it, released an Embercurrent from within, its essence rising like vapor. He leaned forward, breathing in the currents deeply, his chest expanding with the effort.

In mere moments, he changed. His skin, bearing the normal signs of an aging man, turned soft and taut.

His gray temples turned blond, and in seconds, he looked no older than thirty.

Elaris was stunned. She was unable to see more, however, as she was again violently pulled—this time even further upstream.

She came out in the same room, but this time a wrinkled, grey Mordane had a man in his twenties with him. The man looked so like Mordane that she could only guess they were related. Her suspicions were confirmed when he spoke.

"Father. Why have you brought me here?" he asked with a look of disgust.

Mordane smiled patiently at him. "As my heir, you are destined to take my throne upon my death. But I'm afraid I can't let that happen. You see, you have another destiny. To be a placeholder."

The man looked confused. "Father?" he asked cautiously.

"You have served your purpose, my son. The kingdom has seen you grow and mature. They look forward to your reign. It's now time for my rebirth."

A wizard in a dark cloak emerged from the shadows, coming to stand behind his master, placing a hand at his back. Elaris had seen a wizard do this before—with Alec giving her his power so she could use her magic.

In a moment, Mordane had his hands on his son, wrapping them around his neck. The air was charged with energy, and Elaris could feel her skin crawl.

As his son struggled, Mordane held tightly. Suddenly, an Embercurrent emerged, spilling out of the man in streams of green. They wrapped around Mordane, winding up to his face where he inhaled them deeply.

Soon, the currents were depleted and the man dropped, limp, onto the floor.

Mordane closed his eyes, breathing in the last of the energy. His appearance changed rapidly as it had before in the last vision. Within moments, he looked exactly like the man lying on the floor—young and vibrant.

Gazing down at his son, he cooed mockingly, "Draegor—such a good boy."

Elaris's breath caught, and she was pulled again, further back.

She emerged on a desolate plain, no vegetation to be found.

Mordane stood in front of her, his back to her. All around him, bodies lay in heaps. She could smell blood and hear the moans of the dying.

Mordane moved his head slightly to the side. In a flash, he turned to face her, looking intently into her eyes. Elaris gasped. Looking back at her was Mordane—but with intense violet eyes.

"I see you, girl," he growled.

CHAPTER 38

The path to the south entrance of the palace was a narrow one, full of brush and downed trees. Colin grew impatient as they had to stop several times to walk their horses through, for fear they'd get caught in the undergrowth.

Finally, the palace came into sight. Colin had never liked the looks of the place. It was called a palace, but it looked more like a fortress—dark and foreboding.

Dismounting from their horses, the men finished the last leg of their journey on foot, staying low and hidden to avoid detection.

As they approached the back gate, Sergeant Bower ran up to the guard who was posted and grabbed his neck, pulling him down forcefully to the ground and knocking the wind from his lungs.

The guard sputtered, gasping for air, as Colin and Bren dragged him into the trees, tying him to a post that was well secured in the ground.

"Captain… Aedric?" the guard stammered, still gasping for air.

Colin looked at the man but didn't recognize him.

"Sorry, fellow," he said before they knocked him out and ran back to the gate.

The commotion had caused the guard on the interior of the back courtyard to investigate. He was quickly dealt with by Sergeant Keswick, who clubbed him over the head before dragging him out to the trees.

"That was easier than I thought," Bren said with a quiet laugh.

"They always put the guards that are on report in the back." Colin smirked.

As they advanced to the courtyard, they caught sight of several servants working.

"Hewitt, you stay here and post guard. We don't want anyone noticing they are missing," Colin ordered. "Bower, make sure the horses are all gathered for our departure."

The two men ran quickly to their designated assignments.

Colin, Bren, and Keswick waited until the servants were distracted before sprinting to the back doors.

Once inside, they crept down the hall until they found a set of doors that led to a large room. Inside, a long table stood, a map of Ashcar carved into it.

"It's the planning room," Colin said, picking up the flags representing troop placement that littered the table, and throwing one to the side.

"I see we are still at war with the south," Bren muttered as he passed it.

Moving forward, they took another door to the right and came to a main hallway. Looking carefully down the corridor to ensure they were alone, they proceeded slowly.

Stopping suddenly, Bren gazed at the paintings lining the hall.

"The Mordane family…" he murmured, taking a close look at them.

"Why do they all look so similar?" Keswick asked quietly.

"It's disturbing," Bren said with unease.

"Let's move," Colin said softly.

The men continued to progress down the hall, taking cover in rooms nearby whenever someone appeared.

Turning around a corner, they stopped immediately when they saw two guards escorting Lord Mordane himself down the corridor. They were headed straight toward the main hall.

Elaris froze, her heart skipping a beat. She opened her eyes, desperate to get away from the sight in front of her. Seeing her apparent distress, Briggs grabbed her arm and held it firmly. The touch was just enough to bring her back.

She looked around and saw they were almost at the end of the hall, almost to Mordane.

"Sergeant Briggs," she whispered desperately.

Briggs turned his head, hearing the panic in her voice.

"We must turn back," she pleaded, terror gripping her.

Briggs halted mid-step, the other men following suit.

"What is it?" he murmured.

Before she could answer, two guards appeared at the end of the hall in front of them.

"Lord Mordane awaits you, my lady," the taller one said firmly.

Elaris knew they must go forward. Trying to leave now would put them all in danger. She had no choice—she had to continue with the plan.

Walking slowly, they came to the end of the hall and turned, entering a larger room. In the middle of the room stood Mordane. He looked to be in his fifties, but Elaris now knew better.

"My dear girl, you have finally arrived!" he cried sharply.

Walking toward her, he held out his arms to embrace her.

Elaris stepped back, repulsed by the sight of him. The move did not go unnoticed. Mordane stopped in his tracks, a slow smile curling across his lips.

"Sergeant Briggs, is it? I hear you have a report to give me," he said impatiently, turning his attention to Briggs.

Elaris tried to refocus, attempting to find his Embercurrent again. She had difficulty concentrating, the fear of being pulled in gripping her.

Breathing deeply and closing her eyes, she found it—red and blazing. She could feel the pull of his chosen current and tried to fight, but once more was pulled in, as if a hand had reached out and grabbed her.

This time, she went downstream, emerging sometime in Mordane's future. He stood in a room, looking out a window that overlooked the lands. Below, creatures were gathered, the Alari among them. Elaris could see Lumirien standing at the front of a long line of her people.

They were all bound in chains, many wounded and bearing broken limbs. She could see Thistwyn in the back, her face ashen, her wings missing and the wounds from their removal still bleeding.

With a wave of his hand, Mordane gave an order, sending hundreds of soldiers to the creatures, slashing and hacking with their swords.

Elaris tried to look away, but the image was forced upon her. She grew sick at the sight of limbs being severed and the screams that followed.

Elaris summoned all her strength and focus, pushing herself away. Suddenly, she was viewing the currents again. Taking a deep breath, she started her search through the alternate currents, determined to find one that would lead to a peaceful resolution.

The first one she chose opened to another grisly scene, this one with Mordane standing on a battlefield, giving the order to execute thousands of creatures and people who were imprisoned.

The next one she went to was similar, resulting in the deaths of the people of Houck as well as the burning of Vale Forest.

No matter which one she chose, each ended in the destruction of thousands. There was no option—no choice.

Elaris opened her eyes to see that Briggs was giving their story about Colin and Bren turning into traitors and killing Karr and his men.

"And so, you killed them?" Mordane asked, clearly suspicious.

"Yes, my lord. The men and I could not let them live."

"I see," he purred, walking in a slow circle.

Elaris could see movement out of the corner of her eye—Colin. He stood hidden in the shadows of the doorway behind Mordane. She knew he was waiting—waiting for her to act.

Focusing once more on Mordane's chosen Embercurrent, she concentrated on her breathing and manifested it. A red stream, crackling like fire, came from her hands and flowed to Mordane.

His reaction to the sight of the currents came as a surprise to everyone. He laughed.

"What are you planning to do with that, my beloved?" he asked menacingly.

Elaris's memories flashed back to the death of Kaz—the sadness she felt afterwards.

She steadied herself, remembering the visions of Mordane's currents and the devastation he was destined to bring to the people. She swiped her veil back to reveal her face.

In one smooth movement, she pulled at his current, trying to remove it from him, but it stayed firmly in place.

Frustrated, she tried again, pulling harder. The Embercurrent would not give way, crackling in response to her efforts.

Mordane quickly realized what she was trying to do, a look of panic coming over his face.

He stood frozen, waiting for the inevitable. But it never came.

Within moments, he realized that she couldn't do it. His features changed from panic to relief, to amusement in seconds.

Before she could try again, he summoned several guards who had been waiting at the side of the room. They moved quickly to restrain Briggs and the rest of the men.

Briggs fought to protect Elaris, but Mordane moved unnaturally quickly, grabbing her by the neck and pulling her into a crushing embrace.

Colin came from the shadows, followed by Bren and Keswick. Elaris saw him approach and screamed, "Colin, no! He's a Fatewaker!"

All the men froze, stunned by what she had said. Colin quickly recovered, moving rapidly to take down Mordane.

"Move again and she dies," Mordane hissed.

Colin stopped, growling low. A guard approached him swiftly—drawing a dagger and placing it at his throat.

Out of the shadows, a wizard emerged, walking rapidly to Mordane and placing his hands on his back.

Elaris saw what was happening and began to struggle.

"I'm glad you know who I am, my dear—but you only have it half right. I *used* to be a Fatewaker—many, many years ago.

"But apparently, dark magic and the magic of the Embercurrent do not mix. Although I can see and absorb the Embercurrent with assistance, I can no longer manipulate it."

Elaris continued to struggle as she felt his hands closing tighter around her neck. Colin analyzed the room, seeing every one of his men being held with a sword at his throat.

"I have waited for you for a thousand years—waiting for the day we would be joined, where you would willingly give me your power. I fear that I won't be able to gain your abilities the way I had intended, but I'm sure that something of your powers will come to me this way," he growled, as he squeezed.

The wizard behind him closed his eyes, his expression one of deep concentration. Mordane's face twisted as he attempted to draw the Embercurrent from her, but to no avail.

After several moments of struggling, he released her, dropping her to the floor, a look of shock on his face.

Turning to his wizard, he shouted, "Why didn't it work?"

"I... I don't know, my lord!" the wizard stammered in reply.

Colin saw his moment and took it. Slamming his elbow into the ribs of the guard holding the knife to his throat, he gained his freedom. Briggs followed suit, easily overtaking the distracted guard who held him.

Colin ran to Elaris, pulling her up in one smooth movement. Briggs roared loudly and plowed through the opposing guard, releasing the men and allowing them to join in the fight.

Mordane remained standing where he was in the middle of the chaos, shock and disbelief on his face.

"We're leaving!" Colin shouted, pulling Elaris through the door he had come from and down the hall.

The company quickly followed, fighting the guards behind them. Briggs, wanting to slow the enemy's progress, pulled a torch from the wall, and began setting tapestries and furniture ablaze as they ran.

Retracing their steps, the company emerged into the back courtyard, frightening the servants at work there. Bower and Hewitt, standing at the gate, saw them coming.

"Bower!" Colin yelled. "Where are my horses?"

Bower pointed to the tree line outside the gate. "Ready to go, Sir!" he replied loudly.

The two men joined up with the others as they ran through the gates, emerging near the wooded area. Fifteen horses awaited them, all tethered to nearby trees.

"Good work, Bower," Colin said quickly, lifting Elaris onto a horse.

Mounting his own, he led the company quickly away from the palace at a gallop.

Elaris rode next to him, still stunned from her encounter with Mordane.

"It's burning," she murmured, looking back at the palace.

"Good riddance!" Briggs shouted.

Coming to a stop just outside of Houck, Colin called the men together.

"You all performed admirably today. We didn't get our man, but we gained information—critical information that we can use against him in the future."

The men all grumbled their agreement.

"I ride south. The king there may be of some help in our cause. This is your moment to decide your path. You must do so quickly. They will be on us soon."

Colin looked into the eyes of each man. Each man met his gaze with quiet pride.

"I go with you and the Fatewaker, Sir," Keswick said firmly.

"As do I," Corporal Finwick joined in.

One by one, each man made his oath to follow.

Elaris felt tears rise as she heard all of them promise to be with her. These noble men—these friends.

Colin smiled proudly. He had chosen these men for his company for a reason—and he had not been wrong in that judgement.

"Let's move. We have a long road ahead…"

EPILOGUE

Colin stood at the edge of the camp, looking out over the rolling hills that extended to the horizon. The south had landscapes unlike any he had ever seen—lush, wild, and beautiful.

Elaris approached from behind and slipped her hand gently into his.

He smiled to himself, loving the feel of her warmth.

"King Thadius seems happy to have you and the rest of the company here," she said.

"I think he is even more pleased to have you here," he said with a smile, turning to face her.

Elaris looked up at him, her violet eyes shining brightly in the sunlight.

Colin had never felt so at peace—so at home—as he did with her.

Seeing her smile at him, his heart caught in his chest, and he made a decision.

Taking her face in his hands, he leaned down and kissed her lightly, letting his lips linger for a long moment.

Elaris sighed as he pulled away, looking both happy and wanting simultaneously.

Colin beamed at her. He knew they had time.

He spotted Bren approaching from the camp, a grin on his face that made it clear he'd seen everything.

Colin gave him a warning glare before he reached them, causing Bren to laugh.

"Beautiful day," Bren said, a little too cheerfully.

"Yes, it is," Elaris breathed, still blushing.

The three stood still for a moment, enjoying the view.

"Do you think we will ever return?" Bren asked.

"We must. Mordane will cause the destruction of Ashcar if we don't," Elaris said soberly.

"He must be going mad since discovering you two can't affect each other's Embercurrents," Bren said.

"He will be planning his next move. But we will be ready," Colin said, resolve in his voice.

Elaris looked thoughtful. "I know now that I have a part to play. Mordane must be stopped, his children saved. He has a son who is destined to be killed when he grows older. His other children lie frozen somewhere, their Embercurrents captured. And then there are the Alari, and all the other peoples of Vale Forest... and of Ashcar," she said sadly, her voice catching in her throat.

"We will fight, Elaris. All of us—following you. We will ensure he is stopped," Colin assured her, reaching out and squeezing her hand again.

Elaris looked up at him and saw his admiration and love.

Suddenly happy, she grinned and said, "I suppose I should get back to practicing. Do you want to volunteer, Lieutenant?"

"Sure!" Bren laughed. "But do me a favor—look into my future and tell me if there are any tall redheads with pointy ears and wings there."

THE **FATEWAKER** SAGA
HAS ONLY BEGUN

THREE BOOKS. ONE RECKONING.

CONTINUE THE JOURNEY IN

FATEWAKER: FRACTURED

THE WAR IS FAR FROM OVER...
AND SACRIFICE IS COMING.

AVAILABLE ON EBOOK, AUDIBLE,
AND IN PRINT WORLDWIDE

VISIT
FATEWAKER.COM
FOR UPDATES ON THE SERIES AND
FOLLOW ME ON AMAZON
TO GET NOTIFIED OF FUTURE RELEASES

 AUTHORJRMcCULLOUGH

 FACEBOOK.COM/FATEWAKER

ABOUT THE AUTHOR

J.R. MCCULLOUGH SPENDS AN UNREASONABLE AMOUNT OF TIME THINKING ABOUT MAGICAL POWERS, MORALLY GRAY HEROES, AND EXACTLY HOW MUCH EMOTIONAL DAMAGE ONE CHAPTER CAN DO. WHEN NOT WRITING, SHE CAN USUALLY BE FOUND BOUNCING STORY IDEAS OFF HER ENDLESSLY PATIENT HUSBAND OR NEGOTIATING WITH HER TWO CATS, NEITHER OF WHOM RESPECT WRITING TIME. *FATEWAKER* IS HER DEBUT NOVEL—AND THE ADVENTURE IS ONLY JUST BEGINNING.